Can a moment of passion outlast years of secrets and misery?

For Julia Patterson, meeting Luke Buchanan awakens within her a
passion she's never dared dream possible. He claims her body and
and helps her remember what it means to be a woman. But Fate has
a twisted sense of humor. Just when Julia is ready to step over the
threshold into a wonderful new life, her almost-ex-husband is diagnosed
with a heart condition that puts her divorce on hold. Turning her back on
Luke is the most difficult thing she's ever done. But Julia has a secret,
one that Charles discovers and uses against her.

Years later, when Luke walks back into Julia's life, the passion between
them is just as explosive. But Charles is still controlling her from the
grave, and the secret Julia has hidden for fourteen years could destroy
their dreams forever.

I0677672

Books by Desiree Holt

Forward Pass

Finding Julia

Desiree Holt

LYRICAL PRESS
Kensington Publishing Corp.
www.kensingtonbooks.com

Lyrical Press books are published by
Kensington Publishing Corp. 119 West 40th Street New York, NY 10018

All Kensington titles, imprints, and distributed lines are available at special quantity discounts for bulk purchases for sales promotion, premiums, fund-raising, and educational or institutional use.

Special book excerpts or customized printings can also be created to fit specific needs. For details, write or phone the office of the Kensington Special Sales Manager:
Kensington Publishing Corp.
119 West 40th Street
New York, NY 10018
Attn. Special Sales Department. Phone: 1-800-221-2647.

Kensington and the K logo Reg. U.S. Pat. & TM Off.
Lyrical Press and the L logo are trademarks of Kensington Publishing Corp.

First Electronic Edition: September 2014
eISBN-13: 978-1-61650-639-1
eISBN-10: 1-61650-639-3

First Print Edition: September 2014
ISBN-13: 978-1-61650-640-7
ISBN-10: 1-61650-639-3

Printed in the United States of America

To David, who made it all happen.

Writing may be a solitary adventure but no book comes to life without a lot of help. First and foremost to my wonderful dedicated beta reader, Margie Hager. Huge thanks to my friend and writing partner, bestselling author Cerise Deland. Where would I be without our intense brainstorming sessions? And finally to my children who put up with my frantic craziness as deadlines near and talk me down off the ledge. I love you all.

Chapter 1

Julia Patterson put her suitcases in a precise alignment in the front hall and, through the narrow window, eyed the trickles of rain dripping down the pane of glass. San Antonio, Texas might suffer droughts but when it rained it most definitely poured.

Damn.

She hated flying to begin with. Now she worried the flight would be delayed taking off, or worse, they'd run into bad weather en route. Well, nothing to be done for it. She had to make the trip. The anticipated contract was too lucrative to pass up, and her partner in Bright Ideas was tied up on another project.

For the tenth time, she looked at herself in the powder room mirror. Navy slacks sharply creased. Check. Tweed jacket hitting the hips at the perfect spot. Check. White silk turtleneck draped just so. Check. Even the gold hoops at her ears hung in symmetry. If there was one thing she'd learned from Charles, it was to be precise and exact. "Details, Julia," he repeated ad nauseam. "In our circles it's the details that count." Sometimes she felt as if her entire life was a series of checklists.

Charles. His name sent a tiny shiver the length of her spine. One more stroke of a pen and she'd be rid of him altogether. These weeks of torturous haggling and draining telephone calls were coming to an end and his methodical, dictatorial presence in her life would finally be finished. She and the twins, seven-year-old Andy and Beth, could finally move ahead. Luckily, though sadly, Charles had never made himself an integral part of their lives.

There was just today to get through and Thanksgiving, three days from now. The reminder made her stomach cramp. That damn dinner. She was irritated to have it hanging over her. In a moment of total insanity, she'd agreed Thanksgiving would be here at the house. Her house, now. Or almost. The dinner from hell with Howard and Elise Patterson, Charles's parents who made ice cubes look hot, and his sister Evelyn, her husband Mark and their ten-year-old daughter. If Charles was bad, the rest of the Pattersons were worse.

"We have to be civilized about this, Julia." Charles had delivered the pronouncement in his usual clipped voice, still focused on the holiday. "Until you come to your senses."

"I have come to my senses," she'd insisted, forcing herself to be calm. She couldn't let him bait her the way he always did. "Dinner. Fine. Nothing more."

"It's the least you can do," Charles had argued. "You're the one who insisted on this ridiculous divorce. Don't you think you owe something to me? To my family?"

How about a hit man?

His voice gave her the same feeling of discomfort as a hangnail. Too bad she couldn't just clip him away.

Shaking off the anger always lurking beneath the surface, she turned into the kitchen. Miranda Black, her indispensable housekeeper, stood at the counter, making notes on a pad of paper. The woman had arrived a week after the twins were born, agency reference in one hand, suitcase in the other, and she'd been there ever since.

At first Julia had been so grateful, pleased that Charles was thoughtful enough to get her help. Still stunned that a man like Charles from such a rarified privileged environment wanted her. But then the charming prince who'd swept her off her feet turned into a frog. No, a dragon. It was unfortunate she'd gotten pregnant in only the second year of their marriage but he had no intention of letting children upset his life. It was time now for her to involve herself in appropriate community and social activities. Perform in a way demanded by his position in the community.

All Julia had wanted was a stable home and family environment. Her own certainly hadn't fit that bill. Secretly she'd been happy to be living far away from her dysfunctional parents and hadn't argued when little by little Charles cut them out of her life. With Charles she'd been so sure she had her dream, the chance to create a secure family environment. Instead, the courtship, wedding, and honeymoon now seemed as if they'd belonged to someone else. She was left with the villain of the piece.

Without Miranda, she wasn't sure how she'd have survived. She was more family than employee, an anchor in the turbulence of her life.

"I'd like to check the lists again." Julia reached for the pad of paper.

Miranda grinned. "Julia, you've checked them five times today already. I have everything on there for tomorrow's grocery shopping and everything to prepare on Wednesday. This won't be the first holiday dinner I've helped you put together. Let your mind rest, okay?"

But they both knew Julia's mind seldom rested.

She inhaled slowly to center herself. By tonight, she'd be in Boston. Tomorrow she'd be making a key marketing presentation to Hot Ticket, a major sports apparel company, on the proposed plan for their new line. This was the largest bid yet by Bright Ideas. She and Claire worked hard for opportunities like this. As important as this meeting was, she didn't want to leave anything behind because she'd been careless.

What a rage Charles had been in when she'd opened the agency with Claire. But she was no longer the vulnerable young college student swept off her feet by the handsome and privileged prince. It still shocked her to realize he'd married her for that very vulnerability, assuming he could mold her into the wife he expected her to be. She'd certainly tried, despite the fact she began to hate every minute of it. But somewhere along the line, trying to be someone she wasn't, she'd lost herself completely.

Until her friend Claire Westbrook had quite literally dragged her into the partnership.

Somewhere she'd found the strength to deal with Charles and defy him. She was sick and tired, at last, of being little more than his puppet. And angry with herself for allowing it to happen. Even his threats to use his influence to damage the agency, destroy its reputation, hadn't stopped her. Its growing success only angered him more.

And now she was moving on with the rest of her life. Each day was still a struggle but she was getting there, slowly but steadily. If he would just sign the damn papers. She wanted to avoid a three-ring circus in court, if possible. Meanwhile she had to focus on her trip. This account would be a launching pad for Bright Ideas, solidify them, so she had to nail it down.

Yesterday, going over everything one more time in the office, Claire had been full of encouragement. "You'll nail it. I have every confidence in you."

"You have to say that. You're my friend." And one she gave thanks for every single day.

"Have you seen my briefcase and computer?" Julia asked Miranda now, mentally running down her last minute checklist.

"Right by the back door with your luggage. I wanted to make sure you had your things together."

"Oh, thank God." She exhaled in relief. "The car service will be here any minute. It's starting to rain and you know what San Antonio traffic is like in bad weather. This whole area is subject to flash floods. Besides, I want to get to the airport before the weather closes in."

"Not to worry." Miranda smiled at her. "You're all set."

Julia gave her an impulsive hug. "Whatever would I do without you?" She stepped back, grinning. "And don't let me find out. The twins are in the family room?" Miranda nodded. "I'll just say goodbye one more time."

Andy and Beth were planted in front of the television, staring with rapt attention at a cartoon.

"Hey, kiddos." Julia crouched down to their level. "You guys be good for Miranda, okay?"

"Will you be home tomorrow?" Beth asked, sliding her gaze away from the set.

"Not tomorrow, but the day after, and then we'll have fun making Thanksgiving dinner. Okay?"

"Me, too?" Andy wasn't going to be left out, but his eyes remained glued to his program.

"You, too, sweetie. Now both of you give me a big hug and a kiss."

The tap of a horn outside drew her to the door.

"Damn," she muttered. The familiar knot of tension settled into place in her stomach. Of course he'd show up, try to throw her off her game, aware she didn't want to deal with him today. "How the hell did this happen?"

Rather than the dark sedan the car service used, Charles's grey Lincoln sat impatiently in the driveway. In a moment, he got out of the car, slammed the door, and stomped up to the front porch.

Julia pulled the door open. "What are you doing here? I'm leaving in a few minutes. The car service is due any time."

"I canceled them. It's raining. I came to talk you out of this ridiculous trip with bad weather closing in, and discuss ending this sham of a divorce."

Not today. Please not today. She would not let him get to her. Cause her to fall apart.

"I can't believe you took this on yourself to do," she told him. "It's too late to call them back. I'll have to make other arrangements. Damn."

"I forbid you to go."

Flat, cold words, as if what he said was law. For a moment the uncertainty she fought every day flared inside her but she tamped it down.

"Charles." She curled her hands into fists. "I'm going. You no longer have the right to tell me what I can and can't do. And there is nothing to discuss about the divorce except when you're finally going to sign those papers." She turned to go into the kitchen. "Never mind. I'll see if Claire can take me."

"Julia." He used a tone of controlled patience, one she'd grown to hate so desperately. "You are the most irritating woman. Fine. If you insist on going despite everything, I'll take you. But I think it's ridiculous to take chances when we have dinner coming up on Thursday."

Yes, of course. Dinner was the most important thing.

At that moment, the twins rushed into the foyer from the family room. At the sight of their father, however, they stopped so suddenly they bumped into each other. Smiles faded from their faces, replaced by looks of uncertainty.

"Julia." Charles stood in his perfectly tailored black suit and midnight blue topcoat, not a crease in sight, not a wrinkle, not a smudge. Everything was as perfect as the day it came from the tailor. His mouth was set in a thin line as he observed the children, staring at him. "Must they run around the house like common animals?"

"They're just being children, Charles." She ground her teeth. "I should think you'd be glad to see them."

Charles's cold attitude where the twins were concerned bothered the hell out of her, but now was not the time to begin an argument, one she had no chance of winning. She'd discovered the hard way in the Patterson family, expressions of emotion were strictly forbidden. No wonder he'd grown up to be the way he was.

Miranda, eyeing the situation, gathered the twins and ushered them into the kitchen, soothing and distracting them.

"Are you ready?" A muscle jumped in Charles's cheek. "I'd like to get going. It's raining and the traffic will be a mess."

"Yes, I am." Julia picked up her purse, briefcase, computer, and warm duffel coat. The weather report for Boston was snow, snow, and more snow. "If you'll get the suitcase, we can leave."

She hurried to the car and buckled herself into the passenger seat. A dull ache began to build behind her eyes, the result of the tension always in the air between them. Leaning her head back, she prayed for a moment of quiet peace. Raindrops spattered against the windshield, a waterfall parted by the regular motion of the windshield wipers. A good representation of her life, a curtain falling, parting momentarily, then dropping back in place like a shroud.

She felt the anger vibrating from Charles as he navigated the wet streets and traffic. In the nearly ten years of their marriage, he'd become steadily more dictatorial, more autocratic, more controlling. Vulnerable and insecure, she'd allowed it for far too long, losing herself until she no longer had an identity of her own. She'd finally found the courage to break away, but things turned as nasty as she'd expected.

Telling Charles she was divorcing him had been her most difficult task yet. Worse, because he'd fought her at every turn, assuming as an attorney he'd hold the upper hand and emerge the victor. Lucky for her, Claire had found her a shark who could draw blood.

"Once more, Julia, you have made an irresponsible decision." Charles's words interrupted her thoughts now, tiny pin pricks bringing her back to the present. "I don't know why you have to go away during this particular week. You know my parents have very definite ideas about Thanksgiving dinner."

Yes, she certainly did. More than she wanted to. She should have just told him they could have it at their house but it was one more argument she hadn't wanted at the time.

"Charles, I'll be back Wednesday afternoon." She forced herself to bite back her automatic retort. "Miranda is doing the grocery shopping, she'll have the table set by Wednesday night and everything ready for me to finish cooking Thursday morning. I'm only doing this for the children anyway, so don't push me or there won't be any dinner at all."

"May I remind you of the generous monthly stipend your attorney screwed me out of? There are certain conditions for you to continue receiving it."

"As if I could stop you," she snapped.

"My parents like to eat Thanksgiving dinner at three," he reminded her. "It's a tradition. Nothing should disrupt that."

"God forbid we should ever break with tradition," Julia muttered under her breath.

"What did you say?" Charles cast a sideways glance at her.

"I said don't worry, I'd never break with tradition. Dinner will be on the table exactly at three."

Charles made no comment, his attention at the moment riveted on steering through the traffic with precise moves. "I don't know why Claire couldn't have gone instead." A note of petulance tinged his words.

"Claire is doing the Thanksgiving Festival starting Friday, as you well know." Julia was irritated. This wasn't the first argument they'd had about this. "They have no children. This way I can spend the long weekend with the twins."

"I'd rather you didn't work at all and stayed home where you belong."

"I will not have this discussion with you again at this particular moment." She fisted her hands to hold her temper in check. "Your choices are no longer a factor in my life. I'm sick of the whole thing."

"No more than I am. Julia, I'm tired of waiting for you to come to your senses and call off this ridiculous divorce activity."

Slap, slap, slap. The windshield wipers were a metronome keeping time to the throbbing in her head.

"It's not ridiculous, and it's almost final."

"Almost being the key word."

"Charles…" Oh, God, why wouldn't he shut up?

"Never mind." Charles's hands tightened on the steering wheel. "You were right. This is neither the time nor place to discuss this. But trust me, we *will* be talking about this when you get back."

"I can hardly wait," she muttered and moved as close to the door as her seat belt would allow.

They sat in silence the rest of the way to the airport. Charles let her out at the Departures entrance, and confirmed her return time and flight with her.

"I'll pick you up." It was as much an order as an announcement. Would she never have space to breathe with this man?

"Why do you do this?" she asked. "It's over, Charles. Over. I don't want you hovering and caging me in. I'll take the airport limo home. Or arrange for the car service."

A muscle jumped wildly in his cheek. "Any moment now you will come to your senses and stop this ridiculous charade. I may not be able to sleep in my own bed for the moment, but it is my responsibility to make sure you arrive home safely. We have dinner planned for Thursday."

Ah, yes. The dinner again. It would be a damned shame if she killed herself before the obligatory holiday meal.

Tired of the argument, she simply nodded and slammed the door.

Charles pulled quickly away from the curb, water spraying out in a rooster tail from beneath the wheels. The only thing more drenched than the pavement was her heart.

Chapter 2

The faces greeting her in the boardroom were smiling and expectant, the usual eclectic mix of young and old, fresh and worn, male and female, and a wide mix of cultures. She noted Manning had arranged for the equipment she requested, so she hooked up her computer and brought up the PowerPoint presentation. After Howard introduced her, she drew in a breath and began her pitch.

The morning sped by. She passed out two-page handouts for everyone at the appropriate time and answered their questions. But she knew this was just preparation, a briefing if the company bought her plan. Howard ordered lunch sent in for everyone, giving Julia a chance to chat informally with the group and prepare for the afternoon.

"Our executive vice president is tied up in a meeting right now," Howard whispered as the executive staff filed in. "He's the one who says yea or nay. He'll join us as soon as he can."

Great. Would he expect her to do it all over again for him?

She sighed and began her presentation again.

It was well into the afternoon and she was pulling out copies of the proposed budget to distribute when the door to the boardroom opened quietly, and Julia's stomach dropped to the floor. She felt as if an electric surge slammed into her, plucking at every one of her nerve endings.

The man who silently took a seat at the end of the table wasn't necessarily handsome, but he was one hundred percent male. Liquid brown eyes were framed by the thickest lashes she had ever seen on a man. She noticed the strong jaw and the lines of character etched on an incredibly masculine face. Straight brown hair, a hint of silver reflecting in the lights, worn just a little long, gave him a slight rakehell look.

The classic dark business suit barely concealed the power he radiated. More than that, he exuded an aura of self, of authority, of comfort in his own skin few men were able to attain. She could think of only three words to describe him. Dark. Edgy. Dangerous. In her entire thirty years, no man had ever affected her the way this man did. Certainly not Charles. She clamped down on her reaction, forbidding herself to let her thoughts wander into forbidden territory. As she'd learned, her judgment where men were concerned left a great deal to be desired.

"Let me interrupt a moment." Manning jumped to his feet. "Julia, meet Lucas Buchanan, our executive vice president. He's been in another meeting until now."

"I'm pleased you could join us, Mr. Buchanan." Julia pasted on her professional smile and hoped her voice sounded firmer to the others than it did to her.

Lucas Buchanan nodded at her. "Luke, please. Sorry to be late. Please don't let me interrupt."

She struggled to pick up the threads of what she'd been saying, her brain suddenly addled, and her hands unsteady. It took every ounce of personal discipline to keep focused on her presentation.

Somehow she got through it, even managed to answer questions intelligently. Luke was silent throughout, but his eyes never left her. She knew he would remember and file away everything said. A man like Luke Buchanan didn't get where he was by not paying attention.

Then finally, they were finished, and she shook hands with everyone. Howard Manning stood at her elbow like a well-bred guard dog, ushering everyone along. Luke still sat at the end of the table, watching quietly through hooded eyes. She busied herself packing everything back into her briefcase, feeling as if she were surrounded by his presence.

"I hope you'll join me for dinner," Howard told her when she was finished.

"Ms. Patterson will be having dinner with me, Howard. Thanks anyway." Luke suddenly stood next to her, his hand at her elbow.

"Oh, you don't need to—" she began, but he interrupted her.

"We still have business to discuss, don't you think?"

He phrased it as a question, but Julia was positive he was telling her, not asking. Shocked at the electric jolt such a light touch sent buzzing through her system, she wondered if the man sensed how rattled she was. "Yes. Thank you. That would be nice."

The nearness of the man swamped her. She felt as if she were being drawn into a vortex, powerless to pull herself out. Sex with Charles was always…perfunctory. A disappointing crash after what she guessed had been unrealistic expectations. But this man, with one casual touch of his fingers, set bells ringing inside her. She hoped she didn't look and sound as dazed as she felt.

Still lightly touching her arm, he looked at Howard.

"Why don't you carry Ms. Patterson's things downstairs for her and I'll pick her up in front." He turned to Julia. "Five minutes. Howard will help you."

The private elevator doors opened and he was gone before she even knew he'd left her side. The place where he'd touched her still tingled and his absence left her suddenly bereft.

"A good sign," Howard told her. "He doesn't usually do the wining and dining for the company."

"Oh?" Julia raised an eyebrow.

He took her briefcase and computer and led her to the elevator. "If Lucas Buchanan wants to have dinner with you, I'd say you can consider this a done deal."

"Thank you, Howard, but I've learned to keep my expectations under control. We'll see how it goes."

Once outside, Howard ushered her into a black Lincoln, shook her hand, and closed the car door after her.

Luke turned and looked at her. The heat simmering in his eyes, the unspoken message dancing in the air between them, stunned her.

His lips curved in a smile. "Here we go." His deep warm voice was like a caress.

Butterflies fluttered in her stomach and Julia felt an unfamiliar flash of heat suffuse her.

Here we go, indeed.

Chapter 3

"I'd like to take a minute to freshen up, if you don't mind." Julia paused in the hotel lobby.

And take a few minutes to gather her wits about her.

"Take your time." Luke smiled. "I'll get us a table in the cocktail lounge while you run up to your room. I thought we'd have a drink before heading into the restaurant."

"All right. Sounds good."

In her room, she dropped her briefcase and portfolio, leaned against the closed door, and put her hands to her heated face. Her entire body felt flushed, her bones shook, and the oddest sensation coursed through her. What was the matter with her? She didn't even know the man. This was crazy.

There was no mistaking the unspoken message in Luke's dark eyes when he looked at her, no matter how circumspect his behavior. And even three floors away from him, she still felt his powerful presence surrounding her.

What she needed was a cold shower. Maybe the stinging spray would bring her to her senses. She glanced at her watch. Could she do it quickly? She stripped off her clothes, fully aware if she exchanged her business uniform for something more casual, she was acknowledging this was more than a business date. She was equally nervous and aroused. A dangerous combination. Why couldn't she just get on with it? Allow herself to sample life a little?

She hurried through the shower, drying herself quickly, rubbing cream into her skin, spraying perfume on her pulse points, and pulling on the soft slacks and cashmere sweater she'd brought to travel home in. Gold hoops at her ears. She brushed her hair until it shown and swayed with a natural rhythm. And all the while the image of Luke Buchanan burned itself into her vision. Unexpectedly, she wondered what he looked like without any clothes on such a powerful body. Wondered what fantastic things he would do to her. With her.

Oh, my God! Crazy, crazy, crazy.

She sensed she was on the verge of doing the most daring thing she'd ever done in her life, but Luke Buchanan mesmerized her. She couldn't help herself. Maybe it was her lack of experience with anyone but Charles. Maybe it was the need curling inside her to discover what real passion was. Maybe it was a response to having a man look at her as if she was a desirable woman. Whatever it was, it was blossoming inside her like a flower seed buried too long under snow.

When she entered the cocktail lounge, Luke rose from the booth he'd commandeered, his eyes taking in every inch of her body. When he took her arm as she slid onto the bench seat, the same instant shock of electricity she'd felt during the afternoon crackled through her.

"I'd have ordered for you but I neglected to ask what you drink." His deep voice was like a liquid caress.

"Amaretto, please. On the rocks. Thank you."

"Very nice." His gaze took in every inch of her. "I like the outfit. The color brings out the blue in your eyes."

"Thank you." She searched for something else to say, but her tongue seemed immobilized. Compliments were rare in her life with Charles.

She was grateful when the waiter brought her drink, not for the alcohol but for something to do with her hands.

"You're clutching your glass like a lifeline." Amusement edged Luke's tone and his eyes crinkled at the corners. "You aren't an alcoholic by any chance, are you?"

"No. Not at all." She picked up the drink and sipped at it, feeling the warmth slide through her system, praying her hands wouldn't shake. "Just…winding down." Or winding tighter.

Luke studied her face, hot gaze stroking her skin. "Tell me about yourself, Julia Patterson. I know everything there is to know about your agency and absolutely nothing about you."

"You'll find I'm a very boring person, Mr. Buchanan."

"Luke, please." There was that smile again, melting her bones. "And I don't believe anyone who comes up with the creative ideas you do can be boring at all."

"You'd be surprised." She lowered her eyes. His piercing gaze unnerved her, as if he could see beneath her skin.

"Where are you from?" he asked. "What do you like to do?" He grinned. "What's your most secret fantasy?"

Fantasy? Should she tell him she'd been having unbelievable fantasies about him in the quick shower she'd taken to cool herself off?

"Julia?" His amused voice broke into her mental wanderings. "This isn't a test, just nosy interest on my part."

"I'm sorry. I guess my mind drifted." She took another sip of amaretto. "There isn't much to tell. I'm a small town girl living in the big city, with two great kids and a wonderful business."

How could she possibly tell him the truth? She'd rushed into a youthful marriage, propelled by two sets of parents and the social expectations of friends. Now, if not for her agency and her children, she'd be little more than a cipher in limbo. And her sex life wouldn't even be the envy of a nun.

No, she wouldn't tell him that little tidbit.

"Tell me more about your kids," he urged.

"My kids?" She stared.

"Yes. What are they like? Kids tell a lot about the kind of people their parents are."

She laughed nervously. "I don't want to bore you to death."

He gave her a crooked smile. "Nothing about you could bore me."

Her children were an area where she could go on for hours. She forgot to be tense and anxious, forgot about everything as she talked about Andy and Beth. As she talked, she sipped on the wonderful amaretto, its velvety texture soft against her tongue. Wrapped in the growing feeling of relaxation, she barely noticed when a full glass replaced an empty one.. Every so often, she'd catch something dark flashing in Luke's eyes, like a shadow of sadness. She wondered what was in this man's life to cause such hidden melancholy.

* * * *

Luke watched the woman across from him, posture relaxed, careful to betray nothing of his real interest through either movement or facial expression. The cashmere sweater draped softly across her breasts, and when she leaned forward, he could see the rosy skin exposed by the wide neckline. The muted lights of the cocktail lounge caught the golden highlights in her hair and the glint of green in her eyes. Her translucent skin was slightly flushed, and he wondered if it was the alcohol or his presence. He hoped the latter.

The energy he'd felt the instant he met her stunned him, affecting him more strongly than any woman in recent memory. These days, in fact, he'd wondered if he'd burned himself out these past years trying to erase the damage his wife had caused. He'd been hard-pressed to conceal his arousal back in the conference room. The moment he looked into Julia's eyes, he'd wanted nothing more than to take her to bed and fuck her senseless.

He could almost feel the silkiness of her skin beneath his hands, the lushness of her body as he explored it, and taste the sweet essence uniquely hers. He didn't ever remember wanting a woman this badly. From the moment he'd walked into the conference room and saw her standing there, his cock had been so hard he'd had to sit down immediately to conceal it.

And what was that about, anyway? He wasn't a teenager with raging hormones. Or a young man who'd thought he was marrying a princess who turned out to be a witch—a promiscuous one to boot. He'd certainly enjoyed more than enough sex before and after his marriage, yet no woman ever reached deep inside him the way Julia Patterson did just by...being.

She was nervous, and he didn't know if it was him or the situation. He wanted her to relax and be at ease, so he could see if this...*thing*...sizzling between them sparked to life or was nothing more than a hopeful figment of his imagination.

He could tell as much about her from what she omitted as from what she told him. Why no comments about her husband? No enthusiastic description of her marriage? What sort of man claimed Julia Patterson as his wife, but lived with her in a relationship devoid of detail? He saw a woman of great warmth, personal charm, and unbelievable sexual attraction. The man must be a eunuch or a cheat.

His own marriage had been less than desirable, followed by a bitter divorce. The resentment of it all still clung to him and he wished he'd found Julia before someone else had. And before his own life had disintegrated so badly.

* * * *

"You're staring," she told him. "Is my makeup smeared?"

"Your makeup is fine. You're fine." He smiled. "I enjoy looking at you, listening to you. I love the sound of your voice."

She laughed a nervous sound. The longer they sat in the booth, the more overpowering his presence. Could they simply stay here forever? "You must have pretty empty conversations if mine excites you."

"Not at all. By the way, your proposal is excellent. I asked someone to bring me their copy during lunch so I could study it before the afternoon session."

"So you've already seen it?" She was surprised. She'd expected to wait the usual week or so before it made its way to the decision-maker.

He nodded. "If the numbers add up the way they look like they should, we definitely have a deal." He lifted his glass in a toast. "Shall we have another drink to seal the agreement?"

Julia nodded, the almond liqueur soothing her nerves and melting her tension. Luke leaned forward, talking to her in a low, deep voice. She couldn't draw herself away from his eyes, so mesmerizing they locked her in place. Vaguely, she heard soft music somewhere and turned her head.

"They bring in a little duo in the evening." He motioned to the postage stamp dance floor. "What about it?" At her hesitation, he added, "It's nothing more than a dance, Julia. Between colleagues."

A dance. Right.

A shiver skittered over her spine.

What was she doing here? Losing her mind?

Proper, obedient Julia was going to color outside the lines. But she was tempted by the possibility of forbidden pleasure. Of something she'd barely dreamt about. Unknown sensuality she'd heard her friends talk about and silently longed for.

Wordlessly, almost as if her body was on automatic pilot, she slid from the booth and put her hand in his. His fingers closed around hers with a gentle assurance that sent a surge of warmth through her. Despite what he said, she sensed he knew as well as she did things weren't quite as simple as a dance. On the tiny floor, he drew her against him and their bodies fit as if poured from matching molds. They moved in a slow rhythm, his strong arm encircling her, his warm hand holding hers in close to his chest.

She inhaled the scent of him, spicy and musky, mixed with an incredible male essence. Dangerous. The word came back to her again.

She wasn't stupid. She knew what was happening here. Forget more drinks. Forget dinner. She should break away and go to bed. Alone. But she knew she'd already made a choice, and her body began to tingle in anticipation. This was the most daring thing she'd ever done, and she felt powerless to stop herself.

They barely moved from the one spot on the dance floor as the music flowed around them, thighs pressed to thighs, the heat of his body melting into hers. The flexing of the muscles in those thighs as they moved to their own rhythm made hers quiver. Her breasts, pressed against the hard planes of his chest, felt suddenly full and heavy. She wanted to purr and rub herself all over him like a cat. When the song ended and he led her back to the table, she had to blink her eyes to remember where she was.

"You dance well."

"Oh!" The compliment startled her. "Thank you. You make it easy."

His voice melted her. There was a richness to it, like fresh coffee or warm chocolate pouring over her, through her, and around her. She thought she could listen to him talk forever.

When the waiter brought fresh drinks, he smiled at her and they clinked glasses.

Julia lost track of time as they sat in the lounge, sipped drinks, and danced again. They chatted about everything and nothing at all. Luke's natural warmth and charm continued to put her at ease, but sexual tension so intense it was almost palpable electrified the air between them. As inexperienced as she was, Julia still knew she'd have to be dead not to feel it. And wasn't that pathetic; a thirty-year-old woman whose sexual experience wouldn't fill two pages in a book.

At some point, Luke took off his jacket and stuffed his tie in the pocket. Each time he led her to the dance floor, their bodies clung closer together. His arms held her with confidence and assurance, almost possession. Without the extra layer of the jacket between them, she could feel the heat of his body through his shirt. The fine cotton was like a silk caress against her cheek, and thin enough she could feel the hard buds of his nipples. When he moved his head, she could feel the tickle of his breath in her ear and shivered at the tiny fingers of sensation it brought.

His cock pressed against the softness of her through the fabric of his slacks. Her body responded with an unfamiliar intensity, tiny nerves sparking everywhere, the feel of his arousal electrifying her. Her breasts ached with the need to be touched, and her panties were so wet she was sure he could smell her scent. So this was what it was like. This was what other people reveled in and she'd never tasted. She was sure if she went to bed with him, she'd die of pleasure.

If she went to bed with him? Wasn't it already, in her mind, a foregone conclusion?

"I can feel every one of your muscles move against me." His voice was a low hum in her ear. "You have such a graceful body. Soft and warm."

Warm was an understatement. Overheated might be more accurate.

"Do I offend you with my comments?" he asked, his hands tightening on her almost imperceptibly.

"No." She could hardly get the word out. "No, you don't."

"Good. Because I like telling you. Do you know how beautiful you are?" he asked as they shifted their feet almost in place in a corner of the floor.

His words were soft in her ear, a whisper tickling her skin, sending delicious shivers through her.

"Thank you," was the only thing she could think of to say, feeling like a tongue-tied idiot.

"I can feel your heart beating hard against mine," he told her. "Are you nervous?"

"Mmm, I'd say a little…unsure?" She was definitely swimming out of her depth here. "Am I making sense?"

"We don't have to dance any more if you don't want to."

It was way more than dancing. She was sure they both knew it.

The heat of his breath at her ear sent a shiver racing through her. She knew he was slowly seducing her, letting her fall into it in slow increments, giving her plenty of opportunities to change her mind. Pull away.

"You know what I mean, Luke." She took a deep breath. "We're talking about a lot more than dancing."

There. She'd said it. Pulled it out into the open. They might as well stop…well…dancing around it. She lifted her head slightly now and could almost see the message written in his eyes.

"It's about whatever we want it to be." He tilted her head back against his chest. "Right?"

His voice was warm syrup slowly wrapping her in a sensual cocoon.

Did she know what she was doing? Hell, no, but she wanted to do it anyway. Oh, my God. Was this her?

"I don't know how to do this," she finally answered, their bodies almost still, her cheek pressed against his shoulder. "I have no experience."

The squeeze of his hand told her he knew exactly what she meant.

"You don't need experience, Julia. You just go with the flow."

The combination of the music and the drinks flooded her system with erotic sensations, transporting her into an almost hypnotic state. But his next words both thrilled and shocked her, not because she hadn't been expected them but because she had.

"I want you, Julia."

The words, spoken so quietly she almost missed them, made her body contract, her heartbeat kick into triple time, and her pulse race madly.

"I want to feel your naked body next to mine," he went on. "Touch you everywhere with my hands."

She shivered, heat flooding her, the walls of her cunt fluttering, and her nipples throbbing. She could almost feel his hands on her naked skin. So many conflicting emotions roiled inside her. "I'll bet you say that to all the girls." She attempted to lighten the mood.

His grip on her tightened almost painfully. "Now there's where you're dead wrong. I actually say it to no one these days. And haven't for a long time."

And suddenly, curled against Luke's hard, lean body, she couldn't remember why she'd thought even for a minute this might be a bad idea. She was nearly a free woman and the most exciting man she'd ever met actually wanted her. *Wanted her!* And with an intensity she'd never found with Charles. She was practically jumping into this with both feet, without any hesitation at all.

And somehow she felt a rightness to this, a powerful something pulling her and Luke together.

When the duo announced they were taking a break, Luke led her back to the table, still holding one of her hands. "Are you very hungry?"

"No." She was aware of what he asked. "Are you?"

"Not for food," he told her.

Immediate heat flashed through her body again and the pulse beating in her womb reverberated everywhere inside her. One last alarm bell clanged in her brain. If she didn't stop now, it would be too late. But she could have more easily stopped a runaway train.

"This is more than a whim, you know." His gaze was intense. "I want to be totally clear about this."

"Yes." She could barely get the word out.

He paid their bill with efficient speed and guided her to the elevator. As the car glided smoothly up three floors, he held both of her hands, kissing her lightly as if knowing she needed reassurance.

"It will be fine, Julia." Luke moved his lips to her forehead. "Trust me."

What else could she do?

Chapter 4

Her fingers fumbled so much with the key card Luke finally took it from her and swiped it through the slot. As soon as they entered her room, she began to tremble, and he drew her into his arms. Sheltering her. Reassuring her.

"Are you scared to make love, Julia? Does it frighten you?" He brushed his mouth against hers and pressed his warm palm against her back. "What kind of life do you have where sex is such an enemy?"

Illumination from the outside slanted in through the partially open drapes, providing enough light without turning on the lamps. The darkness made her feel more secure, insulated, but still her mouth couldn't form any words to answer him. She was conscious of his maleness, of the feel of his body against hers, of the unfamiliar heat of desire rushing through her. Feelings she'd never known before gripped her and held her. She stood there, wanting his touch more strongly than she could admit.

"I'm going to kiss you," he said. "We'll take it from there."

Slowly, Luke enfolded her in his arms again and began to stroke her back, to kiss the edges of her ear, the side of her neck, the line of her jaw. They were soft kisses, undemanding, and they eased the edge of her nervousness. His hands were warm; wherever he touched, little sparks of fire burned on her skin. He moved his mouth across her cheek to her lips and touched his mouth to hers in a gentle caress. His lips were strong and soft at the same time.

In moments, gentleness quickly flew out the window. He urged her mouth open, savoring her with his tongue, coaxing her to do the same to him. He tasted of whiskey and maleness, an earthy combination that teased her senses. A jolt of electricity sparked as he probed the hot, dark recesses of her mouth, seeking every inch. His tongue moved over every surface, traced a line across the roof of her mouth, rasped against her own small tongue. A different kind of dance took over, a more sensual one capable of fanning her senses to life. She shook with a kind of need she'd never experienced, and he did nothing more than kiss her.

The kiss went on and on. He licked at her lips, his mouth moving against hers as he slanted it first one way and then another. His large hands, with their long fingers, cupped her head with a touch both gentle and commanding. She could feel the imprint of each finger against her skull. His seduction on the dance floor paled compared to the impact of this kiss. Now Julia knew what it meant to be kissed breathless.

With a mind of their own, her arms crept up his back, pulling him closer, sliding her hands against the soft fabric of his shirt. She was in unfamiliar territory here, operating purely on instinct. Her breasts ached even more, silently begging to be touched and held. Her nipples tingled, fire built between her legs, and she didn't know what to do with it. This was so new to her.

Without releasing her mouth, Luke slid his hands under her sweater, caressing the soft flesh with feather-light touches on her ribs and her spine, tracing lines and drawing patterns as he learned the curves and angles of her body. His fingers branded her every place he touched her as he impatiently drew her sweater over her head.

At last! She sighed with relief.

When his thumbs rasped against her nipples, she felt them harden—a delicious shiver ran through her body. With an easy deftness, he slipped the hooks on her lacy bra, releasing her breasts and cupping them at last in his hands. His lips were voracious on hers and the entire time his hands roamed over her upper body, his mouth never left hers. He kept her welded to him as he fed on her taste, stealing her breath.

He drew patterns on her with light touches of his fingers, caressing each bump and space. Pausing for a moment to skim the upper swell of her ass, he shifted his hand to trace a line up her ribs to her breasts.

Aroused by Luke's stimulating touch and desperate to feel his naked skin, she brought her hands around and opened the buttons on his shirt. Yanking the tails from his trousers, she frantically pushed the garment from his shoulders and down his arms until it fell to the floor. She ran her hands over him, exploring his upper body, wanting to touch him everywhere at once. She skimmed his chest with her fingertips, relishing in the feel of the crisp hair curling on his chest and the hard buttons of his nipples.

The thickness of his cock pressed against her stomach, increasing her own heat. Her legs suddenly grew weak and shaky, and she clung to his lean body for balance. His hands dropped to her waist and slowly unfastened the button on her slacks. The rasp of the zipper sounded loud in the room. As he pushed her slacks down her hips and thighs, he lifted his mouth from hers at last. Lowering his head, he closed his mouth over one taut nipple.

"Ohhh." The tiny cry of pleasure rippled from her throat as his lips tugged and pulled on the hardened bud and his fingers kneaded her soft flesh.

In a frenzy of arousal, Julia unfastened his slacks and shoved at them. Clumsy in her efforts, she made small sounds of frustration as she pushed at the clothing.

Luke finally lifted his head from her breasts, pulling one last, erotic time on a nipple and stepped back to rid himself of his clothes. Kicking his shoes off and yanking away his socks, he knelt in front of her. With careful attention, he tugged her slacks and panties down to her ankles, lifting each foot to step out of them. He pulled off her shoes; then he placed his hands on her hips to hold her steady and pressed his head against her mound, inhaling her scent.

"Ohhh." The pleasure of the sensation spiraled through her.

When he opened the lips of her cunt and licked the sensitive tip of her clit, she thought she would melt to the floor. Only her hands braced on Luke's shoulders kept her upright. Again and again he flicked his tongue over the swollen knot, each stroke making her insides quake and her nerves fire. She felt dampness on the inside of her thighs as Luke's wicked tongue did its work. Inside her, the manacles locking her down released with agonizing slowness and her body unfolded, one delightful burst at a time. Luke moved his tongue lower, tracing the length of her slit with the tip of his tongue. She cried out with pleasure at the sensations whirling through her body. It was too much. It wasn't enough. Stop! No, she wanted more.

She clutched at his shoulders, digging her nails into the skin as he took her higher and higher. When her climax exploded, every muscle spasmed in response. The walls of her pussy clenched over and over again, and her body shook so hard she didn't know if she could remain upright. She collapsed forward, leaning into Luke, held in place by his strong hands. His warm mouth whispered kisses over the softness of her belly as she tried to regain some sense of balance.

"Remarkable." His voice was so deep and sensual. "You are the most responsive woman I have ever known."

She was breathless, unable to answer him.

Luke slow-walked them to the bed and reached for the bedside lamp. Julia stretched out her hand to stop him.

"No. Please. I'm… I've had children… I… I'm not a teenager any more, Luke."

"Thank God. Neither am I." He stroked her cheek gently. "I want to see you, Julia, to look at you. Please. It would give me such pleasure."

Reluctantly, she withdrew her hand and he snapped on the light. She would have crossed her arms to cover herself, but he held them at her sides, his eyes raking her body.

"You're lovely," he whispered, drinking in the sight of her. "Why wouldn't you want me to look? You have nothing to hide. Do you know how sexy you are, what a richness there is to your body?"

"My body leaves a lot to be desired, Luke," she protested, still nervous. "Certainly at my age."

"Not for me, sweet Julia. I could feast on you forever."

Now she allowed herself to look at him, to let her eyes take in every inch of his naked body, and she drew in her breath at the sight. As big as he was, his body was still lean but well-muscled, with silky hair on his arms, and a thick mat of curling hair on his chest. A thin line arrowed down to his groin to the most magnificent erection she'd ever seen. She quaked in anticipation.

He carried her down to the bed with him, his lips tracing a path across her breasts and the roundness of her belly to the soft triangle of curls at the apex of her thighs. He captured her mouth again as his hand moved toward her heat, gently nudging her legs apart. The liquid of arousal trickled from her cunt, and she caught her breath. Her body answered his touch with little coaxing. She loved his strong fingers on her, the heat of his mouth, and the feel of his flesh over hard muscles. He dropped his head lower and flicked his tongue on her nipples, then raked them with his teeth. Her breathing quickened and she arched herself into him.

More, more, more!

The demand echoed in her head. She wanted him to touch her everywhere at once. Kiss every bit of her. When his tongued traced a line even lower, a dark thrill raced through her. He shifted positions and his fingers gently opened the lips of her pussy. One swipe of his tongue across the sizzling knot of nerves made her cry out.

"Luke!"

"Right here, baby," he murmured, his mouth busy on her sex.

He traced the line of her slit, lapping at the moisture gathered there. His teeth tugged gently on her pubic curls before nipping lightly at her labia.

Julia was sure she would burn alive from the heat racing through her. As her mind spun out, her only focus was her center where Luke's mouth performed wonders on her. She forgot to worry, to be nervous, or afraid. All she wanted was more of what he was doing. The walls of her pussy fluttered like leaves in a hurricane, grasping hungrily at Luke's marauding tongue.

An unfamiliar ribbon of hot need coiled low in her belly then unwound slowly, pushing her to a sensuous plateau she hadn't even known existed. When his tongue thrust stiffly inside her wet channel, she cried out again and thrust her hips at him boldly.

Magic beckoned, a starburst waiting inside her to explode and thrust her into space. She reached for it, panted for it, but he held it just out of reach, teasing her, demanding she give everything to him. Breathing fractured, her body strained toward the explosion she needed like she needed her next breath.

Suddenly, he pulled away and rose to his knees. She pried her eyes open, her body quivering at the edge of the precipice he'd taken her to, shocked at the sudden absence of his touch.

"What's wrong?" She barely croaked the words, stunned, wondering if she'd done something wrong.

"Shit." He smacked his forehead. "I am the biggest damn idiot."

"What is it?" She was frightened. Was he changing his mind? Now of all times? "Please tell me."

"I have nothing with me," he said, his voice grating. "I didn't carry anything because I didn't expect to need it."

"Carry what?" She blinked. "I don't understand."

"Protection, damn it." He pushed himself away from her. "I don't want to send you home pregnant. That's the last thing you'd need."

Julia reached out a hand and tugged him back to her, desperate to feel his touch again. "It's okay. I'm like the Boy Scouts, always prepared."

"You're taking birth control pills?"

She shook her head. "Couldn't tolerate them. I have a coil. An intrauterine device. I haven't gotten around to having it removed."

"Thank God," he breathed.

"So there's no worry." She tugged again until he lay against her. Her body shook with a desire beyond anything she'd ever known. "Please, Luke?"

Now there was no stopping, no thinking. He began his movements again, this time with a greater ferocity. She wanted to hurry him, so great was her building need, but he took his time, enjoying every inch of her, every response. He grasped both of her hands in one of his and drew them over her head, stretching her out and forcing her breasts upwards. The way he used his lips, his tongue, his teeth on her nipples drove her mad, creating a new sensitivity in her breasts. Lazily, he trailed kisses the length of her body. When she felt his tongue probing at her quivering folds again, she nearly jackknifed off the bed.

"Easy." Luke's voice was husky with desire. "You taste like fine wine, Julia. I could drink from you all night."

He released her hands and placed both of his on her thighs, holding them open for his exploration. Using his tongue, he traced the length of her slit, teasing the sensitive nub of her clitoris, savoring her hot inner sheath. He lapped at her like an ice cream cone before inserting his tongue inside her pussy and fluttering it. She writhed beneath him, her muscles quaking, heat sizzling in her veins and accelerating her heartbeat. As sparks ignited throughout her body, Julia grabbed his head to steady herself, her fingers tangling in his hair, and her hips rising up to meet him.

"Beautiful Julia." When he lifted his head, she could see her cream glistening on his lips. "I love your skin, your hair, every inch of your body."

His words captivated her. They were like an aphrodisiac, inflaming her even more.

"Talk to me, Julia," he rose up and murmured in her ear. "Tell me what you like. What pleases you, what excites you. Do you like my mouth here?" He nipped at her clit. "My hands here?" One long finger pressed into her warm, waiting heat. "Do you like me to stroke you like this?" He slipped another finger in beside it and began a steady in and out stroke. With his voice he urged her on to a greater and greater state of excitement than she'd known could exist.

Desire built inside her, kindled slowly by Luke's patient, expert touching. His mouth worshipped her cunt, sucking and licking until she was nearly mindless. His hands held her thighs apart so she was wide open to whatever he chose to do. In a moment, his tongue was at her pussy, a wicked instrument of arousal. The tension inside her grew almost unbearable in its force. She both welcomed it and feared it, knowing something was about to happen that would change her expectations forever.

At the moment she thought her heart would stop, he moved over her, pulling her hips toward him, and slowly entered her. His cock was so thick and enormous and she was so tight he stretched her to the fullest. He moved slowly, obviously taking care not to hurt her, sliding in inch by inch. When he was fully inside her, the head of his shaft touching her womb, he began moving in and out in an age-old rhythm.

"Look at me, Julia," he commanded.

She opened her eyes and stared straight into his brown ones, drowning in the hot pools of melted chocolate. Her heart, already thundering loudly, stuttered, and a strange emotion rolled over her. Had she known at the start this was more than sex? More than a frantic coupling? More than a sudden itch they'd decided to scratch? Because that wasn't her, and she certainly didn't know if it was him.

"I feel it, too." His voice was hoarse, with the strain of control and... something else. "Keep your eyes on me. I want to see you when you come, watch the pleasure in your face."

She couldn't have torn her gaze away if she'd wanted to.

Now he increased the tempo, and she moved with him, their bodies slick and sliding against each other. He moved his cock in and out of her wet, grasping heat with a steadily building pace. Inside her body, Julia felt pressure building, fighting to consume her entirely. She hung at the edge of a steep precipice, wanting to leap over but afraid. Something held her back. Then Luke slid his hand between them and touched her clit, hard. And she came, shattering in a cataclysmic convulsion, swirling in space, colors streaking around her, the world spinning, spinning. She could feel the spasms as his own climax peaked and he emptied himself into her.

It seemed to go on and on until she thought they both would die. Finally, he collapsed on top of her, his heart slamming into her ribs in time with the loud beating of her own. They lay together, breathing ragged, until calm finally stole over them and their heartbeats returned to a normal rhythm.

Luke raised his head at last and kissed her lightly, nibbling at her lower lip, then her cheeks and her eyelids.

"Can I tell you how unbelievable you are?" he asked. "And what you do to me?"

"This was magic," she breathed, reaching up to hold his face between her palms. "I didn't know it could be this good."

He eased slowly from her body. "I could ask you what you mean, but I won't. I don't want anything to break the spell. Rest, Julia. I'm not near finished with you. But first, a shower." He brushed his lips over one nipple. "I can't wait to shower with you."

Chapter 5

Julia had never showered with another person, not even at camp or in college. Standing under the warm spray with Luke, feeling his hands slick with soap sliding over her skin, was more erotic than she could have imagined—if she'd been able to imagine it. He cupped her breasts and kneaded them gently before rasping his nails over her nipples and pinching them with a light touch. With tender movements, he stroked his way down her stomach to the nest of curls covering her mound, working lather into them before sliding a finger inside her.

She jerked slightly and he caught her gaze.

"Too sore?"

She shook her head mutely, unable to find words as new waves of pleasure swept through her.

"I love how slick you are," he murmured, working his long fingers in and out of her. "And hot. God, you could burn me alive with your heat."

She wanted to touch him, too, wanted to feel him in her hands. She wrapped her slim fingers around his cock, now swollen and erect again. She loved the feel of the velvet skin over steel, the smoothness of the broad head, the fine hair covering the sac holding his balls.

He sucked in a breath when she manipulated him with wet fingers.

"Careful, sugar. I don't want this party to be over before it starts."

She could hardly believe he'd be ready for her again so soon. Everything with Luke was new and different and exciting. She didn't want to sleep, afraid she'd miss some pleasurable experience.

They never truly slept, dozing now and then between wild bouts of lovemaking. For the first time in her life, Julia felt wanton and uninhibited, as if another person had taken possession of her body. She wanted to pleasure Luke as he had done for her, relishing the feel of his shaft in her hand, the silkiness of his skin, the heaviness of the sacs between his legs. She was tentative at first, but urged on by his cries of passion, she became bolder and bolder.

He took her every way possible, each time more creative and inventive than the last, never allowing her to retreat. Nor did she want to. She was drunk with pleasure, her body constantly demanding more. And the words he kept murmuring to her were exciting words, raw, and erotically stimulating.

She resented the inevitable approach of morning, wanting to push back the hours, and extend the night forever. Lying next to Luke was like bonding with strength, but a strength that protected and cherished. When they finally fell asleep for the last time, they spooned together, one of Luke's legs thrown over both of hers, and she slept dreamlessly.

The ringing of the phone with her wakeup call startled her out of sleep, leaving her at first disoriented. Why was there a warm male body lying next to her? Then every intimate detail of the night flooded her brain. She was immediately aroused and anxious. Would he regret everything that happened? Would she? Would it be uncomfortable? What should she say? Do?

Then she felt Luke's morning erection rising against her bottom and snuggled against it.

"Careful," he told her, his voice still drowsy with sleep. "What you feel could lead to dangerous things."

And so it did, wiping away her anxiety.

There was almost no foreplay this time. They were both ready, as if their bodies knew this would have to last until… Who knew when? Luke simply rolled her to her back, bent her knees back to give him full access, and plunged into her pussy. The wet flesh sucked at him, welcomed him, and held him tight. Again he held her gaze, his liquid eyes boring into hers as he plunged in and out of her slick walls. It seemed like only seconds before they both climaxed, bodies shuddering as spasms gripped them. The walls of her cunt flexed and pulsed as she bathed his cock with her liquid heat.

Spent, they lay wrapped together as they'd done during the night, dragging air into their lungs.

"I don't want to let you go," he murmured, his lips against her ear, his warm breath like a soft breeze against her skin.

"I don't want to go, either. I think I'll call home and tell them the rest of the year has been cancelled," she said in a sleepy voice.

The last thing she wanted to do was get up. Maybe she could close her eyes and wish them into Never Never Land.

His fingers brushed against her cheek. "You haven't said a lot about your situation at home," he told her, "and I didn't want to ask you about it."

"Don't. Let's not spoil this."

"Your husband—"

"Is a pen stroke away from being an ex. And no one I want to bring into this conversation." She nibbled on her lower lip, a nervous gesture she'd picked up in recent years. It suddenly occurred to her Luke hadn't addressed his own matrimonial status. "I didn't even think to ask if you're—"

He shook his head. "This is a discussion meant for another time, and I didn't want to ruin what's happening here by going into the sordid details."

"Please don't—"

He touched a finger to her lips. "I've been divorced for two years. It wasn't pleasant and neither was the marriage. Enough said. For now."

He kissed her, long and slow, his tongue slipping into her mouth and teasing hers to dance with him. Then reluctantly, Julia pulled herself out of bed. She stopped, self-conscious in her nudity with Luke's eyes on her, and he laughed.

"I find it delightfully appealing you can still be shy with me after everything we did." He yanked the top sheet from the bed and wound it around her, brushing her breasts and her hips lightly as he wound the fabric like a sheath. "Go take your shower, then I will. I'd suggest we do it together, but you might never catch your plane."

Heat bloomed on her cheeks as memories of the previous night flooded her brain. "Okay."

When she was showered and dressed, she waved toward the bathroom. "Your turn. Shall I order us some breakfast?"

"Please. I think I could eat a horse."

Julia giggled, a sound nervous even to her own ears. "If they don't have any horses, will bacon and eggs do?"

"Sure."

She grinned at him as she closed the bathroom door.

Once she was dressed and packed, she again felt unsure how to act. Was she supposed to thank him for the most stupendous night of her life? Doing so seemed both stupid and inadequate. Should she apologize for being so wanton? No, that didn't seem quite right either. She was caught between wanting his approval of her as a woman and not earning his disapproval of her where their business was concerned.

While she waffled about it in her whirlpool of insecurity, breakfast arrived. She busied herself setting it up on the little table by the window. When Luke came out of the bathroom in slacks and shirt, he walked over to her and gave her a slow good morning kiss. And when he held her chair out for her to sit down, he brushed her hair away from her face and kissed her neck, then nipped the lobe of her ear. Sitting across from her, he studied her as she buttered her toast and took a small bite.

"You look like heavy thoughts are weighing you down." He paused. "Any regrets?"

Was he nervous, too?

Julia smiled tentatively, memories clanging around in her brain, and again she felt her cheeks heat. "How could there be?"

"Will you be okay when you get home?" he asked her. "I sense you have an unpleasant situation waiting for you."

"Yes. I'll get through Thanksgiving one way or another. Then I'll make sure my attorney gets Charles to sign the final papers so they can be filed...at last." She sighed. "I always feel I'm walking on egg shells around him."

"Why does he continue to create a problem for you? He's already accepted the divorce, right?"

Julia shrugged. "I'm not sure he'll ever truly accept it. Not because he loves me, but because he hates to lose. I have an excellent attorney, and he's gotten me an excellent settlement. I had a very—unsettled—childhood and I'm determined my children won't have to go through what I did. I want security for them. And I don't want to uproot them from the only home they've known."

He studied her face, a question in his eyes.

"Someday I'll tell you about the drama I lived with and the uncertainty. Not now. But I don't want my children to suffer the way I did. Charles will look for any little thing to refuse to sign the final papers and find a way to destroy the agreement in place. My attorney won't let that happen."

Luke reached across the table and put his large hand over her small one. "Be careful, Julia. From what you tell me, one wrong move could put you in an untenable position."

He did his best to put her at ease, drinking coffee, chatting as if they'd done this forever. The intensity of last night's lovemaking still clung to her, reaching out to her like a powerful drug. She wanted nothing more than to crawl back into bed and spend the entire holiday weekend wrapped in his arms, offering him her body, giving and taking pleasure, shutting out the rest of the world. Whatever emotion gripped her last night still clung to her.

She stared down into her coffee cup, her mind whirling. Something nibbled at her, a question she was sure would come out wrong no matter how she phrased it.

"Do you do this often?" she blurted out, then felt the heat creeping up into her cheeks. What an absolutely stupid thing to say. She ducked her head, wishing she could dive under the table. "I'm sorry for saying something so inappropriate, not to mention rude."

"Do what?"

"Nothing." She couldn't look at him. "Forget it."

"Julia." He touched her hand. "You can ask me anything you want. So, do I do what often?"

"Go to bed with a woman the first time you meet her," she mumbled the words into her lap.

His fingers idly stroked across hers. "We didn't go to bed, Julia. We made love. There's a big difference. But if it's important to you, I haven't done either one for a long time." He lifted his coffee cup, watching her over the rim as he drank.

She lowered her eyes. "I can't believe women would leave a man like you alone for long."

"Like me?" He laughed. "Horny? Rich? Sexy? What?"

She felt herself blush again. "I should learn to keep my mouth shut. All I do is keep making things worse. It's… I look at you and…"

"It's fine." His tone softened. He put his coffee cup down, reached across the table, and took one of her hands in both of his. "I'm sorry. I didn't mean to laugh at you. It's a…touchy subject for me."

"I'm sorry I brought it up." She looked down at her empty plate, unable to meet his gaze. She didn't want to see the coldness she was afraid would be there.

"Julia." He got up and came around to her chair, lifting her to her feet. Placing a finger beneath her chin, he tipped her face up to his. His mouth brushed against hers, a light touch at first, then deeper…but not passionate. This was affectionate, reassuring. He threaded his fingers through her hair and gave her lips a light flick with his tongue before lifting his head. "You didn't do anything wrong. It was a perfectly normal question. It reminds me of words my ex-wife threw at me, and not in a good way. So I try to make a joke of it."

"Forget I said anything." She chewed at her lip again. "Please. I don't want to spoil this morning."

He kissed her again. "I'm probably sensitive about it because of… history. And for now I'm not saying any more. But don't beat yourself up. You couldn't spoil anything if you tried."

They ate silently for a moment, and then Julia told him in a quiet voice, "I don't, either." Luke looked at her questioningly. "Fall into bed with someone I've just met."

He reached across the table and wrapped her small hand in his larger one. "If I thought you did, it wouldn't be my bed you'd fall into, and we wouldn't be sitting here having breakfast."

Julia stared down at her plate.

"Julia, something special is happening between us. Let's get that out in the open. This is more than a hot night in the sheets." He leaned toward her. "I can't wait until your divorce is final. I want to see you more. Explore what's happening between us. This is sudden and fast. I mean, Jesus. This time yesterday, we hadn't even met. But I think it could be real. And if you're honest, you'll admit it hit us both the same way, right?"

"Yes." She spoke in a low voice. How did she handle this when her heart jumped at what he was saying? "It scares me."

He wouldn't let her look away. "It scares me too. I don't want to do something stupid and kill it before it even has a chance to get started." He studied her face as if looking for answers. "If we sign this contract, you'll be coming back here again. We'll have time together to see where this goes. We can take a good look at the possibility of taking this to the next level. Sound good to you? Am I being presumptuous?"

"No...yes," she whispered, almost afraid to break the spell. "No, you're not and yes, I want to."

"Then let's get you to the airport so you don't miss your plane."

Luke insisted on driving her to the airport, pointing out the scarcity of taxis the day before Thanksgiving.

"Besides, it means I can prolong going home. We close the offices at noon today and I'd hate to be the only one left."

She didn't want to leave him. Luke was right, what they shared went beyond sex. Was it possible to fall in love with someone so quickly? And now, still wrapped in the glow of their night together, she had to leave him.

"Don't come in with me," she said, when they pulled up to the curb.

"I'm not. I'm terrible with goodbyes."

"I guess you'll call me about the contract?"

"Right after Thanksgiving. If I can't get you at your office, I'll try your cell phone."

"All right. Well, goodbye then."

"Goodbye, Julia." He looked as if he wanted to say something else, then simply held her to him tightly and kissed her, a long deep kiss saying more than words ever could.

Julia finally pulled away, turned, and walked into the terminal.

Chapter 6

The plane was late. Naturally. Murphy's Law. It put Charles in a foul mood that never let up. From the time he picked her up until they reached the house, his criticism ran nonstop.

"There was no need for you to pick me up," she finally snapped. "I told you I made my own arrangements. You're the one who insisted, but it doesn't give you permission to chew my head off. You no longer have the right."

"I do until I sign those papers," he reminded her.

For God's sake. Would she never be able to draw a full breath again?

When he dropped her at the house, she tried to stop him from coming in.

"You'll upset the children with this mood you're in. Please try to remember by tomorrow you are their father and they expect a little affection from you."

He simply ignored her, pulled her suitcase from the trunk, and followed her into the house. It didn't matter anyway. The twins were cranky and whining as soon as she set foot inside. The phone rang incessantly: her in-laws, Claire wanting information on the presentation, and play dates for the twins over the weekend. And Charles stood in the hallway getting on her last nerve, still wearing his coat and complaining yet again about the divorce as Miranda continued to prepare dinner.

"It's too late," she said for the umpteenth time. "It's done. And I honestly wish you'd go home and give me some peace and quiet."

"It's not done yet." He repeated what he'd said in the car, his voice like steel. "And maybe it won't be."

Julia stared at him, weighted down by the block of ice suddenly lodged in her stomach. "You said you'd sign the papers," she whispered.

"Perhaps I've reconsidered." His eyes shone with anger.

She knew it was his pride talking, not emotion, but that made it much worse.

Her head throbbed. "I can't discuss this with you now. I have too much to do, getting your perfect dinner ready for tomorrow. I'll have my attorney call yours on Monday." She turned on her heel and headed for the family room, unable to spend another minute in his presence. Not even a bottle of aspirin would take care of the throbbing in her head tonight.

Thanksgiving dinner was worse than purgatory. Her in-laws, always disapproving of her, carped constantly about her trip, chastised the children if they spilled something, and criticized the food. By the time they left, Julia's headache, building since the previous day, had reached blinding proportions. Miranda handed her a cup of tea and she retreated to the bedroom to lie down with a cold cloth on her head.

Friday, with the dinner behind her and no more menacing conversations with Charles, Julia dared to draw a full breath. Her headache finally abated, and she was beginning to think Charles was just making unnecessary noise. She dropped the twins at her friend's house and allowed herself the luxury of a day hanging out in her sweats and curling herself into the warmth of the memories of Luke.

On Saturday, she took the twins to see Santa Claus then out for lunch at McDonald's, where they could exhaust themselves in the PlayPlace. The glow from her night with Luke stayed with her throughout the rest of the weekend, memories she allowed herself to indulge in. By Monday, she allowed herself to hope Charles would sign the final papers quickly and she could get on with her life.

"Next time, you can stay home and I'll go on the trip," Claire said, grinning when Julia walked into the office. A blonde collection of high-energy molecules, she was a good foil for Julia. They balanced each other in both looks and temperament.

Julia lifted an eyebrow. "And you say this because?"

"Because then I'd get the phone calls from the guy with the sexiest voice in America."

Julia turned away, afraid Claire would spot some telltale sign on her face. A blush, at the very least. "I have no idea what you're talking about."

"If you say so, kiddo." Claire's voice held a hint of amusement. "But Luke Buchanan's called three times. He wants you to call him back as soon as you get in."

"It's business," Julia said, hoping to derail whatever Claire was thinking. "And I think it's good news. He told me they'd probably make a decision this week whether to sign with us or not. Maybe they met this morning. It's an hour later there, you know."

"Here's for luck." Claire held up crossed fingers.

Julia went into her private office and picked up the phone, then put it down. This was just a business call. Nothing more. She needed to pull herself together and act like the professional she was.

She looked at the number written on the message slip Claire gave her. The only thing familiar was the area code. Was this his private number? When she dialed and he answered himself, she'd guessed right.

"Luke Buchanan."

"Good morning. This is Julia."

"Good morning."

She promised herself she would be strictly professional when they spoke, but the deep, warm sound of his voice sent shivers along her spine. Instantly, the image of their naked bodies tangled together in bed came unbidden to her mind.

"Claire told me you called earlier."

"I did." She could hear the smile in his voice. "How was your holiday?"

"It was...as expected." The less said about it, the better.

Luke laughed a full, rich sound. "Well, that could mean a lot of things. Did you enjoy yourself?"

Like having a root canal without anesthetic.

"It was tolerable." *Liar!* "And you?"

"I could say 'as expected' also."

She visualized him, imagined him in his office, his big body loose in a desk chair, shirt sleeves rolled back as they'd been Tuesday night. The vision of his face nearly undid her.

"Well, I guess we've taken care of the pleasantries." Now she was laughing, and suddenly she felt easy, relaxed. He was like a balm to her tightly strung nerves.

"I hope not," he told her. "I'm hoping this entire conversation will be pleasant." He paused. "We signed the contract this morning. Everyone agrees it's exactly what we need and you've hit on the mood we want to project."

"Oh, Luke, how wonderful." She wanted to leap from the chair and dance. This was their biggest contract yet. "We'll do a great job for you."

"I expect you to. I've seen what you've done before and I have a lot of faith in your work."

"If you could fax the contract to us, we'll sign it and get it right back to you. Then we can get started fleshing out the outline right away."

"It's on the way right now. But will you be able to get much done with the Christmas holidays coming up?"

"Oh, yes. Claire and I will work on it this afternoon and tomorrow. Then I'll call you with some specifics. But we'll kick into high gear after New Year's."

"Can you get away for a couple of days next week?" He cleared his throat. "I'd like you to see the plant and meet the folks who work there, plus see the samples of the new line. With March as our first target date, I don't want to waste any time."

Get away? Was he kidding? How about right now?

"I think I can make arrangements." Her stomach twisted when she thought of Charles discovering she was once again leaving town. But she'd see Luke again. Oh, God. She'd have to call her attorney and have him force Charles to sign the papers right away.

"Fine. See if you can work it out to be here next Tuesday and stay until Thursday. Call me when you've made your arrangements." He was silent again. "I miss you, Julia."

"I miss you, too," she whispered, so softly she wasn't sure he could even hear her.

But then he answered. "Good." He paused. "How is...everything else?"

The divorce.

"I'm calling my attorney as soon as I hang up. Charles has sidestepped this long enough. I want those papers signed now."

"Will you be okay in the meantime?"

"Yes. I can handle things." She smiled to herself. "And next week, I'll see you."

He clicked off and she sat at her desk, the receiver still in her hand, her heart beating a little faster.

"And exactly what kind of business arrangement did you say this was?"

Julia hadn't even heard Claire open the door, much less enter the tiny office.

"They bought the package," she said, grinning hugely. "We got the contract."

"I know." Claire leaned in the doorway. "I came to tell you the paperwork came through on the fax, but I guess you already know."

"Yes." She opened her day planner and began turning pages. "We need to block out some time together today and tomorrow to go over the outline. They'd like me to come out there again next week."

Claire dropped into the chair in front of the desk. "By 'they,' I assume you mean Luke Buchanan?"

"Well, yes. I mean, he is the executive vice president and the one who would give it the thumbs up."

Claire looked at her for a long time before she spoke again. "We've been friends for what seems like forever, Julia. I love you more than if we were sisters. I don't know what went on in suburban Massachusetts, but you can't hide much from me."

"Claire, I…"

"No. Let me finish. You know what I think about Charles. What I've always thought about him. You have to get him to sign the final papers before he smells something and screws it all up. The faster the divorce is final, the better off you'll be. And I guarantee you it will be better for the children."

Claire was right about their friendship. They'd bonded as college roommates and were attendants at each other's weddings. Claire and her husband were the twins' godparents. And she'd been Julia's rock of support, her confessor, and her comforter through the whole nasty mess. Many days, Julia wasn't sure she would have survived without her friend. Charles was never one of Claire's favorite people and was always aware she detested him for the way he treated Julia.

"I'm calling my attorney right now. Charles still hasn't signed the divorce papers and I'm tired of playing this game."

Claire raised an eyebrow. "What in God's name is it for this time?"

Julia shrugged. "He thinks he can talk me into calling off the whole thing."

Claire's eyes widened. "Is he crazy?"

Julia sighed heavily. "I think so. Probably. I just want this done. Finally. I'm calling Harry Whitaker right now."

"Be careful, sweetheart." Claire's voice carried a warning tone.

"About what? What can he do? He's not going to shoot me."

"Texas law says a man can get a divorce on the grounds of adultery. If there's anything going on between you and Luke Buchanan, and Charles finds out, technically you're still married to him and he can tear up the whole agreement. He can divorce you on his terms."

Julia picked up the phone. "Harry needs to put some muscle into this thing."

"I'm running out of patience, too," Harry told her when he answered the phone. "I'll see if we can't get this finished in the next day or two."

"I want it over with, Harry," she told him.

"As good as done," he assured her.

But even after she hung up, an uneasy feeling wiggled through her system.

* * * *

The next day, she called Luke to tell him she was set for the trip.

"I'm making plans to arrive Tuesday morning. I'll call you back as soon as I make the reservations."

"The company will take care of those, Julia." His voice was firm. "I'll have my secretary arrange things today."

"I'll handle it," she protested. "We're going to be making money on this."

"Don't worry. We can afford it. Besides, I was the one who asked you to make this extra trip. And I'll pick you up at the airport myself."

"Won't people wonder if you do?" She fidgeted. "I don't want to put you in an uncomfortable position."

"Not to worry. I've already mentioned I'd be taking you to the plant to look around. It's much more convenient to leave directly from Boston than to come here first, so they'd expect me to meet you. Relax. We're all business."

But she could hear the smile in his voice.

"Uh huh. If you say so." She smiled herself. "Okay. I'll see you next week."

She hung up the phone, elated, and leaned back in her chair, her eyes far away, and the smile still on her face. How was it possible to feel this way about a man after spending less than twenty-four hours with him? Was she deluding herself? Was Luke just fascinated with her—an equally improbable idea—and she the one making too much of it? She mentally shrugged. It was what it was, and soon they'd be together again.

She was still sitting there, dreamy-eyed, when Claire wandered in.

"Mm-hmm. Do I sniff another phone call with the sexy voice?"

"Business, Claire." Julia waved a hand in the air. "Nothing more than business."

"This is me, honey." Claire laughed, a knowing look on her face. "You might convince someone else but I know you too well. So what's the word today? Are we set for the rollout campaign?"

"I'm going up there for three days next week," Julia said, suddenly busy with folders on her desk.

Claire cleared her throat. "Uh, Julia? What did Harry say about the signing?"

"He's confident we can complete this by tomorrow." She mentally crossed her fingers.

"I sure hope so, kiddo. If he does, I'll be treating you to a celebration like you've never seen before." Claire went over to her friend and hugged her tightly. "Enjoy yourself next week, Julia. You've earned some happiness."

But that afternoon a phone call from Harry gave her a prickle of unease.

"Charles is out of town until next Tuesday," he told her.

"What?" Her fingers tightened on the telephone and she felt as if someone dropped a chunk of ice into her stomach. Did he think this was some kind of punishment? That he could dangle the carrot forever until she changed her mind? "Harry, I—"

"I know, I know," he interrupted. "I said everything to his attorney. But I promise you I'm over it. I muscled the attorney and told him to quit mucking around or we'd go back to court and ask for even more."

Julia allowed herself a tiny laugh. "At least it's nice to contemplate. I'm getting tired of this, Harry. We don't really need his signature. It just makes it a lot neater. I know we agreed it would be best if we could just do this without any more ripples, but it's getting ridiculous. If he refuses to sign let's just get a date, go to court, and get the judge to sign the decree."

Harry's sigh carried to her over the connection. "We could, Julia. Keep in mind, though, we're up against some formidable opponents here. You're not a stupid woman by any means. You know how things work. I like to think I have clout, but Charles's law firm practically owns the judicial system in the state. They dump a ton of money into political campaigns. People do 'favors' for each other. A judge could stall it for any number of trumped up reasons."

"How nice that we have a system where the judges have to run for office." She couldn't keep the bitterness out of her voice.

"Yeah, but they do. It's a fact of life. Unfortunately."

There was a soft knock on her door, it opened, and Claire poked her head into the office. Julia motioned her to come in.

She tightened her grip on the phone. "I guess that's my punishment for making a poor choice to begin with." Damn Charles and his privileged circle, anyway. Damn them to hell. "Listen, I'll be gone for three days next week, but I'll keep in touch by phone."

"Try not to worry. I'll do my best to close the deal while you're gone."

Not worry? Hah! She was sure she'd worry about it enough to give herself a stress headache and make her nerves raw.

"I didn't mean to overhear, but Julia, I swear." Claire shoved her fingers through her curls in exasperation. "I don't know why the hell you let him get away with this. He's a bully who enjoys yanking your chain." She blew out a breath. "I thought Harry was a shark who ate people like Charles for breakfast."

Julia fiddled with a pen on her desk. "He is. I've been trying to keep this as simple as possible. Not irritate him any more than he already is. To get it over with."

"Simple? Over with?" Claire threw up her hands. "Honey, it's been anything but simple. And it's still not over. That asshole has practically made you beg for everything. What the hell has Harry been doing? He should have gone after him with a jackhammer."

"Harry got him out of the house," she reminded her friend, "and worked out the custodial arrangements for the twins the way I wanted them. Charles can't just pop in and ask for them on a whim."

Claire made an unladylike noise. "The only reason he even takes them on his appointed days is because he knows it pisses you off. He doesn't have to worry about winning the Father of the Year Award."

"He can't stick his nose in my business any more, either," Julia said, aware how defensive she sounded.

"Yeah?" Claire studied her face. "How's that working out for you?"

"Fine." Her voice was flat and they both knew she was lying.

Julia worried all week, imagining any number of disasters. Every time the telephone rang, she expected it to be Charles ready to pounce on her for something. Or Luke changing his mind. Or Harry telling her Charles changed his mind. Not to mention the fact time dragged interminably as she counted off the days, one by one. She and Claire spent two days brainstorming the Hot Ticket campaign, an exercise which thankfully forced her to focus. The rest of the time, however, her mind was like a restless nomad, wandering into dangerous territory.

She was a bundle of nerves counting off the days.

Monday night, she packed and unpacked at least three times, then decided to take a bigger suitcase and throw everything on her bed into it. She simply couldn't make a choice. She read the twins a story after dinner, tucked them into bed, and went to bed herself.

The next day couldn't come soon enough for her.

Chapter 7

Luke waited for her at the baggage carousel, ruggedly handsome in his charcoal suit with a dark overcoat folded over one arm. A warm smile creased his face and his eyes danced as he spotted her. She simply couldn't help herself. She threw herself into his arms.

"Hey," he greeted in a soft voice. "I'm glad to see you, too."

He held her so tightly she thought her breath would leave her. He felt so good to her, and his scent wrapped itself around her in a delicious cloud. She'd remembered it every day since the last time she'd seen him.

"I've probably embarrassed you in front of the entire city of Boston." She laughed, pulling back.

"Maybe only half of it," he joked. "Don't worry. They'll tell the other half."

Driving away from the airport, she couldn't get enough of looking at him, staring at his face, memorizing it. Although aviator sunglasses now hid the warm brown eyes and thick lashes she remembered, her gaze took in every line of his face, the strong jaw, and broad forehead. Sunlight glinted on the faint threads of silver in his thick brown hair. He was freshly shaven, and she inhaled the spicy scent of his aftershave.

He reached a hand over to her and she took it, lacing her fingers through his. It felt so good being with him again. Just his nearness made her feel warm and giddy, almost like a teenager. She could hardly believe she was finally here, sitting next to him, touching him.

He squeezed her hand. "I've missed you, Julia. Tell me you missed me a little bit."

"You know I have. More than a little. I feel like it's been forever since we were…together."

"Well, I have a little surprise planned for later I hope will make up for it."

"Oh, good." She sat up straighter. "I love surprises. What is it?"

He laughed the full-throated laugh she loved so much. "If I told you now, it wouldn't be a surprise, now would it?"

And no matter how much she begged and teased, he just smiled and shook his head.

They headed away from Boston, the crowded city soon falling away to a suburban landscape. The landscape was pure New England winter. Pristine white drifts mounded against mostly brick houses and decorated the bare branches of the trees. The brilliance of the sunlight glinted off the surface, making everything look fresh and new.

The plant was just at the edge of a tiny hamlet called Livingston, a two-story brick building with wide windows on both floors.

"We like to give our employees a lot of natural light." Luke gestured at the cars in the parking lot. "Most of the town works here in one capacity or another, and we want to keep them happy."

The plant manager waited for them in the lobby. Behind him, a small reception committee barely concealed the nervousness prompted by a visit from the executive vice president. But Julia watched Luke put everyone at ease, and the tour progressed in a relaxed atmosphere. Lunch was served to them in a corner of the cafeteria.

"I'm sorry," the plant manager apologized to Julia, "but we don't have a conference room or formal dining room of any kind." He looked at Luke and grinned. "The boss says this is a no frills operation."

"As it should be," Julia said. "I'm impressed with the efficient way everything runs. Besides, cafeteria food is my secret vice."

She was amazed she and Luke were able to maintain their professional poise with the sexual tension vibrating between them throughout the day. She worried people would sense it, people who worked for Luke. She couldn't let them speculate on something potentially damaging to him. Once she caught him looking at her, a tiny grin teasing at his lips, and she ducked her head, turning to look away.

At the end of the tour, the plant manager presented her with a Hot Ticket sports bag filled with items bearing the corporate logo. He included samples of the new lines they'd be producing.

"Thank you." She smiled. "Having these things in front of me will help us as we work through the project."

"It was a pleasure having you here today." He held out his hand. "Everyone's excited about the new campaign."

"As are we." She shook hands with him. "My partner and I will be doing our absolute best for you. We're excited about it, too."

She waited as Luke chatted with the man for a few minutes. Then he ushered her back to his car and they drove away. She leaned her head back against the seat and blew out a breath.

"You did great." Luke reached for her hand. "They love you, no big surprise there." He gave her a gentle squeeze. "You're a pro."

"I enjoyed meeting everyone, and the operation is quite impressive." She stretched her legs out. "Are we heading to the hotel now? Are we having dinner there?"

"Not exactly."

"What does not exactly mean?"

"This is where my surprise comes in."

She could hear the smile in his voice along with... Was that a touch of nervousness, too? Luke, nervous? "Don't worry. I told you I like surprises. But how soon will I get to see it?"

"Just relax. I'll give you a little commentary on the Massachusetts countryside and pretty soon we'll be where we're going."

He drove at a leisurely pace along the narrow country highway, pointing out towns they passed. Some were little more than four corners with a general store and gas station. They'd driven for about an hour when he turned off the highway onto a recently-plowed narrow lane and followed it to a clearing.

"Okay." He turned off the engine and put the car in park. "We're here."

Julia stared out the window. A tiny, perfectly shaped log cabin, with a peaked roof and a tall chimney, stood like a jewel in the drifts of unspoiled snow. Evergreens draped in the same snow looked as if moments ago a painter daubed them with his brush. The scene held her enthralled, reminding her of something from Currier and Ives.

"Where are we?" She couldn't take her eyes away from the scene. "Who owns this place?"

"I do." Luke grinned. "Care to come inside?"

Julia was dumbstruck when she walked into the cabin, which turned out to be one huge room. The walls and floor were polished to a high gloss and beams crisscrossed overhead below the peak of the ceiling. One corner of the area was set up as an efficient kitchen while bookshelves and a stereo filled part of one wall. Julia assumed the only inside door led to a bathroom.

A tiny breakfast set, a long couch, two deep chairs, and a king-size bed covered in a traditional quilt took care of the furniture needs. The colors in a thick rug brought warmth into the room, and an inviting fire was laid in the fireplace.

"This is fantastic!" she said. "I feel like I stepped into *Little House on the Prairie*. How did you happen to buy it and what do you use it for?"

"Later." He took her coat and hung it on a hook by the door. "First we relax." He took out glasses, a bottle of amaretto, and a bottle of Canadian Club from a kitchen cupboard. "See." He grinned. "I even remembered what you like to drink." He poured a generous portion into each glass, added Coke to his and ice to both, then handed Julia's to her. "A toast. To us."

"To us," she agreed in a soft voice. She hoped.

They touched glasses and Julia sipped at the smooth liquid, feeling it warm her blood and ease her tension.

"We have steaks for later but we don't need to hurry." He winked at her. "I thought we might find something to amuse ourselves before dinner."

So what now? Did she even know how to do this? Was she supposed to make polite chitchat first while they sipped their drinks, or did they just rip their clothes off and dive into bed? Last time it had happened so naturally she didn't have to think. This was different. Planned. How was she supposed to behave?

Luke picked up on her nervousness. "Did I presume? If this is not what you want, tell me now and I'll take you to the hotel. No harm, no foul."

"No. I mean, yes." She was stammering and she took a deep breath to pull herself together. "You didn't presume at all. I want this too."

He handed her a box from the counter. "I thought you might like this to change into after a long day. It's one of the outfits we shipped a lot of this winter. Usually, there's a logo of your favorite football team on the sleeve, but I don't even know if you like football, so I snagged a plain one."

She opened it and caught her breath. Nestled in tissue paper was an outfit of the softest navy blue fleece.

"It's beautiful." She ran her fingers over the material. "And I love football."

"You look good in blue." He smiled. "You wore blue the night we were…together, and looked terrific in it. Anyway, I figured you might like something comfortable to change into."

"Oh, Luke, thank you for being so thoughtful." She blew him a kiss.

He reached into his pocket and drew out a small box. "I got you something else which I hope you'll wear." He opened it to display a tiny fir tree dusted with snow. When he lifted it out Julia saw that it had a slender chain drawn through a tiny loop at the peak. "Can I put this on you?"

Emotion clogged her throat, preventing speech, so she nodded her head. His fingers trembled against the nape of her neck when he fastened the clasp.

She touched the place where the charm rested against the hollow of her throat and blinked back tears. "Thank you. I don't think I'll ever take it off."

"You could always tell people you bought it yourself."

"I don't have to tell them a damn thing." She drew in a calming breath. She could wear whatever she wanted. Now. "And it means I will have you close to my heart every day and night."

He pressed a soft kiss to her lips. "That's exactly why I got it. A taste of New England and memories of this night."

Julia wanted to take this moment and freeze it in time.

"Now." Luke took a step back and gestured at the box holding the sweats. "Well? Let's see how the outfit looks on you."

"Of course." She set her glass on the counter. "I...I'll just be a minute."

She disappeared into the bathroom, grateful for the chance to freshen up. When she looked at herself in the mirror she saw a woman flushed with sexual arousal and something else. Happiness. She reached up and touched the tiny charm, knowing it would be her talisman until the business of the divorce was settled. God, why couldn't it all be over now?

She smiled as she noted the scented soap and fluffy towels he'd set out for her. As she folded her clothes and set them on the edge of the tub, she gave in to a naughty urge and stripped off her thong and bra, too, slipping them beneath the jacket of her pants suit.

In for a penny, in for a pound.

The two-piece outfit felt as soft as an angel's kiss against her skin as she drew it on, and when she looked in the mirror over the sink, she realized Luke was right. The blue did bring out the brilliance of the color in her eyes. A quick brush through her hair and a swipe of lip gloss, one last look in the mirror, and she was ready.

Deep breath, Julia.

She returned to the room to find a fire crackling in the fireplace. Music played softly on the stereo and Luke, half sitting, half lying on the couch, watched her with hungry eyes. He'd removed his jacket and tie and rolled up the sleeves of his shirt. She loved the play of muscle in his arms and the glint of the firelight on the dark hair of his arms.

"Well?" She twirled in front of him. "What do you think?"

A slow, languid smile spread over his face. "Gorgeous. Just as I expected. How do you like it?"

"I love it." She smoothed a hand over the fabric. "It's like being wrapped in a feathery blanket. No wonder you sold so many of them."

Luke put his drink down, stood up, and took her hand. "Dance with me." He pulled her easily into his arms, nestling her head against his shoulder, their linked hands folded between them. They moved slowly, almost in place, in the same rhythm they'd been caught up in the last time.

Here in this cabin in the middle of nowhere, surrounded by snow and pine trees, warmed by the fire, and lulled by the music, she felt the world fall away. The rest of her life fell away and for the first time since her morning arrival at the airport she relaxed, tension sliding away from her body like a cloak someone thoughtfully removed.

"You smell wonderful," Luke murmured in her ear. "I wish I could have bottled your scent and kept it with me to open every now and then." He pressed her to him tightly. "God, you don't know how much I've missed you, Julia. One night together and I couldn't get you out of my head."

"I missed you, too," she said, feeling the steady thud of his heart against her.

"Did you bewitch me, Julia?" His lips moved against her hair. "Did you cast a spell?"

Her laugh was unsteady. "I'm not sure I'd know how."

"Oh, I think with you, no knowledge is even required."

His words made her feel giddy, excited. It was the kind of nervous energy one got from dancing on a thin wire.

Luke kissed her forehead, then her cheek, sliding his mouth until he found her lips. Gently he pressed his tongue until she opened for him and met him with her tongue. The kiss went on and on as if they were fused together, sensations of heat cascading through her body. The music drifting into the room was a counterpoint to the pounding of her pulse.

Luke slid his hands beneath the knitted band of the top, drawing a sharp breath when he realized she had not put her bra back on.

"Tempting me already?" His voice was just a tiny bit unsteady.

"Hoping to." Hers was underscored with the same slightly shaking timbre.

He cupped her bare breasts in his warm hands, caressing the soft flesh, lightly rubbing his thumbs across the nipples. They hardened almost painfully at the contact, and the same needy ache she'd felt the first time he'd touched her sizzled through her again. He gently squeezed the flesh of those mounds, his palms bearing their weight. His touch was so exquisite she could barely stifle the tiny moan vibrating in her throat.

As they danced, he continued to stroke her breasts, rubbing them, and teasing her nipples. The fire he'd lit in the fireplace was nothing compared to the one he ignited deep inside her. He brushed tiny kisses over her forehead, down the side of her face, along the column of her neck. He moved his mouth everywhere, tasting the sensitive spot on her neck that made her nerves tingle, trailing kisses along the line of her jaw, dusting her eyelids. His swollen cock pressed against her like heated steel and desire surged through her, enveloping her in a scorching grip.

The touch of his hand as he skimmed her ribs and the flat of her tummy and slipped into the waistband of her pants liquefied her bones. His caresses were like magic, turning every part of her body into an erogenous zone. And when he cupped her buttocks, sliding his fingers into the warm cleft between the cheeks she caught her breath on a rush of need. Another moan escaped her. A sigh. The more he drew his fingers through that hot place, the more rapid her breathing grew. Every pulse point throbbed with hunger, every sensitive spot begged for his attention. She wanted his touch everywhere before she exploded with need.

When at last he moved the hand around to touch her between her legs, she gasped at the electric shock coursing through her.

"You're wet." His voice was almost guttural. "Slick. Very slick. And your sweet pussy lips are so swollen, Julia. I remember how they looked when we were together, the lamplight glowing on their deep pink color, your little clit so swollen and just peeping out."

His words stimulated the nerves in the walls of her cunt, making the flesh quiver with need and anticipation. She clung to his arms, steadying herself against the erotic onslaught. When he probed her folds with one finger, her pussy clenched around him and she made a strangled sound in her throat.

"You're killing me," she moaned.

"But it's so sweet, isn't it? So hot and wet inside. You grip my finger the way you grip my cock. You like my fingers inside you."

She could barely nod her head. Her bones were already turning liquid and her muscles threatened to give out on her.

Luke withdrew his hand and licked his fingers, eyes darkening. "Sweet," he repeated. "The best taste there is. *Yours* is the best."

Despite the trembling in her fingers, she managed to undo his buttons, her gaze locked with his as he continued to run the tip of his tongue over his fingers. His nostrils flared as he inhaled the scent of her sex. He laughed softly when she fumbled with the fabric of his shirt, yanked it out of his slacks, and tossed it aside. His breath hissed at the touch of her fingers on his chest. God, she loved the silky feel of the thick matte of hair and the hardness of the muscle beneath.

When she skimmed her fingers over his nipples, he wrapped his own fingers around hers and pressed them hard against his chest. She was thrilled she could arouse him so quickly and easily. Experimentally, she dragged her fingernails over the flat buds, then put her lips around one of them.

Luke grabbed her shoulders, his grip almost bruising in its possession.

"Careful." His voice was hoarse with rising hunger. "I want to make this last for you, but I've been on the edge wanting you since you left here."

Julia looked up at him. "But I love touching you. Feeling how you respond to me."

"We'll have plenty of time for me. This is for you." Gently he moved her hands to her sides. They'd stopped dancing and stood still, the firelight warming them, the music weaving a soft cocoon of sound around them.

Sliding the soft fleece of the pants past her hips and thighs, he knelt to help her step out of them as he'd done in the hotel room.

* * * *

Jesus!

His dick was rock hard, vibrating with the blood flowing through its veins and begging for the soft feel of Julia's hands, mouth, and incredible pussy. He skimmed his hands over her velvet-soft skin, gritting his teeth to hang on to his rapidly fraying control. More women than he liked to think about had passed through his life—probably far too many—but none had ever affected him like Julia Patterson. With her, everything was new and fresh. He felt like a different person. It was just as he'd told her before. This wasn't sex. This was making love.

He wanted to take her every way possible. Plunge into every opening of her body and fuck her until she didn't even know her own name, taste every inch of her body until it gave up its secrets. He wanted things with her he'd never wanted with anyone else.

He pressed his face against her soft pubic curls and inhaled her scent, the tang of it flowing through his system. Prying open the lips of her cunt, he exposed her clit and pulled it into his mouth. Julia balanced herself with her hands on his shoulders. When he grazed her tender knot with his teeth, her body shook and delicious sounds of pleasure exploded from her lips.

He licked in earnest, pulling her labia back further to expose the slick pink flesh of her slit. He feasted on it, lapping and sucking, using his thumb to keep her clit in a constant state of arousal. Her entire body was trembling now as he ran his tongue over her sensitive flesh and drank in her sweet cream.

The moment he slid two fingers into the hot well of her vagina she climaxed, clenching around his fingers. A low throaty sound vibrated from her, body convulsing, fingers digging into him as she desperately tried to maintain her balance. He stroked in and out and sucked again on her clit until he'd wrung the last drop from her.

Then he rose, pulling her against him tightly and pressing his mouth to hers so she could taste herself on his lips.

"I love you," he murmured against her open mouth. "It's quick, it's fast, but I know what I feel."

"M-Me, too." Her voice trembled as much as her body did.

"Good." He lifted his head to smile at her. "It's always nice when it works out that way."

He broke away from her long enough to toss some of the pillows from the couch onto the floor, then laid her down on them in front of the fire. He felt his groin tighten even more as he looked at her naked in the firelight, flushed and wanton. She was sated, yet the message in her eyes plainly told him she wanted him again.

With swift movements, he discarded the rest of his clothes and lowered his naked body to the cushions next to hers.

* * * *

Julia lay there, warmed by the flames and the look of pure desire in Luke's eyes. She was too aroused to even care her body might be less than perfect for him. Watching him shed his clothes, she trembled in anticipation of his touch again, the feel of his body against hers. Her hands itched for the solid feel of his muscles, the crisply curling hair on his chest, the thickness of his visibly engorged shaft. An unfamiliar sensation gripped her, one she couldn't ever remember feeling. Pure lust.

Lordy! He'd just brought her to a climax so instantaneous there was barely time to catch her breath, yet here she was craving him again. More cream seeped from her pussy at the images conjured up in her mind.

In seconds, Luke's mouth was on hers again, a voracious kiss drawing from deep within her soul. She felt his hands skimming her body, lightly touching her everywhere. Without urging, she opened her legs for him, felt him cupping her mound, opening her folds, sliding first one, then two fingers into her again. She moaned and moved against his hands.

"You feel so good," he whispered. He moved his moistened fingers down into the cleft of her buttocks again, rubbing them against the skin in the hot, tight place. Placing his lips on her already swollen and sensitive bud, he sucked and nibbled as he slid and probed, and her nerves exploded like firecrackers.

"Easy, easy," he crooned, withdrawing his hand and placing one of hers on his throbbing erection. "See what touching you does to me?" She closed her fingers around him and he pulsed in response. "I want to make this last for you, sweet Julia, but I want you too badly."

"Please," she begged, moving her hand up and down on him. "Don't wait." She wanted to feel him inside her again, feel the length of him filling her, stretching her. Her body ached for the fulfillment he gave her.

He pulled her hand away, moved over her to position himself, and thrust slowly. At last he was inside her, and it was the most incredible feeling in the world. She was so ready for him he was buried to the hilt almost at once. He probed her mouth with his tongue, mimicking the movements of his body as he drove slowly in and out of her. She clutched at him, raking his back with her fingernails. Their bodies were slick with sweat, skin sliding against skin.

"More," she cried. "More. More, more." In an agony of frustration, she moved her hips against him, trying to draw him in deeper. She was so close, almost there, hanging on the edge. "Harder. Please. Please."

"Julia."

She opened her eyes wide to look at him, saw the tension in his face, the sweat beading his forehead. Their gazes locked and she felt as if he stared right into her soul. Her tremors intensified, her sheath grasping at his hot shaft. With a hoarse cry, he gave her the release she sought and carried them over the edge. Waves of pleasure washed over her body, intensified by spasm after spasm. Julia clenched around him, milking him, as he poured into her, filling her. On and on it went, until she thought her heart would stop altogether.

Finally, spent, skin slicked with sweat, they collapsed in a tangle of boneless limbs.

Julia didn't know how long they lay there. The weight of his body on her was heavy, but nothing could have induced her to move him. She had the feeling something momentous had just happened. And, in fact, it had. Even more than the one night they'd spent together, she'd given herself completely to Luke Buchanan.

"Jesus." He barely raised his head. "You make me wish I was sixteen again." He touched his forehead to hers.

As they lay there, waiting for their breathing to return to some semblance of normal, she was stunned to realize what began their first night in the hotel had now blossomed into something real.

"I've been thinking about this since the last minute we were together," Luke told her.

"Me, too." She bit her lower lip. "I can't seem to shut my brain off."

He held her to him in a tight grip. "Mine, Julia. No matter what. You'll always be mine. Do those words scare you?"

"Maybe. A little. I don't know." She drew a shaky breath. "How did we get here so fast? What's happening to us, Luke?"

"I don't know. It just sort of snuck up on us, I guess." He looked at her. "We have to talk about it, you know."

She nodded. "I want to."

He stood up and reached a hand out to her. "But first, I'm famished. I think I worked up a good appetite."

Julia grinned at him. "I'd say so."

Luke threw on jeans and a T-shirt he pulled from a dresser drawer and began taking things out in the little kitchen area. In the bathroom, Julia found a washcloth to clean herself then slipped the soft fleece outfit back on. She carried her drink to the kitchen table where she sat watching him broil steaks and slice tomatoes. They kept conversation light as they ate, and after Luke cleaned up, they took their drinks and sat in front of the fire.

"How is it you have a cabin way up here in the middle of nowhere?" she asked.

"It's a long story. And messy. Are you sure you want to hear it?"

"It's about you, and I want to know everything I can about you." She leaned against him, cuddling against his body when he put his arm around her.

He took a long swallow of his drink. "Long story short, my marriage began to fall apart the day after the ceremony and I never quite figured out why. Not even two children could patch the cracks." He finished the drink. "Then I found out my wife was sleeping with every willing candidate she could find. If it had a pulse, she fucked it."

"Oh, Luke." The pain in his voice sliced through her, and she wished she knew what she could do to ease it.

"I wanted to keep things together because of my boys. I have two sons who are very important to me, despite the fact my ex does her best to turn them against me."

"It's always hard when kids are caught up in a bad situation." And didn't she just know that.

"I changed corporations twice, always moving up. I might be a failure at marriage, but not in business. Somehow, I have a knack for looking at a company and figuring out what it needs to do to remain profitable and increase the bottom line. When Hot Ticket recruited me to be executive vice president, I thought it would give us a fresh start."

"It didn't?"

"No, and it was important to do something before everyone in the company knew about it. Even though the boys were only nine and fifteen I couldn't let things go on one minute longer. So I filed for divorce and sent her back to Alabama with the kids."

"But you get to see them, right?"

He shrugged. "As often as I can work it out. My ex is not exactly too accommodating," He rubbed a hand over his face. "I can feel them slipping away from me every time I see them, but there doesn't seem to be much I can do about it. She's done her best to poison their minds against me."

"Oh, Luke." Tears burned her eyelids.

"I bought the cabin shortly after we got here, as a place I could go to hide from everything." He rose and looked down at her. "No one's ever been here with me except you. It's important you know that."

His words made something pull at her heart. He'd deliberately chosen to share his most private space with her, something she took as a gift.

"I'm glad." She smiled up at him. "And thank you."

One corner of his mouth turned up. "I sound disgustingly sorry for myself, don't I?"

"No." She shook her head. "Just painfully lonely and shortchanged by life."

He fixed himself another drink and sat down beside her again, staring silently at the fire. Julia waited for him to speak again. When he didn't, she rested her head on his shoulder and reached down with one hand to link with his.

Luke raised their joined hands and kissed her fingers.

"Whatever you tell me is part of who you are," she said, breaking the silence. "The person I love is the one you've become. People say the past is always with us, but now we have a chance to make a new future." She leaned over, touched her lips against his, and was rewarded by an answering pressure.

He opened his mouth and eased his tongue inside her, setting her on fire.

"Works for me." He gave her his crooked smile as they broke apart.

He pulled her with him as he stood up, took their drinks and set them carefully on the coffee table, and led her to the bed. His moves were deliberately precise as he removed the fleece top and bottom, kissing each part of her body as he exposed it, his mouth hot and wet and open. He placed her naked body on the bed, his gaze hungry. He ripped off his jeans and T-shirt, tossed them to the floor and then he was beside her.

This time they made love in ways too numerous to count, their minds inventive. Every joining, every sensation, was wrapped in words of love, of the new feelings surging through them. Finally, sated and exhausted, they spooned together, bodies nestled comfortably.

Julia drifted off to sleep, completely spent by the intensity of their lovemaking, content to feel his body around her. Her last thought was how wonderful it would be if they could do this forever. She was impatient to be free, so they could make the dream a reality.

Chapter 8

Julia was proud of them the next day. Through the entire schedule of intense meetings at the Hot Ticket headquarters, the small conferences, the explanations, she and Luke were very professional. Somehow they managed to act like two businesspeople, keeping the sexual tension under control.

"We could always get jobs as actors," she teased Luke when they were alone. They sat in the corner booth at the Holiday Inn lounge, the place where they'd spent that first momentous evening. "We played our parts pretty well."

"You were the consummate professional," Luke told her with affection.

"What's wrong?" A feeling of apprehension washed over her. Was he regretting everything? Wondering if he'd made a mistake? Why couldn't she just quit always second-guessing?

"Nothing." He reached for her hand, squeezed it gently. "Not a thing. What could possibly be wrong? I'm sitting here with the most beautiful woman in the world anticipating yet another night of unbelievable sex."

Julia blushed. "I don't know if we can possibly top last night." She looked around the room. "I'm curious why we're staying here tonight and not the cabin? Aren't you worried some of your people might wander in here for a drink and see us?"

"Not a bit." He shook his head. "Taking you to dinner is expected, and the choices are limited. I didn't want to chance it at the cabin in case we get snow. While being stranded there with you is very appealing, it might present problems neither of us wants to deal with."

"You know, Charles should have signed the divorce papers by the time I get back."

"Yes." His grip on her hand tightened. "Another reason I don't want you to be delayed. You need to be there in case there's a problem. I don't know the bastard, but from what you tell me, he's going to go to the mat on this. I'd like to keep you locked away until it's a done deal, but I know you have other responsibilities. The twins, for example. And I don't want anything to go wrong to delay this one more day."

Julia nodded her head slowly. "I've been checking my messages. Harry texted me Charles still wasn't back from his trip, but he was supposed to be back today. Harry called the other attorney and demanded a firm appointment for tomorrow morning. If things go well, by the time I get off the plane, Harry should be at the courthouse filing the papers." She didn't want to let him know how worried she was, tell him about the feeling of unease tickling at her like the rake of the claws of a beast. Damn Charles to hell, anyway.

Luke's deep brown eyes captured hers and held her gaze. "I wish I could promise you everything will be fine, but you're a strong woman, Julia. You'll survive whatever happens."

She exhaled a long breath. "I didn't use to be, you know. I let Charles bully me for years so he thinks he can get away with it now." She leaned forward and smiled. "Somehow I lost myself along the way, but you're helping me find the real me."

"A warm, smart, funny, wonderful woman," he told her. "You know you can call me whenever it gets rough, right?"

"Yes." She smiled at him. "But this is my mess. I want it over and done with and not slopping over onto you. The next time we're together, I want it to be without any strings still dangling."

"It will be," he promised her. "I have faith. We couldn't have something this good happen to us and then lose it for some stupid reason."

The musical duo started their first set of the evening and Luke wordlessly led Julia to the dance floor. She allowed him to pull her body in close to his and tuck their clasped hands against his chest. They moved slowly to the rhythm, his arousal hard against her, nudging at her, calling her senses to come out and play. Resting her head against his shoulder, she was filled with an incredible sense of déjà vu.

"I can't believe how hard I am," he whispered in her ear. "By every law of nature, I should be dead by now."

"I love it." He couldn't know what a sense of new power it gave her.

They barely moved, shuffling their feet in place to the notes of the soft ballad until it ended.

"Hungry?" Luke led her back to their table.

Julia shook her head. It sounded like a repeat of their first night. She was hungry all right, but not for food. "No. Thanks."

They looked hard at each other for a long moment; then Luke nodded and signaled for the check.

They rode the elevator in electric silence, and at her door she gave Luke the key card to open the room. He flipped the light switch and the two bedside lamps poured their golden color into the bedroom.

"Let me just look at you." Luke ran his gaze over her. "Feast my eyes on you. I want to memorize every single inch of your body." One piece at a time, he peeled away her clothes, not kissing her or touching her in any other way, just absorbing her with his eyes. When she stood completely naked, he took a step back and carefully looked at every inch of her body. His hands flexed and naked desire flared in his eyes.

"God, you take my breath away," he told her. "You are so gorgeous."

"You must have a distorted view of me." Her voice trembled. "My body certainly shows the wear and tear of motherhood."

He shook his head. "Only to give you a warmer, richer look." In an instant, he divested himself of his own clothes and stood before her, just as naked.

Now it was Julia's turn to look, to devour him with her eyes, storing up memories to take home with her. For whatever reason—maybe because she didn't trust good luck—she sensed something disastrous was about to happen. She wanted something to hang on to. When she fell asleep, she would dream of his strong chest with its crisp, curling hair, the flat brown nipples on his chest. Of his hot, hard erection and its remembered presence in her body She wanted this for a lifetime. Would fate be so cruel as to jerk it away from her?

Then there was no more time for thinking. They were kissing, deep, voracious, carnal kisses, where their tongues did an erotic dance and probed every inner recess of their mouths. Luke guided her to the bed, pausing only to reach down and rip away the covers. Lying side by side, they fused their mouths together, hands reaching for each other.

Luke tore his mouth away, trailed kisses along her cheek, then grasped both of her hands in one of his and stretched them back above her head.

"Tonight, my love, I'm going to show you what it's all about." And he proceeded to be as good as his word.

For Julia, it was the most sensual experience she'd ever had. His hands on her skin seemed to burn against her, plucking at her nerves, leaving little fires in their trail. He laved each breast until she thought she would go mad with the sensation, then drove her even crazier as he plucked on each nipple with his teeth until they were swollen and aching.

The touch of his lips on her stomach was like a feather, teasing her with the lightest of touches. Then he used his tongue to draw circles on her skin, knowing exactly how to convey the most carnal invitation. He shifted his body and dipped his tongue lower, nudging her thighs apart with his hand. When she felt him kiss the soft curls at her vee, then move his tongue along the length of her slit, she nearly came off the bed.

"Easy," he whispered. "We have so much time. I want to enjoy you completely. Remember me when you go home and you're caught up in your work and your children."

As if she could forget one minute with him.

He parted her already throbbing folds with his thumbs, laving every inch of her cunt, finally tasting the inside of her. She jerked against him and he used both hands to hold her in place. God, his tongue was a live wire, searing her every place he licked. Blood pounded in her veins, her heart thudded, and she couldn't get enough air to breathe.

"Please, please," she moaned softly. "Oh, please."

"Not yet," he whispered against her skin. "Not yet, my love."

He used his mouth and his fingers expertly, bringing her to her peak and then drawing back, holding her right at the edge of release. He held her hips firmly, bringing her back to his mouth, and began again. He brought her to the edge so many times she lost count, each time taking her a little higher, a little further. On and on it went, Luke using his mouth and fingers to play her body like a fine instrument.

Finally, when she had reached the point of sobbing, begging, pleading for her release, he captured her nub between his teeth, slid two fingers into her slippery sheath, then three, and took her over the edge. She climaxed with huge shudders, bucking against his hands and mouth, biting her lips to keep from screaming his name.

* * * *

Before the spasms even subsided, he moved into place over her, his shaft so hot and hard it nearly caused him pain. He thrust into her, slowly at first, feeling her liquid heat surround him, then harder until he was buried to the hilt. The walls of her pussy still quivered and clutched around him and he nearly lost what was left of his control.

Julia gasped then moaned softly. Lifting his head, he saw her eyes glazed with pleasure, her face hot and flushed with passion. He paused to gather himself, then began moving within her, slowly at first, then faster and faster. She answered his rhythm, thrusting her hips at him, wrapping her legs around him to pull him closer. Their sweat-drenched bodies moved slickly against each other.

He slid nearly all the way out before thrusting hard into her, repeated the movement again and again until she pled once more for release. He felt her orgasm building and he gritted his teeth to hold on to his control as long as he could, until he couldn't stop. Neither of them could. He slammed his mouth against hers, swallowing her moans. They spiraled together into space, bodies shaking, hearts pounding in tandem, falling, falling, until they were spent.

It was a long time before either of them spoke. Finally, Luke raised his head and cleared his throat. "Are we still alive?"

"I don't know." Julia wet her lips, her breathing uneven. "I actually think I've died and gone to heaven."

Luke rolled to the side, keeping one arm around her and bringing her with him until she was nestled close to him. "Julia, I…"

She reached up and pressed her fingers against his lips. "Don't say it. Whatever it is. For tonight, let's not talk, okay?"

"I'm not sure I'm good for much more right now." His chuckle had a rusty sound to it.

"Oh, I don't know. Give me a minute and we'll see." She trailed her hand softly down his body, feeling each muscle with the tips of her fingers. "It's amazing what a few minutes of rest can do."

"Not at my age." He laughed. "Don't let your expectations exceed reality."

He wanted to ask her where they could go from here. They'd said things to each other, opened their hearts, but was it possible for them to blend their lives together? She had young children and obligations. He had a career here. Could she drop everything to come here? Could he go there? How could he give up perfection when he'd just found it?

Pulling her against him, he added in a low voice, "Julia, I wish…"

She leaned over and kissed him, effectively stopping any conversation. "Don't say it. Not right now. Okay? Whatever it is, I want to believe we will work things out." Then she curled against him and closed her eyes.

They didn't sleep, just dozed. Luke woke to find his body doing things he'd thought impossible just a while ago. Warm sensations flooded him, snapping him to attention. He tried to clear his head, and suddenly realized what was happening.

Julia looked up at him, her eyes hot and demanding. Wrapping her fingers around his shaft, she slid them up and down the skin covering the hard core, coaxing a response, as her lips swallowed the tip. Watching her was one of the most erotic experiences of his life. Luke could not have protested if he wanted to. The sensation was exquisite torture, rousing him when he'd thought no reaction was possible again.

"Just lay back and enjoy it," she told him. "Now it's my turn."

And so it was. As he'd done for her, she took her time, drawing it out as long as she could, letting her hands slide tantalizingly along his erection, cupping the heavy sac between his legs, her tongue sliding across the soft velvet tip.

When she licked the tiny drops of moisture seeping from the slit, he nearly lost it altogether. If he'd been able to, he'd have reached up, moved her on top of him and thrust inside of her. But she was too determined. He finally gave himself up to the sensation, and when she drew him over the edge, he lay there shuddering in unbelievable ecstasy.

* * * *

They slept spooned together, but not restfully, despite being spent physically. They were glued skin to skin, unwilling for space to come between any parts of their bodies. When Julia woke, it was still dark and she snuggled back against him, wanting just a few more moments of his warmth and the feel of his wonderful body.

His arms held her tight, his arousal pressing against her. He stroked his hands over her and they made love one last time, slowly, gently, savoring every moment.

Eventually they dozed. When the phone rang, Julia cursed wakeup calls in general and this one in particular. She fumbled for the receiver and mumbled, "Hello?" two or three times before realizing it was her cell phone ringing.

She sat up with a quick movement, swung her legs over the side of the bed, and punched the talk button.

"Yes?" The readout on the bedside clock said four in the morning. Who would call her at this hour?

Oh, God, not the kids. Please don't let something have happened to one of the twins.

"Julia?"

"Who is this?" She rubbed her face, trying to wipe away the vestiges of sleep and make her brain work.

"It's Claire. Julia, are you there?"

"Claire?" Why was Claire calling her at this hour? Fear grabbed at her heart. "Oh my God. Claire. The children. Are the twins okay?"

"Yes. I didn't have another number for you, so I called your cell. I know it's always on."

"What's wrong? Why are you calling?"

Luke was awake now, sitting up on the edge of the bed next to her, his big, warm hand soothing as he stroked her back and shoulders.

"Miranda called me a few minutes ago and asked me to get hold of you. She thought it would be easier if I told you about this rather than having it come from her."

"What do you mean? Damn it, Claire, what's going on?"

"It's Charles. He's had a massive heart attack."

Chapter 9

"What?"

At her shriek, Luke tightened his grip on her and pulled her close to him.

"Apparently it happened around midnight," Claire told her, "but it wasn't until a little while ago one of his partners, who happened to be with him, thought to get hold of you."

"Of course." Her voice was bitter. "Everyone knows about the divorce. I guess they didn't think his children needed to know." She raked her fingers through her hair. "Oh God, Claire."

"I came right down to the hospital so I could find out what's what." Claire made a sound like a snort. "His asshole partner acted like I was carrying cyanide or something. Anyway, the doctors are with him now. I'll see what I can find out and call you back."

"The children." She could think only of them at the moment. "I'll have to tell them."

"Let's find out what's going on before you do. How soon can you leave? Can you come right to the hospital when you get here?"

"Of course. Absolutely. I… I'll have to call the airlines. I'll have to… Oh, God."

"Call Miranda, then call me back when you have your reservations. And pull yourself together, kiddo. We'll get through this."

She sat with her cell phone in her hand, trying to process everything.

Tell Luke. Make plane reservations. Pack.

She turned to face him and everything spilled out in disjointed sentences.

"I'll call the airlines then order you some tea." Luke held her gently, trying to ease the tension gripping her body. "Go take a shower."

"It's my fault." She felt such a heaviness she almost couldn't breathe.

"Stop it." He tilted her face to look at him. "Nothing is your fault, and I refuse to allow you to take the blame for this."

"But…"

"We'll talk about it after you're dressed. Go on." He patted her gently on the rear end, urging her toward the bathroom.

By the time she was dressed, Luke had confirmed new reservations for her and a pot of tea waited on the nightstand. She gulped the hot liquid gratefully. While Luke showered quickly and dressed, Julia called Claire back with her flight information, then spoke to Miranda.

"The children are still sleeping." The woman sighed. "I'm just glad he wasn't here when it happened."

"Me, too." Julia could imagine how affected the twins would have been. "I'll call you when I get to the hospital and find anything out. Why don't you try to go back to sleep?"

Miranda laughed, sadly. "As if. Just call me when you get there. Do you want me to keep Andy and Beth home from school today?"

Julia nibbled her lower lip. Should she? "No, let's keep everything as normal as possible until I have some answers."

"You take care of yourself," Miranda admonished before she hung up.

"I think I should take a cab to the airport," Julia told Luke, zipping up her suitcase. "You don't need to go running me around in the middle of the night."

"No." Luke was emphatic. "Out of the question. I'll drive you to the airport. I won't have you taking this ride by yourself. Julia, this thing with us isn't some little quickie, where I run out when the going gets tough. I'm here for you. I care for you and about you. Hang on to what I'm telling you, okay?"

She smiled weakly. "How did I get so lucky as to have you walk into my life?"

"I'm the lucky one." He hugged her quickly. "Finish your tea."

The hot drink settled her stomach but she didn't think anything would help her heart. Guilt, misery, and expected loneliness fought for possession of that fragile organ, and at the moment, guilt had the edge. Still, one thing was certain. Leaving here was going to be hell.

She put on her coat and waited by the door with her suitcase, feeling like the victim of an earthquake. An emotional one. Luke took her face between his palms and kissed her, a long, deep, soul-satisfying kiss.

"Remember this when you fall asleep at night, sweet Julia," he said. "I know I will."

"Yes," she whispered, her throat tightening.

"I love you."

"I love you, too."

The hotel bill would be sent to Luke's office so they went directly to his car. They tried to make small talk on the ride into Boston, but Julia's mind was too preoccupied. Discussing business wasn't even an option. Both of them avoided the elephant sitting in the car with them.

Finally, Luke let her be.

"Don't worry about the contract," he told her. "I'll get in touch with Claire and we'll work things out."

"Oh, Luke. The contract." *Damn.* "I didn't even think about how this will impact my time."

"Hopefully not much," he told her. "Charles is out of the house and the final deed is almost done, whatever happens with this latest crisis. I know you'll be wound up getting your kids through this. Claire and I will take care of whatever has to be done."

When they pulled up to the curb at the airport, Luke killed the engine, undid his seat belt, and reached for her. "I can't let you go like this, with everything still so unsettled between us. I wanted time to make plans, to think of a future together."

"Oh, Luke. Me, too." Tears spilled from her eyes and etched tracks on her cheeks. "This is so damn unfair."

"Damn right it is," he told her roughly. "Go on. Go home and see to your kids. They're what's important right now. Call me, okay?"

"I will."

"We'll get through this, Julia. I'm here for you. Don't doubt that for a moment. This isn't the end, it's a beginning."

"Oh, God, how I want to believe that." She fisted her hands. "This is a terrible thing to say, but it's just like Charles to find a way to screw things up for me."

Luke's laugh was without humor. "I'm sure he didn't give himself a heart attack just to punish you."

"He's capable of anything." Damn him. "Alright. Let me get home and see what the situation is and go from there."

He got out of the car, opened her door, and took out her suitcase. They stood for a moment looking at each other and she drank in the sight of him. A light snow began to fall and the soft flakes dropped easily on their heads and faces, but neither of them seemed to notice.

"There is so much I wish I could say to you right this minute," he told her. "There just isn't enough time."

"Me, too." She touched her fingers to his lips. "But don't. Please. It's hard enough as it is. We'll have time when things settle down."

"Let's hope," he muttered. "All right. Be sure to let me know how things are. I'll be worried about you. Here. Give me your cell phone."

She pulled it out of her purse and handed it to him. He punched some numbers and gave it back to her.

"There. My private number's in there. I'm speed dial number one. I'll have my phone on all the time. Call me whenever."

"Oh, Luke." Her voice broke and she dug deep to get control of herself. "Why couldn't we have met fifteen years ago?"

"I don't think we would have been ready for each other then." He kissed her one last time, then enfolded her in his arms. "Just remember. No matter what happens in your life, you will always be mine."

"Yes, I will." She fought tears and clung to him as if she'd never let him go before taking a step back. "Goodbye, Luke." And then she couldn't help herself. "I love you." She yanked up the handle of her suitcase and nearly ran into the terminal, dragging the luggage behind her.

Julia went through check-in and security as if in a fog. She bought herself another cup of tea and sat in the waiting area, sipping at the hot liquid, hoping it would ease the sudden chill invading her. The man sitting next to her was kind enough to nudge her when the call for boarding came. She entered the plane and took her seat like a robot, buckled in and leaned her head back.

Images flashed through her mind: she and Luke dancing, bodies moving slowly to the music, their first night together, the wonder of exploring each other's bodies, the night in the cabin, warmed by the flames of the fire, their kiss at the airport, more poignant than sensual.

What a mess. The damn divorce papers still unsigned and now she had no idea when or how they would be. Luke had said he would wait but for how long? And how would the twins handle this? Their relationship with their father left a lot to be desired yet surely this would affect them emotionally. Her life was slowly being flushed down the toilet and she was left with a very inadequate plunger. Tears begin to trickle from the corners of her eyes, and her stomach knotted.

"Excuse me." The flight attendant was leaning towards her, over the empty seat next to her. "Forgive me for asking but is something wrong?"

"No." Julia sniffled, then tried on a smile. "Just fighting a cold is all."

"Can I get you anything?" The attendant was obviously concerned.

"Some hot tea would be nice, if you could. And thank you." Maybe she could drown herself in an ocean of the stuff.

"Tea it is. Coming right up."

She realized as she sipped the hot liquid, she would now always associate it with Luke. She hoped she would still be able to drink it without crying. The tea seemed to settle her still-jumbled stomach enough so she could relax a little, but it did nothing to rid her of the feeling of despair creeping over her. Would she be punished if she wished Charles in hell? Because that's exactly where he kept sending her.

When the plane landed, she pushed her way through the lines, apologizing as she went, and raced for ground transportation and a cab. She needed to assess the situation and try to make some plans.

"Methodist Hospital," she told the driver. "And please hurry."

* * * *

The snowstorm demanded Luke's attention as he headed out of Boston, but not enough to keep thoughts from clogging his mind. Julia's face kept floating in front of him. His lips still burned from their kisses, his skin branded by her touch. Watching her leave, walk away from him, was like having his heart ripped out of his chest.

Knowing Julia, sharing himself with her in more ways than the physical, made returning to his solitary life a difficult task. When he'd walked away from his wreck of a marriage, solitary seemed like the best choice. It had taken him far too long to realize what a shallow woman he'd married. By then their two sons were born and the chain around his neck was firmly in place. He'd stayed believing whatever the cost, no other man would raise his children.

But things hadn't worked out quite the way he'd expected. His sons were in Alabama with Patty and she'd done her level best to ruin any relationship between them. With Julia, he saw hope for the future. A life he'd never thought he'd have.

Damn Charles anyway.

The closer he got to his condo, the more uptight he felt. Life had apparently decided to kick him in the teeth again and he needed to figure out how to handle it.

* * * *

Julia paused at the entrance to the Cardiac Intensive Care Unit waiting room. Forcing herself to breathe slowly, she slowed the accelerated pace of her heart, wet her lips, and swallowed. For this, she needed to be in control of herself. Every available seat seemed to be filled, but she spotted

Claire in a corner, leaning back, eyes closed. She walked over to her and touched her shoulder gently.

"Oh!" Claire startled, then focused her eyes as she recognized Julia. "Oh, my God. Julia." She stood and hugged her friend. For a moment, the two women took strength from each other.

"Why are you still here?" Julia asked. "You must be exhausted. Not to mention the fact your husband is probably wondering where you are."

"Brad's fine. He was here, too, as a matter of fact, but I finally sent him home. I figured you'd rather have just me."

"Thank you for that." Julia motioned toward the doorway with her hand. "Can we go into the hallway and talk?"

Claire nodded. They walked to the far end of the corridor and paused near a tall window, wet with the rivulets of rain skating down the surface.

All of her crises seemed to occur on rainy days.

"All right." She touched Claire's arm. "Tell me everything."

"Okay. I had to pry this out of the jackass he was with." Claire rubbed her forehead, an effort to sort out her jumbled thoughts. "He and Rod McGuire apparently were having dinner at the Downtown Club, then ran into a couple of clients and sat in the bar talking with them for a long time. Charles got up to say goodbye, grabbed his chest, and fell down in terrible pain. McGuire called an ambulance and they brought him here."

Rod McGuire, of all people. *Damn.*

Not only Charles's partner, but his oldest friend. They had been friends since they were toddlers, playing together, supervised by one nanny or the other. They'd gone through boarding school, college, and law school together. Now they were law partners, in practice with their fathers. Julia knew strong friendships formed under those circumstances. The first time she met Rod, however, she'd sensed an allegiance that went beyond that. A loyalty from Rod that might be admirable if she knew what brought it about. Something stronger than normal friendship, that was for sure. The man was also a consummate snob, as was everyone else in their circle. When Charles married Julia, Rod had made it patently clear he thought she was a poor choice and he'd never bothered to mask his dislike.

"Oh, God." Julia bit her lip. "It's the divorce. I know it is." A feeling of blame surged through her, trailing nausea in its wake. Apparently, she was one of those people destined never to have real happiness in their lives. When she reached for it, everything else went to hell.

"Stop it." Claire's voice was sharp. "Get this through your head. Nothing you did caused what happened. Nothing. Are we clear? This would have happened no matter what."

"If you say so." Julia took a deep breath and let it out. "All right. Go on."

"About three in the morning, McGuire finally figured someone should call the house and let you and the children know what was happening."

"Charles didn't know I was out of town," Julia told her in a low voice. "I'm glad they brought him here. His doctor is on staff."

"McGuire filled out the insurance papers. He sure wasn't happy to see me. Told me bluntly he'd handle everything and I could go home." She made a sound of disgust. "Said I didn't have any business here but it would be nice if Charles's wife showed up."

"He knows about the divorce." Anger crawled up her spine. "Everyone does."

"He was just being an arrogant ass. Ignore him."

"I don't know how to thank you for coming down here." She hugged Claire again.

"I didn't want you to walk into this by yourself with no one but the Ice Man for company."

"What have you been able to find out?"

"By the time Dr. Vinoy got here, Charles was in Emergency and stabilized. Then Vinoy called in a top cardiologist. I have his card here someplace." She dug around in her purse, produced a thin piece of pasteboard. "Insisted he give it to me. Rombauer. Ethan Rombauer. He left a message for us to page him when you got here."

"This is my fault." Julia chewed at her bottom lip again. "God is punishing me, I just know it."

"Julia." Claire's voice, though heavy with fatigue, was sharp. "I won't even allow you to go there. God doesn't hand out heart attacks or anything else as punitive measures. That's your father talking in your head, bullying you and your mother. Stop it right now. In no way are you responsible for this." She shook her head. "I was surprised to discover Charles has a heart at all."

"Claire! My God!"

"I know, I know. Don't speak ill and all that garbage. But I will not permit you to take this on yourself. Charles is a big boy. He knows enough to take care of his health. Whatever happened is on him. And you deserve to have a good life without him."

"But not this way." An image of Luke flashed in her brain, his warm smile, his dark eyes. She'd been so excited at the possibility of a future with him. Apparently, Fate had decided to punish her for looking to a new future. Her emotions were a mixture of anger and depression. *Why me?*

she wanted to cry out. Hadn't she done enough penance for making such a poor choice the first time?

The weight of guilt pressed heavily on her. She'd gone from one man's loving, virile arms to another's critical condition in a few short hours. She couldn't separate her stolen happiness from the unfolding disaster.

"What's going on now?" She looked around for someone to ask. "I need to find out what his situation is. Can I see him?"

"Come. I'll take you to the CICU. Then we'll get them to page Rombauer."

But before they could enter the CICU, they were confronted by Rod McGuire, looking like a thundercloud come to life. He planted himself in front of Julia, rage burning in his eyes. She had a feeling if he could get away with it he'd kill her on the spot.

"It's about damn time," he ground out. "I stayed until you finally got here. I'm just thankful Charles was with someone when this happened."

Just what she needed, the devil himself. Julia clenched her fists, digging for some semblance of control.

"Thank you for taking care of things, Rod. I appreciate it."

He glared at her. "Maybe if you'd been here with him instead of who the hell knows where, none of this would have happened." His eyes were like twin flames. "They won't let me in because I'm not family, but I told the cardiologist I'll be calling regularly for updates. *Someone* has to make sure Charles is being cared for properly. And you'd better not shirk your damn responsibilities."

"Rod, I—"

"Stop it, Rod." Claire took Julia's arm and dragged her away. "She doesn't need this right now. We'll keep you informed."

"Oh, God." Julia was glad for Claire's physical support. The force of Rod's verbal attack nearly fractured her.

"Forget him," Claire told her in a furious whisper. "And pay no attention to anything he said. He's a jackass, just like I always thought. Come on, let's find out what's going on."

The CICU was a row of cubicle-like rooms. Each one glass-fronted, to give the nurses at the central station an unimpeded view of the patients. Nurses in scrubs of various colors either sat at the long central console or moved about in the patients' rooms performing required tasks. Unconsciously, Julia wrinkled her nose against the acrid, medicinal smell—common to hospitals—permeating the area.

"May I help you?" One of the nurses approached quietly, and without seeming to, effectively blocked their path.

"This is Julia Patterson, Charles Patterson's wife." Claire waved sketchily in the general area of Charles's bed. "She's just arrived from the airport and would like to see her husband."

"Of course." The nurse turned to Julia. "We've been expecting you. Dr. Rombauer left a message to page him as soon as you arrived. Let me take you in to your husband, then I'll make the call."

"Thank you." Julia bit her lip. "Will... Will he know I'm here?"

"He might." She smiled. "Even if they're heavily medicated it helps for them to have human contact. Touch his hand. He'll sense it. Come on. I'll take you to him."

Claire squeezed Julia's arm. "I'll wait outside. I don't want to see him, anyway. I might be tempted to finish him off myself."

"Claire!" Julia protested.

"Go on, sweetie. Do your thing. I'll wait for you over there." Claire indicated some chairs against a far wall.

"Okay. And...thanks."

Charles was in the cubicle at the absolute center of the area. The nurse led Julia to a place beside his bed and slid a chair over for her to sit in.

"He looks so still."

The nurse nodded. "He's been given a lot of medication to keep him sedated. Right now it's best for him. I'm sorry, the most we allow for visiting is five minutes at a time. The doctor should be here by then, however."

Julia stared at him, lying there silent and pale, surrounded by a variety of machines that beeped, dinged, or fed fluids into his system. His blond hair was uncharacteristically rumpled, his face drawn and darkened by an emerging stubble of beard. He looked almost shrunken in the ubiquitous hospital gown, as still as if life had already left him behind. She might not love him any longer but seeing him in this condition she could at least have empathy for what happened.

Tears threatened to spill from her eyelids. Fatigue, she told herself. And despair at the downturn her life had taken once again. She'd stopped crying over Charles years ago.

His chest rose and fell evenly, and if not for the lines of pain etched deeply on his face and the vast array of technology keeping him alive, she might have thought him simply sleeping. How difficult it was to realize, less than twenty-four hours ago, the man who lay like death in the hospital bed was a domineering force in her life. Even a frightening one. God surprises us all, she thought.

"Charles?" She wet her lips and tried again. "Charles, can you hear me? It's Julia."

No response. Not even a twitch of his fingers.

She forced herself to sit quietly, speaking softly to him, hardly even aware of what she said. It seemed only moments passed before the nurse was beside her again, signaling her time was up.

A tall, cadaver-thin man waited just outside the glass door.

"I'm Dr. Rombauer, Mrs. Patterson." He shook her hand. "Let's find a place to sit down so I can fill you in on your husband's condition. You look exhausted."

"I've just flown in from Boston. I was there on a business trip." Not to mention the most incredible pleasure she'd ever experienced. "I don't understand how this happened. Charles always seemed in excellent health."

"Unfortunately, that's often the case."

Claire rose as they came toward her. "I'll wait in the hall so you can talk."

"No. Please stay." Julia needed the support of Claire's presence. She turned back to Rombauer. "You've already spoken to Mrs. Westbrook and I'd prefer to have my friend here with me."

"Your call." He nodded.

Julia perched tensely on the edge of her chair watching Rombauer open the chart in his hand.

"I'll try to explain this as clearly as I can," he began. "What your husband suffered is what you call a heart attack and we call a myocardial infarction. In some cases it's mild, in others it's a lot more severe."

"And in Charles's case?" she asked.

"I'm afraid his is in the latter category."

He went on to explain in detail about Charles's condition. Hands gripped tightly in her lap, throat dry, Julia listened, but after a few minutes, the words seemed to blend. She could barely distinguish one fact from another.

"I appreciate the abundance of detail, Dr. Rombauer, but can you just give me some kind of simple prognosis? My mind isn't functioning too well right now."

He closed the chart and looked at her carefully, a clinical assessment. "Of course, forgive me." He paused. "Were you aware your husband was being treated for high blood pressure?"

Julia tried to conceal the shock she felt. "I was not. Charles never mentioned a word to me." And how like him to conceal any evidence of imperfection lest it be seen as a chink in his armor. "But we're separated. I don't know if anyone's told you. Our divorce is practically final."

He raised his eyebrows. "No, I wasn't made aware of that. Maybe I should be meeting with someone else?"

"No." She shook her head. "He's still the father of my children and a part of the family circle."

"All right, then." He leaned back in the chair. "I've discussed this with Dr. Vinoy. Apparently, Mr. Patterson's been taking medication for three or four years. When he was diagnosed, his blood pressure was dangerously high and Dr. Vinoy stressed to him the importance of keeping it under control."

Julia tried to process what he said. Rombauer droned on about the high blood pressure as the underlying cause of the heart attack, the loss of blood to the heart muscle, and its subsequent damage. Scar tissue. Restrictive blood flow. Congestive heart failure. She felt as if she'd been dropped into a medical drama without the benefit of a script.

Swallowing twice to wet her dry throat, she asked, "How long will it take him to recover? Will this be a long process? What kind of care will he need?"

The look of kindness in Rombauer's eyes was the signal, and she braced herself.

"I'm afraid there is just too much damage to the heart." He shook his head. "There is no way for it to recover."

Shock ran through her. "He's going to die." A statement, not a question.

"Probably within six months."

Julia's head spun, making her dizzy and faint. The room spun slightly. Only Claire's hand on her arm steadied her.

"Surely with the number of advances in modern medicine," she protested, "there's some way to fix this."

Rombauer shook his head. "More than three quarters of the heart is damaged. The only option would be a transplant, but even if we could find a donor match, your husband is not a good candidate for the surgery."

"I don't understand."

"The lab tests revealed a rare blood condition making surgery of any kind risky, and cardiac surgery prohibitive. The best we can offer Charles is medical attention to keep him comfortable."

Rare blood condition? How had she never known this? What else had he kept from her in his drive for perfection? Something else suddenly jumped into her mind.

"Has anyone called his parents?"

"I did," Claire told her. "I waited until it was light. I know how they hate having their sleep disturbed." She could barely keep the distaste from her voice.

"Are they coming to the hospital?" How on earth was she going to deal with them?

"Oh, sure." She made a face. "On their schedule. They told me they needed time to compose themselves first."

Julia refused to imagine the scene she'd face when the elder Pattersons arrived. They would blame her, of course. Normal behavior for them. Everything wrong in their lives could be laid at her doorstep. Of course she'd never hear the end of her trip out of town. A wife's place is with her husband. She should have had it tattooed on her backside. Well, her place wasn't there any more, even if they chose to ignore the divorce proceedings.

Their arrival would be an intrusion into the routine of the hospital. Without concern for other patients and their families, Howard would demand attention in his loud, authoritarian voice. Elise would stand like a carefully placed wax mannequin, totally unmoving, nodding her head to punctuate each of her husband's words. He would use his power to threaten doctors and nurses with dire consequences if they didn't rush to do his bidding where his son was concerned. As a former member of the hospital board, whatever he said carried a lot of weight.

She fervently hoped they didn't expect her to take him home with her. The Pattersons, with their huge home and abundance of money, were far better equipped and could hire whatever care he needed.

She tried to focus on what Rombauer said, but her brain simply shut down. The room spun, the air suddenly like cotton fleece sticking to her. The doctor caught her just before she slipped from the chair to the floor.

* * * *

When she opened her eyes, she found herself in an unfamiliar room, sunlight pouring in through a large window. Apparently the rain had stopped. The room was strange, the bed unusually high. Claire sat in a chair next to her, flipping through a magazine. Brad, Claire's husband, stood at the window, staring through the open drapes at the brightness of the day.

"Where am I?"

Claire closed the magazine and leaned forward. "Rombauer asked them put you in a vacant hospital room."

She realized she now wore a hospital gown. "What's wrong? Am I sick?" She tried to sit up, but the spinning of the room made her nauseous.

"No, just exhausted and emotionally drained. Everyone was quite worried about you."

"Charles." The memory stabbed at her. "How is he?"

"Doing fine. He's being well taken care of."

"We're much more concerned with you, Julia." Brad turned from the window to look at her. "Charles is receiving the finest care his money and his insurance can provide. You have to think about yourself. You have children who need you, now more than ever."

He was right. It was just so hard to think. Too much. Too many things to deal with.

"What time is it?" Her brain felt fuzzy.

"About three o'clock," Claire told her. "You took a nice nap. I'm glad. You obviously needed it."

"I haven't called Miranda yet." She sat up, moving slowly. "Can I make calls from here?"

Claire picked up the receiver from the bedside telephone. "I already spoke to her, but I know she'd like to hear from you personally." She put her ear to the instrument, spoke briefly, and handed it to Julia. "You have a dial tone now. Go ahead. Would you like us to wait in the hall?"

Julia shook her head. "No. Please stay." She looked at both of them. "I'm not sure I can get through this by myself."

Brad moved to stand beside her. "We're here for you, kiddo. Start to finish."

"I'm so glad to hear your voice." Miranda's relief, when she answered the phone, was evident. "You doing okay, Julia?"

"Yes. Fine," she assured her. "How are Andy and Beth? You sent them to school as we discussed, right?"

"Yes. They just got home but I haven't said anything yet. I thought it would be better coming from you."

Another difficult task, but one only she could handle. "I'll be home later. Before I leave here I should know more about what's going on." She hung up the phone and looked at Claire and Brad. "What about Charles's parents?"

Claire made a face. "They were here this morning. Threw their weight around. Complained about everything. Didn't seem too happy about your situation. Then they left."

"Left?" She was stunned.

"Yeah. Howard said Elise is quite delicate, you know."

"Like a praying mantis." Brad snorted.

"They'll be back tonight," Claire warned. "Are you ready?"

"As much as it's possible to be."

"I have your suitcase here." Claire pointed at it against the wall. "Do you need anything from it?"

"Not now. I need to do something with it, though."

Brad pulled up the handle. "Since we'll take you home I'll go put it in the car."

"I can take a cab," she protested. "You guys have done enough."

Claire hugged her. "That's what friends are for."

And wasn't Julia just damn glad for them now.

She found the clothes she'd been wearing in the narrow closet and took them into the bathroom with her. A long, hot soak sounded like heaven but that would have to wait until she got home. She splashed cold water on her face instead and looked in the mirror. What she saw frightened her. The face staring back at her was familiar, but it was bleached white with dark smudges beneath eyes filled with anguish.

Luke!

No. She mustn't think of him now. If she hadn't let herself…

Let herself what? Be a human being for a change? Respond to a man who made her feel like a woman? Intellectually, she knew neither her impending divorce nor her connection with Luke bore any relation to Charles's heart attack. But the enormous guilt gene Charles fed throughout their marriage smacked at her. It cracked its whip and jammed her back into the dutiful wife mode.

Somehow the fact the final divorce papers weren't signed appeared as some kind of omen to her, a sign her penance for pleasure was to stand by Charles during this terrible situation. Nausea bubbled up in her throat. With a heavy heart, she pushed away thoughts of Luke and headed back to the CICU.

She checked in with the nurse before beginning her allotted five minute visitation. Again, she tried to coax a reaction from him but he lay wax-like in the bed, unresponsive, his chest slowly rising and falling as the machines beeped and dinged. When she left the room Claire led her to the CICU lounge where Brad waited, holding a cup of hot tea for her. She clutched it with hands not quite steady, grateful for the warm liquid as it seeped through her still frozen body.

The elder Pattersons chose that moment to arrive, taking in the little tableau with barely concealed scorn.

"I hold you responsible for this, Julia." Howard delivered his opening salvo. "If you spent your time taking better care of Charles instead of running God knows where around the country, this wouldn't have happened. Rest assured we will see that you pay for this. You have no idea the power of this family or our connections."

"We expect you to stand by Charles in this," Elise sniffed. "He is, after all, the father of your children."

Claire, like a warrior, rose fierce and angry against the invader. "You might want to rethink what you're saying, Howard. Julia has been a damn good wife and mother. Perhaps it might have helped if Charles had told her he was being treated for high blood pressure, among other things."

"Too bad your day was so busy you couldn't get back here until now." Brad snorted. "How do you suppose that looks?"

Howard placed a hand on his wife's shoulder, his face a mask of controlled fury. "Elise was so distraught I wouldn't allow her to leave the house again until she'd rested."

"Mmm hmm." Brad turned away from them. "Julia, I think you need to lie down again."

She shook her head. Running away from this wouldn't help. "I'm fine, Brad. Honestly. But I could use another cup of tea." By the time this was over, she'd probably never be able to drink it again, but right now it sustained her.

"Coming right up." He slid past the Pattersons as if they weren't even there.

"I demand to see the doctor." Howard's authoritarian mantle now sat firmly in place.

"The nurse will page him for you." Claire was not about to leave Julia's side for a moment.

"You know the divorce brought this on," Elise accused, her face pinched. "There's never been a divorce in this family. Charles was mortified."

"Mortified?" Claire was furious. "Maybe if he—"

Julia put her hand on her friend's arm. "Leave it alone, Claire. It's a losing battle."

"There will be no divorce," Howard stated. "I will see to that. Try to go ahead with it and you and your children will be sorry."

Julia tried to speak but a boulder had lodged in her throat.

Claire opened her mouth to speak again but Rombauer's arrival interrupted whatever she planned to say. Howard planted himself aggressively in front of the doctor and barked his questions. In his dictatorial fashion, he gesticulated, demanded, ordered, and excoriated. Rombauer listened patiently, providing information in a calm, controlled voice.

Watching him, Julia saw assessment and recognition flare in his eyes. He was no fool. Quietly, he assured Howard he was free to call in as many specialists as he wanted, but pointed out before he did anything he would have to consult with the patient's wife.

"Wait a moment." Julia froze at his words. "What?"

Rombauer turned to her. "Mr. Patterson has a medical directive and power of attorney. His partner brought them in this morning. You're listed on both of them as the person making every medical decision."

"That must be what Rod was so ticked off about," Claire murmured.

Julia was so shocked she struggled to put words together. "B-But that's impossible. Charles and I were...are..."

"Nonsense," Howard thundered. "We are responsible for his care. Before this happened they were all but divorced. That's in the wind but no way is his care in the hands of anyone but us."

Rombauer shrugged. "I'll be happy to show you the documents, if you like. But until Mr. Patterson is able to make any changes, whatever actions are needed will be her choice and hers alone." He paused. "You are, of course, free to consult with her and give her your input. I'm sure she'll be happy to consider your wishes."

Julia could have sworn a smile flirted with the corners of his mouth. His face was his normal impassive mask, but his eyes quite clearly stated he did not like Howard and Elise Patterson. Claire and Brad struggled to keep their own faces impassive.

Howard's face twisted in contempt as he turned on her and delivered a speech that would have stripped the skin off someone who cared. But in the years of their marriage, any good feelings Julia harbored for her in-laws had disappeared. The thick shell she'd developed where they were concerned insulated her from any pain they might now inflict, and she hoped they'd get out of there before she told them to go to hell.

At a time when normal families pulled together and surrounded each other, the Pattersons' single purpose was gaining control and shutting Julia out. If things hadn't been so dicey—the destruction of her marriage, the separation, the impending divorce that now seemed on hold—she might even have laughed. She was caught in a trap she didn't want, yet it was her only weapon against a familiar enemy.

Howard was infuriated at his inability to intimidate her, and the presence of Claire and Brad only increased his rage. Through it all, Elise sat without moving, avoiding so much as a glance in Julia's direction. The only words she spoke were to demand Claire find her some coffee.

"Preferably with hemlock," Claire muttered, then touched Julia's shoulder briefly. "I know, I know. I'm going."

If not for Brad's intervention, Julia knew she would have said things best left unspoken. Forceful in his own way, he thanked Rombauer for everything and asked if the Pattersons could see their son. Elise waited for her coffee, but Julia followed the nurse as she led Howard down the hall to Charles's cubicle.

"My God." Howard's eyes swept the room full of machines and his son lying immobile in the bed. A muscle twitched in his cheek. He didn't approach the bed, simply watched from the doorway. Julia waited outside until the nurse came to tell him his time was up.

Elise still sat on the hard plastic chair drinking her coffee. She raised her eyes to Howard's as he walked toward her. He simply shook his head.

"He's still not awake, my dear. Perhaps tomorrow will be better."

Elise stood up, mouth set in a grim expression. "We'll arrange our visits so we needn't collide with each other," Howard told Julia. "We'd prefer to visit in the evening."

Good. She'd work it out so she could avoid them altogether. "Actually that will work out well. I'll be home then with the children."

"Oh. Yes. The children." As if they were belongings with no place to be put at the moment.

"Well then," Howard continued, "we'll be leaving. Elise needs to get home to lie down. This is quite an ordeal for her."

He took the coffee cup from his wife and handed it to Claire, as if she were the maid. Without another word they made their way down the hall, backs stiff as starched sheets.

"Ordeal, my ass." Brad twisted his lips in a grimace. "I noticed they didn't once ask how you were, Julia, or if there was anything you needed."

"What a couple of cold fish," Claire added.

"They just don't know how to deal with a situation requiring emotion. Nothing has ever disturbed the smooth surface of their lives. And I don't expect them to think of me. The minute they discovered they didn't have me under their thumb, I became the enemy." She rubbed her forehead. "It's fine. But I don't know what to do about the medical power of attorney. The last thing I want under the circumstances is to make those kinds of decisions."

"Well, honey." Brad gave her a lopsided grin. "I hate to tell you, but you're stuck until Charles is alert enough to appoint someone else."

"Maybe if I sneak in and pull out his tubes and wires, we won't have to do anything," Claire teased.

"Claire!" Julia was shocked her friend could call up gallows humor like that.

"Just kidding." Then she winked at Julia. "But it would solve a lot of problems."

"Right now I think I'd like to go home and see the children. I've done what I can here for the moment."

"I'll get the car and meet you two downstairs." Brad strode toward the elevator.

They were all silent on the drive to her house. Julia was too exhausted to form words and she was sure Claire and Brad were giving her space. All the house lights were on and Miranda opened the door for her as Brad helped her and her suitcase up to the porch.

"Thank you," she told him. "I... Just thank you."

"It's okay, kiddo." He kissed her cheek. "We're here for you, whatever you need."

"The kids are across the street with their friend, Charley." Miranda closed the front door and took her coat. "I told the Greggs what happened and they invited the little ones over to play. Give you a chance to get yourself together before you have to tell them what happened."

"Oh, thank God." She hugged Miranda.

"You go on upstairs. I'll bring this suitcase up in a bit."

Gratefully Julia made it up to her room, closed the door, and threw herself across the bed. What a mess. What an incredible mess. Just when she thought she'd finally gotten things under control and could move forward, fate knocked the pins out from under her. All the pent-up tension finally exploded and sobs burst from her throat. Hot tears burned her cheeks. She reached up and touched the tiny charm at her throat, wrapping her fingers around it. She could almost feel Luke there with her, encouraging her. Telling her how strong she was. As her tears finally subsided and her heartbeat slowed, she realized she had the strength to get through this, for her children and for herself.

Chapter 10

It hardly seemed possible it was only five o'clock in the afternoon. The day seemed as long as a year since Claire's early morning phone call. Cried out at last, she washed her face and drank a glass of water. Then she sent Miranda to fetch the twins. They were wildly glad to see her, hugging her with great ferocity and pressing their bodies against hers.

"Why do you look so sad, Mommy?" Beth plastered herself against Julia's side.

"Did we do something wrong?" Andy's voice had a plaintive sound to it.

"No, babies. Not at all." Julia dug up a smile. "You are my wonderful children."

"They know something's wrong." Miranda shook her head. "Kids sense those things."

"I missed you guys so much." Julia hugged both of them at the same time. Fear of the unknown bloomed in their eyes. She knew exactly how they felt. How would she tell them from this moment on their lives would be dramatically altered?

They would be her salvation in the difficult days ahead. Their love for her and their needs would keep her sane and grounded when the urge to run away became too strong.

"How come you didn't come home this morning like you said?" Andy demanded.

Julia swallowed. "Some…things came up. Let's have dinner first and then we'll talk about them."

"What things?" he demanded in his child's voice.

"After dinner," she insisted.

"Will you eat with us, Mommy?" Beth begged.

"Please?" Andy added. "We didn't see you for three whole days."

Julia's head throbbed and her stomach was doing a war dance again, but no way could she deny these adorable imps.

"Yes." She hugged them tightly. "I'll eat with you. But just some soup and tea," she told Miranda. "I think it's about as much as my system can take right now."

"Why don't you change into something more comfortable and I'll get something on the table. Come on, kids."

Miranda herded the twins toward the family room. "Give your mama a few minutes to herself and then you can sit down together."

Bless Miranda. Life would be abysmal without her.

Julia unpacked, showered, and opened a drawer to take out sweats. Charles hated for her to sit around the house in them, but right now she needed the feel of comfort they gave her. Her hands hovered over the set Luke had given her for just a moment. She recalled how his eyes lit up when he saw it on her, and darkened with passion as he'd slowly removed each piece. She was just finding herself and now she was being swallowed up again. She needed Luke.

But Luke was an impossibility at the moment, and who knew for how long. Depression settled over her. Stop it, she told herself. No time for tears or self-indulgence now. Her children needed her. And Charles, damn him, Well, she'd do what she had to for him to get stabilized and then she'd tell Harry to get the damn papers signed one way or another. Her life had been on hold for long enough.

Resolutely, she dressed in another pair and headed downstairs.

Miranda fixed her chicken noodle soup and tea, so she sipped and chewed as the children ate spaghetti and told her everything about school. She wanted to keep them distracted as long as possible.

"I got to do the puppet for story hour," Beth bragged.

"But I got to help on the playground," Andy countered.

And they were off, playing Can You Top This, but in a giggly way, anxious for their mother's approval.

She couldn't avoid the topic of Charles for long, however. Miranda helped her with bath time and when they were in their pajamas, she took them both into Beth's room and sat on the bed with them.

"You know Daddy hasn't been living here for a long time," she started. They nodded solemnly.

"He's divorced, like Mitchell's daddy." Andy's tone was so matter-of-fact it hurt.

"Well, almost." What a screwed-up social circle, she thought, where the idea of divorce was so commonplace with children.

"That doesn't mean he doesn't still love you as much," she told them.

Beth and Andy exchanged a look.

"Okay," Beth said. Her tone of voice told Julia what she needed to know. At seven years old, the twins had already accepted the fact their father found it impossible to love them, or maybe anyone. How terrible. Damn Charles anyway.

"Well, one of the reasons I'm late is because I went straight to the hospital." She looked from one to the other. "While I was gone, Daddy got very sick so I went to see him right from the airport."

Again, they exchanged a look. Sometimes Julia wondered if they weren't one person split into two bodies.

"Will he get better?" Andy asked after a long pause.

"I don't know." Be truthful, she told herself. Lies never helped. "Right now the doctors are trying to figure out what to do to help him."

"What's wrong with him?" Beth wanted to know.

Julia took one hand from each of them. "It's his heart. He's had a bad heart attack and there's a lot of damage."

"Heart disease is the number one killer in America," Andy recited in a solemn voice.

Oh, my God. What were they teaching second graders these days?

"You may be right," she said slowly, "but right now we have to wait and see what the doctors say."

"Can we see him?" Beth asked.

Julia shook her head. "Not just yet. He's still in a special part of the hospital where children can't visit. But the minute the doctor says it's okay, you can see him."

"Mommy?" Andy's voice suddenly sounded very small. "Are you going away, too? Are you sick?"

Tears stung her eyelids. "Oh, no, sweetie. Mommy's just fine. And I'll always be here for you."

She gathered them close to her and hugged them against her body. A fierce protective feeling came over her, even as her life unraveled. She hadn't a clue how to prepare them to see the man who'd projected such strength, now lying white and drawn, surrounded by a myriad of machines monitoring his every bodily function.

Before leaving the hospital, she'd discussed it with Rombauer. He'd advised her as best he could, but he was, after all, a cardiologist, not a pediatric psychologist. He had referred her to one in the office tower next to the hospital, even called the doctor himself. The man had taken the time to come to her at the CICU and evaluate the situation. He'd been unbelievably kind and told her what he could in the abstract. He had, however, predicted the suddenness of their father's illness and his impending death would require professional care for the twins, and she'd promised to schedule appointments.

Now she made a mental note to see about that tomorrow.

The nausea was creeping up on her again, but she gritted her teeth until the twins said their prayers and were tucked in bed. Then she pulled on a warm nightgown and collapsed in her own room, forcibly quieting her unsettled stomach and falling asleep with images of Luke unwinding across her dreams.

* * * *

The days passed as an unending train, one after the other, linked together. Julia woke early each morning to eat breakfast with the twins and give them the security of her presence to start the day. When the school bus left them at the door each afternoon, she was there to greet them, answer their questions, and eat an early dinner with them.

In between, she was a haunted-looking wraith moving between Charles's bedside and the CICU lounge, waiting for the brief visits she was permitted, and fighting the nausea and fatigue she couldn't seem to shake. Each night, she crawled gratefully into bed, falling into a dreamless sleep.

Rombauer made sure to spend a few minutes with her each day, always pragmatic but in his own way supportive. Undoubtedly Howard put him through intense grilling sessions in the evenings, but he never mentioned a word to her.

Miranda was a rock. She grounded them, coddled them, and made them laugh when tears threatened. She was the one constant no matter what happened. Julia was just glad that Charles had not lived at home for some time. His absence wouldn't be such a rude shock to them as they grappled with the ways their lives were changing.

Julia's visits to the hospital became divided into five minute and fifty-five minute intervals. Each time she was allowed into the cubicle, she sat beside Charles's bed, watching him sleep, watching the machines, searching for any sign of response. But she had no intention of sitting there all day. She couldn't do him any good and the only feeling she had for him was a remote kind of sympathy. What she'd feel for a stranger.

Her call to her parents was less than satisfactory. Her father was just as much a bully as ever and still enraged that Charles had disdained them and cut them out of her life. And the circle of privilege, she thought to herself. Her mother refused to come to the phone. As she'd done all her life, she followed whatever dictates her husband laid down. How disappointed

Charles must have been that Julia wasn't a carbon copy of her mother, addicted to social demands and obedient to every wish of her husband's.

Her days became a manageable routine, mornings at the hospital with Charles, late afternoons and evenings at home with the children. The hours in between she spent at the office, her only sanctuary. Feeling guilty that so much of the load was falling on Claire, she drove herself in a frenzy, trying to accomplish a full day's work in a few hours. Claire finally sat her down one afternoon, told their secretary to hold their calls, and shut the office door.

"Enough," she said. "You're not Superwoman, nor does anyone expect you to be. The Hot Ticket campaign is moving along and only requires maintenance at the moment. Believe it or not, I can handle the rest until things settle down."

"I just feel so guilty dumping all this on you." Julia stared at her friend, misery wrapped around her like a cloak.

"I'm happy to be dumped on. Right now, everything's under control. Save your strength for when I really need you. Take some time for yourself and spend the rest with the kids."

"I'm taking them to see Charles on Monday, when they move him into a private room. I think it will be less intimidating for them."

"Let's hope Charles will be less intimidating."

"Claire, for God's sake. The man is dying. Cut him some slack." Yet the same thought rattled around in her head.

"Honey, regardless of his physical condition, Charles has a lot to make up for in the way he's treated you and the kids. Just keep that in mind while you're running yourself ragged with this." She scanned Julia's face carefully before she spoke again. "Luke's been calling."

"Luke." She drew out the syllable. God, how she missed him.

"Yes." She grinned. "You know, the man with the sexy voice." The grin disappeared. "He's concerned about you, sweetie. He wants to talk to you."

"I can't, Claire." Julia felt tears gather behind her eyelids. No matter how she tried, she couldn't push away thoughts of Luke, his warmth, his tenderness, his passion. "What can I say to him? I feel so damn guilty about everything as it is. I'm afraid if I hear his voice I'll want to dump everything and run to him. I have to think about the twins. I certainly can't ask him to come here, in this unholy mess."

"You can dump the guilt, Julia." Claire made a sound of disgust. "I heard what Rombauer said about Charles's physical condition. Nothing you did precipitated this attack. Or its aftereffects. Nothing."

Julia looked up at her friend, pain lancing through her. "Then why do I feel like it's my fault?"

"Probably because Charles has you conditioned to accept the fact happiness isn't something you deserve. Call him, honey. Call Luke. He desperately wants to hear your voice for himself."

Julia shook her head. "I can't. I couldn't handle it. I'll call him when Charles is out of the hospital, my life is somewhat back on track and I can get back to making plans. You talk to him, okay? Please?"

"And what exactly shall I say?"

"Tell him I love him and I'm sorry," she whispered and fled to the powder room.

Despite her continued fatigue and the incipient nausea that never seemed to ease, despite the ache in her heart for Luke, whom she forcibly banished from her thoughts, she somehow managed to prepare herself to be compassionate with Charles. He was ill, he was dying, and she was ready to provide whatever support he needed. From a distance. She would forget the emotional wasteland of the past eight years and do her best to give him aid and comfort. Perhaps the heart attack would make drastic changes in his personality, give him a new outlook on life.

Yeah, right. She knew that only happened in fairy tales.

Those first couple of weeks turned out to be the easiest. Charles remained in CICU and heavily sedated. Their communication consisted mainly of him squeezing her fingers whenever she placed her hand in his. Besides, what could happen in five minute visits?

When they moved him to a private room, the heavy sedatives were cut back. Charles grew more alert, and she discovered if anything, he was more irascible and domineering than ever. He criticized everything, bullied the nurses, and bemoaned his situation. Julia, of course, was the repository for his venom.

"Why do you do it?" Claire asked. "For all intents and purposes, you aren't even married to him anymore."

"I feel so guilty," she cried for the hundredth time. She blew her nose. "Jesus, I'm turning into a whiner and a dishrag. Smack me, will you?"

"I would if I thought it would do any good." Claire studied her, eyes filled with sympathy. "Julia, Luke calls every single day. The man is in torment. Please, please, please just give him one call."

"I can't." Julia turned away. "If I hear his voice, I'll lose it."

"Honey, he'll wait for you until this is over. You know it. All he needs is one word from you. Why are you so insistent on punishing yourself? This is not your fault."

Maybe she didn't deserve any happiness. She'd made such a poor choice in her hungry need for a family and stability. Now she was paying the price.

"I'll see."

"Charles will probably be dead in six months." Claire's voice was hard. Pragmatic. "Are you going to give up what appears to be the best thing ever to come into your life for some idiotic notion of wearing a hair shirt?"

"And exactly how would I explain to my children when their father was dying, I was planning my future with another man?" she snapped.

Claire threw up her hands. "I give up."

When Julia finally brought the children to see Charles, it was emotionally exhausting for everyone. Despite her careful preparation, walking into the room and seeing the reality of the situation was a terrifying experience for Andy and Beth. The smell of antiseptic and the lingering odor of illness permeated everything.

Their fear of the situation was palpable, and Charles, totally self-involved, did nothing to ease their panic. Julia forced herself to keep her voice and attitude cheerful and reassuring, but she was happy when they could escape to the car. Beth and Andy were deathly silent on the drive home, and not even Miranda could coax a smile from them.

She spent the remainder of the afternoon and evening at home with them. When she called Charles to tell him she wouldn't be back until the next day, he simply growled, "Fine," and slammed down the phone. But Julia knew the twins needed some guarantee their lives hadn't crumbled away and left them adrift. She would have to be their anchor, their refuge, their source of comfort. But she couldn't do it alone, and Miranda wasn't the answer.

The next morning she called the pediatric psychologist and scheduled appointments.

Charles resented the time she spent away from him with the children and didn't hesitate to let her know it. He dealt poorly with his situation, finding fault with everyone and everything. Julia realized one day with sudden clarity he was terrified of dying. She knew the death sentence pronounced on him paralyzed him with fear. She tried to convince him to seek professional help, to have someone more qualified than she to guide him through this, but he turned a deaf ear.

Religious support was out of the question. The last time Charles was in church was for their wedding, and then only under protest. He considered organized religion a challenge to his self-control. Rombauer recommended two therapists he deemed excellent, with extensive experience with dying patients. Charles took the slip of paper with their names, tore it into shreds, and dropped the pieces into the bedside wastebasket.

"Can they give me back my life?" He vibrated with anger. "Unless they can I'm not interested in seeing them. It's a waste of time."

It was obvious he was looking for an assurance that wasn't there, a guarantee he was immortal, had been misdiagnosed and would wake up the next morning sitting at his desk reviewing a legal brief.

His partners visited in a preselected rotation, usually in the afternoon so she was spared any contact with them. Rod McGuire and Carter DeWitt were carbon copies of Charles—autocratic, dictatorial, and unmoved by the bumps and hurdles of life. The qualities making them good litigators also made them unlikable human beings. Julia was sure they blamed Charles for disrupting their perfectly oiled legal machine. Rod, especially. His longtime personal connection to Charles made him a bitter adversary. Sometimes she wondered if there wasn't something deeper than just friendship, some event or series of events that bonded them together.

She was late leaving one morning and Rod showed up early for his visit. He stepped out of the elevator as she stood waiting for it and blocked her from moving.

"Charles could have done a lot better than you." Venom scored every word. "I'd actually be happy for him to divorce you, but his parents are scandalized by the thought."

"Why?" She raised her chin in defiance. "They hate me as much as you do."

"For the same reason Charles has refused to sign the papers. The legal entanglements with the children would be enormous. You screwed him out of a lot of money, Julia, but there's a lot more where that came from and he's not about to let you get your claws into it."

Her jaw dropped. "But the children. He has to provide for the children."

"Yes, and if he could do it without providing for you he would. People in our circle don't divorce, Julia. They swallow shit and move on. Trust me. If I could find a way to wash you out of his life, I would."

She stepped into the elevator as the doors closed, trying to absorb everything that had been said. Her life had turned into a B movie, so absurd normal people wouldn't believe it. She was still trying to make sense of it all when she walked out of the hospital lobby.

She brought the children on Christmas Day, bearing perfectly wrapped gifts, but it was an ordeal they were happy to be done with.

She was about as far from the holiday spirit as it was possible to get. Fortunately, Miranda took care of all the holiday things at home, to keep the twins distracted. She even put up the tree and had Andy and Beth help decorate it. She took them to see Santa Claus and chauffeured them to children's holiday parties. It kept them occupied and gave Julia breathing room.

Her balance, however, tipped over the morning she found Rombauer waiting for her at the nurses' station.

"Mr. Patterson is napping right now," he began, "so I thought this would be a good time for us to chat."

"About?"

He walked her to an alcove where a couple of chairs and a table had been placed.

"Can I get you some coffee or tea?"

"No, thank you." She tightened her grip on her purse. "I'd prefer it if you just said what's on your mind."

"All right." He dropped into the chair across from her. "It won't be much longer before we've done everything for your husband we can do at a hospital. His status will change to long term care and he'll need to be discharged."

"Discharged?" Where was this going? "But… I mean, his condition…"

The doctor nodded. "Yes. His condition. He needs to be in a place where his medications can be monitored and he can get the kind of daily care we don't provide here. I can recommend excellent home health care services that can help you."

Panic surged through her, nearly choking her. "Dr. Rombauer, despite what's happened, Charles and I have been separated for months. Our divorce is nearly final. What about his parents?"

God knew they had plenty of room and money to care for their precious son.

"I've spoken with them, but Mr. Patterson explained to me how delicate his wife is and what an emotional strain this would be for her."

Delicate? Elise? Julia wanted to laugh hysterically.

"His condition will continue to deteriorate," Rombauer continued. "His organs will fail. He will be bedridden for whatever time he has left. They feel even with help it would be more than they could deal with."

"B-But what am I supposed to do with him?" The nightmare kept getting worse. Every option she imagined was unpleasant. "I cannot take him home."

Oh, God. The thought of it made her dizzy.

"I had that feeling." His understanding smile brought tears to her eyes. Deliberately she blinked them back. No crying now. "Under the circumstances I'm recommending he go directly into a nursing home from here."

Nursing home? Of course. The best solution. The wave of relief washing over her shamed her. Yes, it was appropriate, Charles could be in a place where he could get the right kind of care.

"As his medical representative," he went on, "it will be up to you to choose the place and make the arrangements."

"Dr. Rombauer." She swallowed hard, trying to ease the panic rushing up to consume her. More decisions. More challenges. All of which Charles would argue about. He resented his crippling condition almost as much as he resented her, and what he referred to as her "defection." "Charles is alert now. I think he should remove my name from those documents and make his own decisions."

Rombauer shrugged. "I spoke to him about it, but he was adamant it still be your responsibility."

Punishment. He was going to continue to punish her. She wanted to laugh hysterically, because he didn't even know what he was punishing her for.

"I have no idea where to start looking for one."

"Not to worry. There are two or three excellent ones I can recommend. If you like, I can check with them, let you make the selection, and take care of the arrangements when the time comes."

"Oh, please." Relief surged up. "I'd appreciate it." She took a sip of her tea. "Have you spoken to Charles about this?"

Rombauer frowned. "Yes, and I have to warn you, he's not happy with the idea. I've tried to explain the necessity as best I can. Perhaps you can help with this."

Not happy. She'd bet that was an understatement.

Discussing something with Charles he'd already closed his mind to was not her favorite activity. She rubbed her hands over her face, feeling drained.

"All right, I'll do my best. Thank you, doctor."

She excused herself and raced for the restroom as her stomach heaved its contents back up into her throat.

* * * *

"I will not be locked away in some medical prison like a drooling old man." Charles glared at her as she walked into his room.

Julia forced herself not to react. "Hello, Charles. I'm glad to see you feeling a little better today."

"I am *not* feeling better and I'm quite sure you're not glad to see me."

Julia sat down in the chair beside the bed. "Dr. Rombauer said he'd explained to you why you need to be someplace where skilled care is available twenty-four/seven."

"I'm sure you'd be happy with that." His bitterness was evident. "Out of sight, out of mind."

"Charles." She gritted her teeth. "All I want is to make sure you have the best care possible."

"A comfortable place to die, right? How nice for all of you. Even my parents have explained how difficult it would be for them to have me at their home."

For one brief moment, Julia felt a stab of pity for the man nobody wanted. But then she steeled herself. She was losing herself again, and she needed to hang on to whatever shreds were left.

She dredged up every scrap of patience, but it was like trying to dam a tidal wave. The entire time she was there Charles drowned her with his self-pity. Her nausea was worse than ever and Charles wrinkled his nose in disgust whenever she raced for the bathroom. Whatever bug she'd picked up wasn't going away. She'd probably have to make time to see a doctor.

Sitting in a chair by the bed, even for short periods of time, wasn't doing her body any good, either. These days it didn't seem as if it belonged to her, with its variety of protesting twinges and soreness. She was angry at herself for this physical weakness at a time when she needed to be at her strongest, but her body seemed to have a mind and will of its own.

The morning stretched interminably. The discussion of the nursing home options only precipitated Charles's worst explosion yet. The outburst caused his machines to beep and ding, nurses to rush in, and medication to be administered. When he dropped off to a sedative-induced sleep, Julia left to go home. Tonight she would make a telephone call requiring every bit of her staying power. She'd have to draw Howard and Elise into the nursing home debacle. She dreaded that conversation but maybe Charles would listen to them.

* * * *

Luke replaced the handset on his telephone and sat back in his desk chair, watching Mother Nature dump her latest deluge of snow outside his window. The flakes fell so fast they resembled a white curtain hanging from the sky. The atmosphere was dull grey, matching his mood.

Four weeks since he'd left Julia at the airport and the best he'd been able to accomplish was conversations with Claire. Much as he tried to push thoughts of her aside, she was a constant resident in his mind. How was she doing? How was she handling things? Most importantly, what did the future hold for her? For them?

He regretted more than anything the unfinished feeling they'd parted with. Foolishly, he'd assumed they would have plenty of time to explore a future together, to see if one was even possible. To see if the blossoming love was real. Would the obligations that weighted them down be an effective blockade, or could they weather the predictable storm and forge a life together? He hadn't expected life to intrude so roughly, leaving them like a book with no ending.

"She's doing as well as can be expected," Claire told him during this latest call. "But you know our Julia. She's determined to martyr herself for Charles's condition."

"Damn it, why won't she at least get in touch with me?" Luke could barely keep the frustration from his voice. "Maybe I could find some way to help her."

"Luke." Claire's voice was quiet. "You're the only happiness Julia's found after nine years of emotional hell. She's consumed with guilt about it. Unreasonably, she wants to blame this whole mess on what she calls her selfish indulgence."

"Ridiculous," he snapped.

"I know. But there it is." Claire was silent a moment. "I've talked until I'm blue in the face. But she's trying to bolster the twins as well as herself."

"I've half a mind to just get on a plane and show up." He had to force back the anguish consuming him.

"Please don't. She'd crack and fall apart."

"Just keep me in the loop, okay?"

More than anything, he wished it was possible for him to be there to hold her in his arms and soothe away the pain. If only she would call him or take one of his calls. He wanted to smash something, throw something, rant and rave. He hated the fact she blamed herself for this, as if the brief happiness they'd shared was undeserved.

He closed his eyes, remembering the silken feel of her skin, the delicate floral scent she wore, the velvety texture of her hair.

God, how he missed her.

Chapter 11

Pregnant!

Julia lay on the examining table in the doctor's office, listening to the confirmation of her own fears. She'd done whatever she could do to get through the holiday season, hoping afterward she'd begin to feel better. When she didn't, pestered by both Miranda and Claire, she finally called her doctor. Except by then she was sure of the diagnosis. Something she should have known right away. The immediate and constant nausea, the dragging fatigue, every one of the symptoms mirrored those with the twins almost from the moment of conception.

"No question, Mrs. Patterson." Dr. Berlin looked up from the foot of the table. "A little less than two months. Does that jibe with your calculations?"

Unfortunately, yes.

"Mrs. Patterson?" he repeated.

"I'm sorry. Yes. Yes, it does."

"Well, I hope this is good news. I know you were disappointed when you couldn't take the birth control pills, but usually we have pretty good luck with the coil." He chuckled slightly. "Although they do fail once in a while."

"Well, it seems this is one of those times," she told him.

"You'll need to be cautious," he told her. "Miscarriage is sometimes a problem with the coil in place. No strenuous exercise and, I hate to tell you, no sexual activity. I hope your husband won't mind too much."

"I can assure you that won't be a problem. My husband has suffered a severe heart attack and his health isn't good."

"Oh. I'm so sorry." He paused. "Is the situation such you might consider terminating the pregnancy? This may not be the best time for you to be giving birth."

"No!" She nearly shouted the word. "No," she repeated more quietly, "that's not a consideration." She touched her abdomen as if to protect the growing child from harm.

"I'll take your word for it. But if you do change your mind, you'll need to decide soon."

"I won't be changing my mind, Dr. Berlin."

"Fine, then." He stood up and reached out his hand to help her sit up on the table. "I don't need to tell you what to do, but because you're past thirty, we'll want to watch you a little more carefully this time."

"I understand. I'll do my best." And how exactly would she accomplish this under the circumstances?

"Make your next appointment on the way out. You're nearly through the first trimester and I'd like to see you every two weeks from here until the ninth month."

Julia was still in shock when she climbed behind the steering wheel of her car. She'd suspected as much with the nausea then the first missed period, but initially chalked it up to stress. There was certainly plenty to go around. She rested her hand against her lower abdomen. A child! Luke's child! Something of his she would always have to cherish.

How the hell was this going to play out with Charles? God! Could things possibly get any worse?

She had stopped visiting him every day. There was only so much she could tolerate. She believed he'd be grateful for her absence. Instead, when she made herself show up, he lectured her on the propriety of appearances. What would people say? What would they think? She wanted to tell him she didn't give a damn about any of that. She was sick to death of him and his family and his friends. If he'd just sign the damn divorce papers she'd be out of his hair and he could tell everyone whatever he wanted. She didn't care. Harry assured her the financial settlement was ironclad so she could rest assured the children would be provided for.

Now she knew for sure she couldn't talk to Luke. If he knew she was pregnant, he'd be here on the next plane and try to take charge of the situation. There'd be holy hell to pay, with Rod McGuire leading the charge. Luke had thought his ex-wife's behavior would scandalize his employers and affect his job. Rod and the Pattersons would make that seem like child's play.

Needing time to absorb her situation, she drove to her favorite café, ordered a pot of tea and the butter cookies she loved, and spent an hour examining her situation. A combination of dread and elation filled her. A good plot for a movie: marriage falling apart, wife takes a lover, husband lies near death from a heart attack, wife is pregnant with another man's child. What a melodrama.

Unconsciously her hand drifted to her abdomen again and a soft smile curved her lips. Luke. The thought of his child was a life raft in a sea of despair. Would it be a boy or a girl? Would it have his wonderful eyes, his thick hair?

She shook herself. She was in no position to be daydreaming. She didn't want to think what would happen when she couldn't conceal it from Charles any longer. Maybe if things worked out Charles would be… gone…before she began to show.

Terrible. Awful. How could she think that?

She waited another day before heading to the hospital again, gripped by a feeling of dread when she walked into Charles's room. Carefully composing her face, willing her nausea to go away, and pasting a smile on her face, she greeted him with as much pleasantry as she could muster.

He tossed aside the magazine in his hand. "What's wrong? You look like hell?"

"Nothing, It's…nothing at all."

He studied her with a critical eye. "You've been sickly the last few times you were here. You should take better care of yourself. The children need you. Before long I will need you."

For a moment she was that insecure young woman again, unsure of herself in the strange world she'd been dropped into, starving for approval and affection. God. If she could just hide away somewhere for a while. Recharge her energy. The way she felt at the moment, she had no strength to deal with anything.

"I'm sorry. I… You're right. I'll see the doctor." She started to sit down but nausea gripped her with a tight fist and she raced for the bathroom. Her stomach emptied itself, leaving her drained. She rinsed her mouth and patted her face with a damp towel then girded herself to face Charles.

His eyes stared daggers at her. "You're pregnant."

Julia recoiled in shock, as if from a physical blow. "Pregnant? W-Why… I mean…"

"Don't try to lie to me. You never were very good at it."

"H-How did you know?" She instinctively looked down at her still-flat stomach.

"No, you aren't showing." His smile was nasty. "It wasn't hard to figure out. Did you think I'd miss the signs? The vomiting every time you're here? The changes in your body? The fatigue you never could hide? We've been through this before, remember? I don't know why you couldn't have neat pregnancies the way other women do."

"Neat…pregnancies." What the hell did that mean?

"My heart may be damaged," he went on, "but my brain is still fully functional." When she was silent, he asked, "Have you no comment to make?"

"What shall I say, Charles? Yes, I'm pregnant."

"I can hardly believe this," he said. "I've been fighting a heart condition and you've been whoring in some man's bed."

His words hit her like brickbats. If only she weren't so tired and achy. If her head didn't hurt so much as she tried to deal with one crisis after another. If only she could run away and hide. She dug her nails into her palms to keep from crying. "You're wrong."

"No?" He lifted an eyebrow, a scornful look on his face. "Then what was it like? An immaculate conception? It certainly isn't mine."

"Charles, I…" She swallowed, took a breath.

"Anyway, I thought you were using one of those devices." He vibrated with rage.

"Yes, and it's still in place. But Dr. Berlin says they have a greater rate of failure than the pills."

"Which your *sensitive* system couldn't tolerate."

"A lot of women can't take them, Charles." She would not apologize. She would not be on the defensive.

He stared at her from the hospital bed with the most malevolent look she'd ever seen. "Get rid of it."

"What?" She turned clammy with shock, her heart first racing then threatening to stop altogether.

"You heard me. Get rid of it. Right away."

Oh, my God. Get rid of Luke's baby? They'd have to kill her first.

"This is not your decision to make." She sounded braver than she felt, but she would fight for this child.

"For God's sake, Julia, for once in your life will you think of someone besides yourself? How will the children react when they find out you're carrying someone's illegitimate brat? Or my partners? Or my family, for that matter."

"What?" She nearly fainted, collapsing into the chair before she fell to the floor.

"I'm appalled you would prostitute yourself in another man's bed. Before long, everyone will know. How do you think this will play out for a man with a damaged heart?"

Prostitute? *Oh, Jesus.*

The nausea roared back with a vengeance, threatening to overtake her. She made a dash for the bathroom, reaching it just in time. She took a minute to splash cold water on her face and try to pull herself together. She still shook, but not as badly, when she went back into the room.

"There." His face was set in the smug look she hated. "Exactly what I mean. Here I am practically an invalid, and I have to listen to you retching every day."

"I'll try to keep the vomiting contained to the hours I'm away from you." She couldn't help the sarcasm.

"I hope you didn't pick someone my friends might know. I don't need everyone smirking at me behind my back."

"He's not from here and he's no one you know. He's a wonderful man who gave me the most pleasure I've ever known in my life." The words were out before she could stop herself.

Charles clenched his jaw, and suddenly one of the machines behind him began beeping rapidly. In seconds, the nurse was beside the bed. Julia stood aside, waiting for the woman to check his vital signs and reset the machine.

"Just a little irregularity." She smiled and patted his hand. "Nothing to worry about, but you mustn't let yourself get excited."

After she left, Charles looked at Julia, his face set in an expression of disgust. "I suppose you would have been more than happy if your news managed to kill me and I was out of the picture completely."

"Please don't say that." She was back in control again. "I don't wish anything to worsen your condition. But I am keeping this baby, Charles, so forget about suggesting a termination again." Unconsciously her fingers touched the tiny tree charm nestled at the hollow of her throat. It was her only contact with Luke and bolstered her courage as her life continued to deteriorate.

"What on earth is that piece of junk you're wearing?" Charles snapped, his gaze focusing on her. "Where did you get it? I don't remember giving it to you."

Julia swallowed. "I saw it in the airport and it appealed to me. Besides, you no longer have the right to tell me what to do or wear."

"Really?" He lifted an eyebrow. "Now that's where you're wrong."

"Excuse me?" Now what?

"You may not realize it"—he smirked—"but you may have just handed me the keys to the kingdom."

She frowned. "I don't understand. You'd better explain."

"Not now. Right now I'd like you to leave." His voice was cold, like chipped ice. "I have a lot of thinking to do and I'd rather do it alone."

"Fine." Julia gathered up her purse and jacket. "I'll be back in a few days. It's obvious you're fine without me and I have things to do."

"I want you back here tomorrow," he snapped. "But in the afternoon. I'm going to have Rod come by in the morning. Then we're going to have a discussion about the future. Everyone's, including mine and yours."

Outside the room, she leaned against the wall, her legs threatening to collapse under her.

"Mrs. Patterson?" One of the nurses stood next to her. "Can I get you something? A drink of water?"

Julia drew a breath and exhaled slowly. "No. Thank you. I'm fine now." She walked to the elevator on rubbery legs, her mind whirling. She felt guilty enough about Charles's condition without nearly hastening his demise, but she was not getting rid of this child. Charles wasn't going to live forever. Was she a terrible person because she clung to that thought like a lifeline? And then she could make a life with Luke.

* * * *

She had avoided telling Claire about her situation, but in fairness to her friend, she couldn't stall any longer. She called the office from the car. "Can you stay a little later today? I need to talk to you."

"Sure. Of course. What's up? Is Charles worse?"

"No." Not exactly. "I just need to chat with you a few minutes."

"No problem. Come on. I'll wait for you."

All the way to the office, she rehearsed how she would break the news to Claire. It should have been easier than Charles, but for some reason this was worse. When Julia walked in the door, her practiced speeches failed her, and she simply blurted out, "I'm pregnant."

Claire stared at her, open-mouthed. "It's his, isn't it," she said, eyes flashing.

"Whose?" Julia tried to keep her voice level.

"The deep voice. It is, isn't it? Come on, Julia, we've known each other forever. 'Fess up."

Julia was silent and Claire laughed.

"How fascinating. A love child. Our proper Julia. Good for you."

"Claire!"

"Don't 'Claire' me. You needed a little spice in your life, being married to an ice cube. And I won't help with the hair shirt you insist on wearing by condemning you for this."

"Charles is just...reserved."

"Ha!" Claire barked a laugh. "Reserved, my ass. How are you going to tell his majesty, anyway? The man you're all but divorced from?"

"He guessed. The nausea and vomiting, and the fatigue, gave it away. He remembered."

"You could have been upset about this whole situation. Emotionally distressed."

Julia flapped her hand. "I'm all that, for sure. But his eagle eye zeroed in on the symptoms from my last pregnancy. It might have been a shot in the dark but he scored a bull's-eye. We had an unpleasant little conversation today." She dropped into the chair in front of Claire's desk. "I don't think I'd like to repeat the process."

"I can't imagine what he said." It was a statement, not a question.

"No. You can't. He wants me to have an abortion."

"What?" Claire was nearly speechless. "What a bastard. That's harsh even for him."

Julia twisted her hands. "He knows it's not his. That's reason enough."

"But... You're practically divorced. And would be if he hadn't been such a prick. It's none of his business." She shook her head. "Let him go to the nursing home and rot there."

"I...I just..." She felt herself sway.

"Oh, my God. Stop." Claire came out from behind the desk. "You need some tea. Sit down and let me fix you a cup." She literally pushed Julia onto the couch, pulled a tiny footstool over to prop her feet on, and plugged in the kettle in the powder room to heat water. In minutes, she handed Julia a steaming mug of fragrant liquid. "Drink. So. The baby is Luke's."

Julia nodded. "Yes. It is." Her hand automatically went to her stomach.

"What happens next? I'm sure you didn't agree to an abortion."

"No way. I told him I'm keeping this child and nothing he said could change my mind."

"Good for you. Who knows how long Charles will be around, anyway?"

"Claire!"

"Julia, you can't run away from the truth. His heart condition is acute and Rombauer told you the prognosis is not good."

Julia shoved her hand through her hair. "This couldn't be happening at a worse time."

"Are you going to tell Luke?"

"Are you out of your mind?" Julia's jaw dropped.

"The man has a right to know."

"The man also knows I have a husband who is dying, twins who need my love and support, and an uphill battle no matter how you look at it. I know Luke. If I tell him, he'd hang up and jump on the next plane to San Antonio. How would I possibly keep this little secret from him? And then we'll be in a bigger mess. You think Charles flexed his muscle to hold up the divorce? You ain't seen nothing yet."

"Secrets have a way of coming out, Julia. One of these days it will come back to bite you."

"Well, this one has to remain well-hidden. At least for now." Until Charles was gone and she could pick up the frayed edges of her life. Then if Luke didn't hate her for keeping this from him and still wanted a life with her, she might finally be able to embrace happiness.

"When are you due?"

"August."

"You're going to have to make some preparations. For one thing, you need to tell the twins. And by the time another month rolls around you'll be in maternity clothes, so it won't exactly be a secret."

"I know, I know. Oh, God." She looked into the mug as if it held the answers she was seeking.

"You should go home and get some rest. You look like hell and this is no time to neglect yourself."

"Thanks so much."

"Don't go back to the hospital tomorrow. You've been cutting back on your visits. He won't miss you."

Julia shook her head. "He has something in mind. Whatever it is involves Rod McGuire so you know it can't be good. I'm to report back tomorrow afternoon."

"Oh, sweetie." Claire gave her a hug.

"I wish to all that's holy I knew what the bond is between those two."

Claire giggled. "You don't suppose they're both closet homosexuals, do you? Maybe they've had a thing going all these years."

Julia stared at her. "What? No. I may be stupid about a lot of things, and Charles may be a dud in bed, but I never got a hint of that. Especially when they were together. There are always signs. No, it's something else. Something that makes a bond thicker than blood."

Claire nibbled on the edge of a nail. "I'll tell you what. I'm going to find out what it is."

"Leave it alone, Please. Besides, who would you ask?"

"Leave it to me. I promise you I won't make any waves and it will never get back to either of them."

"Good, because I've got all the stress I can handle right about now."

"You're right. Go home, take a hot bath, and cuddle your kids. That's an order."

"Yes, ma'am." A ghost of a smile chased itself across Julia's face. "Whatever would I do without you?"

"I'm not about to let you find out. Don't you worry. I'm going to coddle you like a piece of china. No traveling and no late events. I'm happy to do it all." She hugged her friend. "Something special in your life. You need it."

* * * *

Charles sat propped up in bed when Julia entered his room the following morning. His face still held the same implacable look and anger still simmered in his eyes. She wasn't sure what to say to him. *Hello? How are you feeling? Rotten, I hope.*

"Sit down," he snapped. "We have business to discuss."

She took the chair furthest from the bed. "Then let's get on with it." She was proud of the controlled tone of her voice.

"I've given this entire situation a great deal of consideration. I don't have much else to do, as you well know."

"Yes, Charles. I'm aware of your incapacitation."

"At its best, your—situation—is still a problem. Even if the child were mine, this would not be the best time for you to be pregnant."

She said nothing. Silence was her best tack right now.

"Since you insist on keeping this bastard child, there are only a few options. It would create more embarrassment than I'm willing to endure to have you parading around fat and swollen and have to deny the child was mine."

"Yours?" She raised her eyebrows. "B-But…I mean, the divorce… everyone knows…"

"Yes," he spat. "The stupid divorce. Another manifestation of your childish behavior."

Anger surged through her. "Childish—"

Charles held up a hand. "Please let me finish. I discussed everything in detail with Rod this morning. He's only too happy to help me carry out my wishes."

I'm sure he is, she wanted to spit out, but pressed her lips together.

"Under the circumstances, divorce is no longer even a consideration. Especially since my signature is the one holding up the process and I have no intention of signing now. Or ever. Oh, yes, I know a judge can force the issue but you'd have to find one willing to do it. And at this point I'm prepared to contest it."

"But—" Julia felt the nausea creeping up again. Every word was like a body blow.

"So, what to do," he went on, as if discussing some errant business problem. "What solution would be a fair compromise for the parties concerned? Having looked at the entire situation from every angle, I've decided to offer you a bargain."

"A bargain? How magnanimous of you." She forced herself to be calm although inside she was shaking like watery Jello. "What do I have to do, cut my heart out?"

"Here are the terms if you don't want to lose your present children and be thrown out in the streets," he went on, ignoring her remarks. "Rombauer made it quite clear my days are numbered and my condition will continue to deteriorate. He is recommending I be moved to a nursing home."

"Yes. He went over everything with me."

"I refuse to accept it as an option. For whatever time remains to me, I choose not to spend it in the care and company of strangers."

"Then what's the alternative?" Julia frowned, puzzled.

"I want to go home."

"Home?" She was sure her voice squeaked.

"Yes. We can turn the den into a room for me, a hospital bed can be brought in, we can arrange for home health care. Everything can be done quite simply."

Bring him back into the house? Where she'd never have a minute's peace?

"And?"

"And the rest of my care will fall to you."

"You're out of your mind." She clenched her fists at her sides. "You want a pregnant woman to be at your beck and call twenty-four seven, taking care of you? How will I even manage?"

"That will be up to you. You have Miranda to help you. Let her earn the outrageous salary we pay her. However you do it, I expect the finest care and attention. Are you listening?"

She nodded, gritting her teeth.

"We will tell everyone the child is mine. We tried a…reconciliation we hoped would work."

She goggled. The only word for it. "Are you out of your mind?"

"There is nothing wrong with my mind. I have been over this from every angle and discussed it thoroughly with Rod. I will allow this child to have my name and share equally in my estate. The public would expect it."

The public. Of course.

"You will say nothing of this to anyone," he told her. "For the next few months you will be the loving, dutiful wife I always hoped you'd be, sharing with me the joy of the coming birth."

"As if anyone would believe you wanted another child."

He held up a hand. "Please. It will be up to you to make them believe it."

"And if I say no? What possible advantage would this be to me?"

"If you don't agree, I will countersue for divorce. Some proceedings can be dragged out for a long time. And while that's going on I'll have you declared an unfit mother and the twins will be removed from your care and custody."

For a terrifying moment she was afraid she'd faint. "Un-Unfit? But you can't—"

"Of course I can. Rod is prepared to parade a number of witnesses who will testify to your inability to care for your children. How you leave them for hours to pursue your own pleasures. How I was forced to hire a housekeeper because I feared for their welfare. How I—"

"Stop!" She pressed her hands to her temples. "Those are all lies. Every one of them."

"Are they?" His features settled into a smug expression. "Who will argue against them? Your little friend Claire? Your support circle is very small, Julia, while mine is large and powerful."

"You can't do that," she whispered. But she knew he could. She'd heard of so many situations where people lost everything, from their families, to their businesses, to their lives because people richer and stronger and more influential pulled the right strings. Right now, she barely had the strength to get from one day to the next, never mind fight a battle she would probably lose. People in Charles's circle never lost anything.

"No? It happens all the time. Watch television. Look on the Internet. Read the newspapers. Push me and you'll find out." He fiddled with the sheet. "When we married you told me more than anything you wanted a stable home and financial security. I gave you that and you made a mockery of it."

"You made a mockery of our marriage," she cried.

"Quiet. There's no need to broadcast this all over the floor. So..." He paused. "You will still have that security you wanted, only under certain terms."

"Such as?" She was afraid to even ask.

He paused to steady himself with some deep breaths. "This man, whoever he is, will never become a part of your life again. Ever. That's not negotiable. It would pain me greatly to think as soon as my body was cold, you'd be running off to a love nest."

"And how will you insure that, you bastard?" *Luke!*

"I discussed this at length with Rod McGuire. He'll serve as my executor. He has sealed instructions to follow if you break your promise. He will activate the charge of unfit mother and have my parents sue for custody of the twins."

"Your parents? I don't see them as having two children invading the discipline of their lives."

"They don't have to. They will immediately ship them off to boarding school."

"Boarding— What? Are you serious?"

"He'll have all those witnesses lined up, ready to go at any time. You will only see the children for limited amounts of time each year."

Her heart was galloping. Lose her children? "I'll fight you."

He waved a hand at her. "Feel free. But it's a long and expensive process. Under these circumstances, your financial settlement would be null and void so you'd be penniless before long. And of course unable to provide a suitable environment for the children. As I pointed out to you many times Julia, power and money control the game. Nobody fucks with me and gets away with it."

Julia thought she would faint. This was worse than a nightmare.

"I also plan to leave a letter to be delivered to Andrew and Elizabeth detailing exactly what kind of woman their mother is. Instead of staying home taking care of them, she was out whoring in some man's bed."

"But you don't even know who he is."

"It doesn't matter. I don't want to know." He twisted his lips in a caricature of a smile. "And don't think the future holds any hope for you. Whore. Rod has promised me any man who tries to make a place in your life he'll methodically destroy. We have the resources to do it. A word to the man's employer. Clients. Friends. Again, the power of money and influence. I hope it was all worth it, Julia."

"God, you are the cruelest man I know." She felt sick and shaken.

"Cruel? You call me cruel? You're the one who ran off to another man's bed."

She curled her hands into fists, fighting for control. "If it weren't for the twins, I'd tell you to go to hell, heart condition or not. But I won't put their security with me in danger. They love me, the only parent who has shown them affection, regardless of what your lying friends might say. I will not jeopardize that."

"Well, Julia, those are my terms. Take them or leave them."

The most important thing was the children, all of them, including Luke's child. She must safeguard its future no matter what it cost her. And she could not put her children through a public scandal.

"I'm waiting, Julia."

She nodded. "You win. Now excuse me so I can throw up."

Chapter 12

Bringing Charles home was the easy part. The mechanics of preparing the den for him, of arranging for home health care, of listening to instructions from Rombauer were accomplished with a minimal amount of stress. She'd scheduled the ambulance to deliver him during the time the children were in school. She was unwilling to subject them to the distress of watching him being carried in and arranged in bed, seeing a nurse hook up his monitors and his medication.

The first afternoon when Andy and Beth came home from school, Miranda swept them into the kitchen where Julia explained over cookies and milk what their routine was now going to be and the importance of being quiet. She thanked God for the size of the house, the distance of the family room from the den where Charles was set up, and the intelligence of her seven-year-olds who seemed to absorb everything without too many questions. She also blessed Dr. Grenfeld, the therapist working with Julia to help the children adjust to this drastic alteration in their lives.

One week dragged heavily into the next and now it was April. She and Claire sat in the family room, the late afternoon sunlight slanting in through the big picture window. Julia's pregnancy bump was growing, although certainly not as much as with the twins. She insisted on at least doing desk work from home, so for weeks Claire brought her projects to work on. It kept her mind occupied, distracting her from the disaster of her situation.

"You're exhausted," Claire said.

"I'm fine." Julia pushed her hair back from her face. She'd cut it shorter, something else for Charles to express his displeasure about, but it made it much easier to care for.

"No, you're not." Claire grimaced. "You've got to let Miranda take up more of the slack."

"She's already doing a lot. Anyway, Charles won't even let her in the room."

"What a total shit he is." Claire twisted her lips in an expression of distaste. If you'd come to me about this Brad and I would have helped you. We'd never have let you agree to this."

Tears burned in Julia's eyes. "I could never ask you to do that. We're talking about a fortune here. Money they all have and we don't."

"Honey, Brad's a well-paid engineer and we have resources. We'd gladly do whatever it takes. Then or now."

Julia reached over and grasped her friend's hand. "Thank you. Knowing that helps more than I can tell you, but this is my mess and I have to live with it."

"I want you to promise me that once Charles is gone we'll reevaluate the situation. Please."

Would she have the courage to do it then? Right now she just wanted to get past her two immediate crises—Charles and the baby.

"We'll see." She lifted her tea and took a sip.

"He's determined to make your life as much of a living hell as possible," Claire pointed out in a caustic voice.

"The weaker he gets, the more fearful of death he becomes. This is just his way of expressing it."

"You're making excuses for him."

Julia knew that, but it helped her deal with his demands and unreasoning rages. The months were dragging interminably, a leaden weight stretching every minute into hours.

Claire leaned forward, an earnest look on her face. "Just remember, it won't do either the twins or this new baby any good if you're out of the picture too."

"I know, I know. I wish he'd leave Miranda alone. That woman is a saint."

"No sainthood here." Miranda walked out onto the patio carrying a fresh pitcher of iced tea. "Only the devil has thoughts like the ones running around in my head."

"He must be in mine, too," Claire laughed.

"I'm sorry he yells at you." She took Miranda's hand and squeezed it. "Maybe you should just stay out of the den."

"And let him yell at you?" Miranda sniffed. "Don't make no never mind to me." Miranda waved a hand. "I just close my ears and my mouth when I walk into that room. You just need to keep the twins away from him."

"If only his rages didn't carry through the house."

Just last night the children, frightened by Charles's latest outburst, had huddled against Julia, bravely swallowing tears.

"Let's close the family room door when they're in there," Miranda suggested. "They can have supper in there, too. They'll like playing picnic. Then you can take them upstairs, supervise their baths, and read to them."

"That ought to work," Claire agreed. "Do it, Julia. Whatever you have to in order to get them—and yourself—through this."

* * * *

April turned into May. The twins celebrated their eighth birthday, a subdued celebration, under the circumstances. Charles still clung to life, well past the doctor's predictions, although it was obvious any day could be his last. Julia was barely hanging on to her sanity.

"He's stopped calling." Claire made the announcement when she dropped by the house one afternoon.

"Who?" Julia wrinkled her forehead. She sat in the family room with her feet up, fanning herself. She'd gone to the store and the heat of the Texas summer had undone her in the few moments she was exposed to it.

"Who do you think? Mr. Sexy Voice."

"Luke?" The thought of him was like the painful stabbing of a sword. She'd lost track of the nights she'd lain awake in her bed, longing to feel his hands on her just one more time. His mouth on hers. His cock inside her. As his child grew within her, the longings became even more acute. "I thought he stopped ages ago."

"He's persistent, the asshole. But I think he finally got the message."

"He's not an asshole," Julia protested.

Claire just smiled.

"He needs to get on with his life." She felt such sadness at the thought of him in a solitary existence, waiting for something that could never happen. "All I'd bring him is a mess."

"Don't you think that's his choice to make?" She leaned closer to Julia. "You know, despite Charles's diabolical plan, there's nothing to prevent you from calling him when this is finally over. With Luke beside you, anything is possible. And at least then it's his choice to make."

Julia shook her head vehemently. "No, I can't. And please don't ask me about it anymore. If you're my good, good friend, you'll leave it alone."

"Well, I also stopped by to tell you that Brad's done a little discreet digging and we know why Rod McGuire is so willing to take up the sword for Charles."

"Please tell me he didn't put himself in a vulnerable position to do it. I'd hate it if this mess spilled over into your lives and damaged it some way."

"Trust me. He was the soul of discretion. But he has some clients who were in college with Charles and Rod. He casually brought up the names while they were all at dinner the other night." She grinned. "And maybe he led them to believe he was a lot closer to him."

Julia sat up straight, nerves vibrating. "And? Don't keep me in suspense here."

"It seems in his younger days Rod had a gambling habit. A bad one he acquired in prep school."

Julia waved a dismissive hand. "Some of Charles's friends used to joke about it. They all did it."

"But I'm sure none of them became addicted to it the way Rod did."

"And?"

"He loved to bet. Horses. Race cars. Sports events. Anything. In college he got in pretty deep with the wrong people. His father had already threatened to cut him off after paying off two huge debts, so he couldn't go to him for money. Whoever these guys were, they beat him up pretty bad. He managed to call Charles, who picked him up and wanted to take him to the hospital."

"That bad?"

"Oh, yeah. Rod refused to go so Charles booked them into a cheap motel, went to the drugstore for supplies, and nursed him back to decent condition. He also took his own money and paid off the bookies, told them they better not ever take a bet from Rod again. Then, until they graduated from college and law school and even when they joined their fathers' law firm, he made it his business to keep Rod out of trouble."

"Damn!" Julia sucked in a breath. "That's why he feels so loyal to him."

"Yeah. He owes the guy his life. Literally."

"No wonder it's such a blood vendetta." She leaned back in her chair, rubbing her forehead.

"Honey, don't make yourself sick over this. We'll figure out how to handle this."

Wouldn't that be nice. Unlikely, but nice.

That night when she crawled into bed, for the first time in months she allowed herself the luxury of tears. The enormity of what Charles had set in motion made her physically ill. Stuffing the pillow against her face so her sobs would be silent, she wondered if the rip in her own heart would ever heal. How cruel life was to offer her the golden ring and then snatch it away with such violent abruptness.

During the following week, Charles began sleeping most of the time. By the weekend, he quietly slipped into a coma and then he was gone. The funeral home picked up what was left of the man she'd once thought she loved. A crew from the medical supply company disconnected machines, packed up supplies, and returned the den to its original state. Claire, as always, came in response to her call and supervised the process. Miranda had taken the children upstairs and was absorbing their sorrow with her usual kindness and unflappability. Although, as Julia sat in the kitchen numb in every extremity, she wondered how they could mourn for a man who had treated them so coldly.

One hour later, it was as if none of it happened, except for the wreckage of her life strewn in its wake.

"Here, drink this." Claire set a fresh mug of tea in front of Julia.

"I think I'm turning into a tea bag."

"It's herbal and decaffeinated. Dr. Berlin said there's nothing in it to harm the baby, and maybe it will do you some good." She waited a heartbeat. "I hate to bring this up, but have you thought about funeral arrangements?"

"I didn't even have to give them a moment's consideration." Julia snorted. "Charles was thoughtful enough to take care of the preparations with his parents and his partners. The service will be at the funeral home, and he'll be buried in the family plot at the cemetery. I don't have to do anything but show up."

"I'd take that as a relief, rather than an offense. You don't need to be entangling yourself in those details right now. The baby's due in a month."

"I know, I know. I just feel like I'm on the outside looking in on everything."

"Sometimes it's a good way to be," Claire told her in a soft voice.

The day of the funeral was blazing hot. She was sure everyone in the crowd of mourners was conscious of her advanced pregnancy. She sat at the graveside clutching the hands of her children. Her face was shadowed by an enormous black hat that barely protected her from the broiling sun. She chalked up the lack of sympathy for her to the obvious shunning by Elise and Howard. And Charles's partners, especially Rod McGuire, who always made his hatred and distaste for her blatantly evident. Both at the funeral home and the cemetery he'd kept as far from her as possible. The expression on his face, however, left no doubt about his feelings.

Most of the people at the funeral were clients or friends of the elder Pattersons or the partners. Without Claire, she'd never have gotten through the day. The service itself seemed endless, and at the cemetery, the minister droned on interminably, unaware that everyone surreptitiously blotted at their perspiration. Julia felt as if she'd been stuffed into an oven in a tight corset. By the end of the graveside service, she could barely breathe.

With Andy and Beth beside her, she took one white rose and placed it on the casket. Then she gladly let Claire lead them away to an air-conditioned car and home. All the mourners were invited back to the senior Pattersons' after the service. Howard and Elise gave her a token invitation but she begged off, using her condition as an excuse. She certainly had no intention of subjecting the children to such a depressing environment. It was time for them as a family to move on with their lives. It wasn't as if either Charles or his parents had a warm, affectionate relationship with the twins.

"They should be coming to your house." Claire's anger was sharp as the car pulled away from the graveside.

"Forget it." Julia removed the uncomfortable hat and brushed her hair away from her face. "Let Howard and Elise play the grieving parents. These are their people anyway. I just want to be done with it."

She spent most of August secluded at home. She never asked about the agency, never ventured outside. Every moment of her time was devoted to the twins and the child about to be born.

Her seclusion was interrupted, however, by one unpleasant call from Rod McGuire.

"Per Charles's instructions, I've deposited a significant sum in your checking account," he told her. "But we do have some important things regarding the estate to handle." He cleared his throat. "I'd like to wait but Charles was quite specific with his instructions."

"Yes, I'm sure he was." She sat in the big chair in the family room, her swollen feet propped up on a footstool. "Just tell me when you'd like to do this. I'd rather you came to the house, if you don't mind. Going out is not as easy for me these days."

"Yes. I understand." The censure in his voice was hard to miss. "Then it's important we meet. I'll have my secretary call and schedule it."

"Fine. Thank you." What else could she say?

He clicked off, without a goodbye.

She dreaded the meeting, knowing every one of their secrets along with his anger was now in his hands. However unpleasant, she couldn't avoid it.

A week later, McGuire sat facing her in the den, the scene of Charles's final days. The acrid odors of medicine and illness were gone, banished through Miranda's elbow grease, but the miasma of death still hovered. Julia seldom came into the room now, but she'd determined it to be the most fitting place for this discussion. She sat at the desk, McGuire across from her.

"I find this somewhat uncomfortable, Julia." He opened his briefcase and extracted a file.

"I'm not too happy myself," she said.

"You must admit, considering your…um…situation, Charles was more than magnanimous."

Julia gritted her teeth. "My pregnancy…" she stressed the word, not caring if it embarrassed Rod, "is something that happened. We can at least call it what it is."

"Nevertheless, Charles was disturbed about it. I'm sure you were aware of his feelings."

"Rod, can we stop tap dancing?" She shifted uncomfortably in her chair. Lately she couldn't seem to find any place to put herself. "I don't have time to listen to a lecture. You and I both know why I brought Charles into the house for those last months. My pregnancy was an unexpected turn of events, and Charles chose the path he did so he could save face. My feelings were never part of the equation."

"I admired him for the way he handled it." He eyed her swollen body with evident condemnation. "I'd have just tossed you out into the street."

Yes, and now Julia knew why.

She took a deep breath to steady her voice. "Let's just get to the heart of the matter here. I'm well aware of the terms of the will and of the letters you hold, so what else is there to discuss?"

Rod's mouth thinned in disapproval. Julia knew full well being Charles's executor was a distasteful problem for him but only because it meant dealing with her. He extracted a sheaf of papers from a folder and placed them on the desk.

"This is the deed to the house. It and all of its contents are left specifically to you. Charles wanted to insure a proper home for Andrew and Elizabeth to be raised in. I've arranged for the name on the deed to be changed."

The house was larger and more ostentatious than she'd ever been comfortable with, more a symbol of Charles's image than anything else. But it was the only one the twins had known and she knew what it was like to have that stability ripped away from you.

"I'll be sure to cancel the rental on the mobile home." Acid dripped from her voice but she didn't care.

McGuire ignored her remarks. "There was substantial life insurance, payable to the estate, as well as Charles's investments." His smile was cold. "He was blessed with an incredible mind when it came to those details."

"Yes." What was she supposed to say?

"At his direction, I set up a fund to provide monthly income for the care of Andrew and Elizabeth. Individual trust funds have been set up for them, which they will receive when they're twenty-five, as well as separate trusts to pay for their education expenses." He raised his eyes to look at her. "He was far more generous than I felt he was obligated to be."

"Obligated to?" she nearly shouted. "You can bet he was obligated, whatever you think. Those are his children and he damn well better have provided for them."

"Julia." Rod frowned at her. "There's no need to curse."

She took a deep breath, aware she was rocketing out of control. "And the baby? That was part of the deal from hell."

"I'm getting to it." He frowned. "I must tell you I advised Charles against this but he was determined to honor the agreement he made with you." His disgust was obvious. "So yes, you'll be interested to know he established a substantial enough sum to include support for this bastard child as well."

Julia ground her teeth. She'd get through this. She had to.

"Would I be assuming too much to think he made some kind of arrangements for me? I was technically still his wife."

"Technically being the operative word." Rod glared at her.

"So am I the pariah who gets left out in the cold?" She'd find a way to make things work if such turned out to be the case. She hadn't expected to be taken care of, anyway.

Rod sneered, the only word for his expression. "I'd say you're a lucky woman, Julia. Charles was far more generous with you than he should have been and again I advised him against it. The twins are taken care of. You and your bastard child deserved no more than a pittance. However, he wanted his children to retain a good memory of him. He thought doing what I advised him would taint that image when they were old enough to understand it."

"Suddenly he was worried about what his children thought?" Julia barely held on to her temper. "Too bad he didn't care about it when he was alive."

Rod's face turned so red she was afraid he might have a stroke. "Damn it, shut up, Julia. You've been overcompensated for the whore that you are. Charles left you what I would call a significant sum of money." He handed her a sheet of paper. "This is your current bank balance, and the other is the investment account we've set up for you. It will generate a nice income each month. Of course, you're free to move the funds if you choose."

Julia was stunned at the amounts on the sheet Rod handed to her. She'd hoped there would be trust funds for the children, but the additional support money would allow her to do many things for the baby, which might otherwise not be possible. Claire was still taking a minimum salary from the agency, and in fact, Julia had refused to draw anything for herself. Her choice. She couldn't justify it as long as she contributed so little to the effort.

"Thank you." She broke the uncomfortable silence. "And thank you for handling this for Charles. I realize he put you in a difficult situation, but he placed confidence in your ability to see his wishes carried out." She'd be polite if it killed her, damn it.

"Charles and I were friends since boarding school." He stiffened his posture. "I told him not to marry you, but he refused to listen. You turned out to be exactly what I thought. A piece of trash." He stared at her pregnancy bump. "And to get pregnant with another man's child was just the frosting on the cake. I must tell you he was devastated by the situation, something I'm sure hastened his heart problems."

"I doubt it." Before she could stop herself she blurted out, "You must have a heart before you can have problems with it." Turning away from Rod, she picked up a pen from the desk. "I think our business is concluded. Just show me where to sign and tell me which copies of everything are mine."

When they finished, McGuire swept a thick stack of papers into a pristine manila envelope with her name printed in neat block letters and handed it to her.

"Everything else deals with charitable bequests. I assume you don't feel the need to be involved in those."

She nodded and started to rise from her chair. "Then we're done."

"Except for the letters."

She froze. "I don't think we need to discuss the letters, Rod." She gave a slight gasp as the baby chose that moment to kick. "We're both aware of them, and of the terms. You won't have to open them."

"This won't go away." His voice was colder than winter.

"Eventually Andy and Beth will be of age," she pointed out, "and the threat of custody or guardianship will no longer be a factor."

"No matter how many years pass, Julia, or how old the children get, it will be my great pleasure to destroy any chance at happiness you might try to have. You ruined Charles's life. I will enjoy ruining yours."

She kept herself together until he was out of the house, into his car, and out of the driveway. Then she walked into the kitchen, sat down at the table, and for one last time gave in to the tears threatening to choke her. When she stopped at last, she felt as if she'd cried for hours, her throat raw and her eyes burning. She touched her stomach and felt the baby kick again.

At least I'll have this, she told herself, her heart so full of despair she didn't know if she'd ever smile again. What a terrible mistake she'd made, even though at the time she thought it was right. If only she'd had more courage.

She didn't know how to deal with the grief that was more of a release than anything else. She felt guilty someone might see into her mind and read her thoughts. Only Claire knew the real truth about her marriage and she wanted to keep it that way.

As her due date approached, she was petted and cosseted to the extreme by Claire, Miranda, and the twins. Andy and Beth were enthralled with the idea of a baby brother or sister and Julia was grateful for the distraction from their sorrow.

On August twenty-fifth, Julia gave birth to a gorgeous baby girl, Courtney Emily Patterson. When she held the baby in her arms for the first time, she whispered to her, "Your daddy would love you if he could see you."

Luke had a right to know about his beautiful baby girl. How had she thought to keep this from him? It took her two days to get up the courage but finally, touching the charm she still wore around her neck, she tried his cell number. The mechanical voice telling her the number was no longer in service set her back on her heels. No longer in service? Why? What happened? Infused with a strength and confidence she hadn't known she had, she called Hot Ticket. Bright Ideas was long finished with the original project. The two additional campaigns they'd subsequently been hired for were very short ones that Claire handled.

"I'm sorry, Mr. Buchanan is no longer with the company," the impersonal voice told her.

Julia was stunned. "But—where is he? Where did he go?"

"I'm sure I don't know, ma'am. Would you like me to transfer you to Human Resources? They might be able to help you."

"No, it's fine. Thank you."

She could just imagine the gossip and speculation if the whole company knew of her efforts to track him down. Why had he left? Where on earth had he gone? And how would she ever find him again? Despair washed over her like an icy shower. She cuddled the baby close to her, pressing her cheek against the downy head as tears filled her eyes.

Chapter 13

Thirteen years later

"Courtney, I will not ask you again. Where did you go after school today?"

Julia stood toe to toe with Courtney in the foyer, trying hard to control her frustration with her thirteen-year-old daughter. As usual, though, the belligerent teenager reveled in making it difficult for her.

"I went to Laura's house." The tone was both petulant and hostile.

"Try again. I called there looking for you."

"What difference does it make? No one cares what time I come home, anyway." She turned to leave the room.

Julia grabbed her arm. "Not so fast. You're not leaving here until I know where you were. And exactly what did you mean by your remark?"

"You're never here when I get home." Her tone contained a mixture of anger and self-pity. "Beth and Andy have their own places. They hardly show up here except for a command performance. And Miranda just bitches at me."

"We are lucky to have Miranda at all, let me tell you. And Beth and Andy work. They were both lucky to get jobs when they graduated. Plenty of kids are out of college and can't find work at all. We see them as often as they can make time."

"Understood. They're wonderful. Can I go now?" Courtney stood with hip cocked and arms folded defiantly across her chest, glaring at her mother.

They stood there in what Julia could only think of as a face-off. She made herself take a deep breath before she said something she truly regretted. As she prayed for the wisdom to know what to do next, the front door opened and Beth breezed in. She stopped and looked from one to the other.

"What's the deal, guys?"

Julia forced herself to speak calmly. "Your sister missed school again this week."

"Big deal," Courtney sneered.

"Courtney, it is a big deal," Beth put in.

"She hangs out with people two or three years older," Julia continued. "Kids who look like ads for 'Just Say No To Drugs.'"

"There's nothing wrong with them." Courtney uncrossed her arms and stood with clenched fists, face set in anger.

"They're nothing but trouble," Julia seethed. "You shouldn't even have anything to do with them."

"They're my friends," Courtney shouted. "They don't judge me and they think I'm wonderful."

"Who—" Beth tried to interrupt.

Julia held up her hand, her focus still on her younger daughter. "Of course they do. You spend your money buying them food and other things." She blew out a breath of exasperation. "Fine. Hang out with them. But I'm cutting your allowance. A lot. See how they like you when you don't have pockets full of money."

"That's my money. I heard you tell Miranda that Daddy left it for me."

"To use wisely." Julia held on to her temper by a thin thread. "We'll talk again when you can learn to manage it better. End of discussion."

"You hate me," Courtney shouted, and stamped upstairs.

Trembling, Julia blew out a breath to steady herself and turned to her older daughter. "Sorry about that, sweetheart."

"Well, that was pleasant." Beth gave her mother a hug. "She seems to be getting worse."

"Tell me about it." Julia bit her lip. "I just remember what a sweet child she was and have a hard time believing she does the things she does."

Beth looked at her mother steadily. "Take it from me, she does."

"Have you talked to her?" Maybe Beth could get through where Julia couldn't.

"Of course. So has Andy. She doesn't hear a word we say. Listen, Mom, I stopped by to see if you wanted to grab a bite to eat with me. I think getting out of the house would do you some good."

"Maybe." Julia smiled at her older daughter. "That's probably just what I need but I don't think I should leave right now."

"Mom, she's going to sulk in her room, you know that. Maybe if she sees she's not upsetting you she'll calm down. I love my sister, but I think at least half the time she does this to get a rise out of you." She paused. "To see if you care enough about her to worry."

Julia was startled. "You think that? Why? She has to know I love her."

"I'm sure she does," Beth assured her. "But think about it. She's a teenager with raging hormones, emotions all over the place, and—don't get mad at me—growing up in a one parent household. Not that you haven't been the best parent in the world," she added quickly.

"Lord, Beth." Julia stared at her. "I guess I never looked at it that way. I've tried to be both mother and father to her—"

"And you have." Beth gave her a hug. "I'm not smart enough to have answers here so I guess just keep loving her and doing what you think is best." She grinned. "You did just fine with Andy and me."

"I know. You two are my brightest hope."

When Beth left, she gathered herself and went upstairs. She'd made a decision that she was sure would precipitate another outburst of anger. Courtney was in her room, the door closed as usual. Julia could hear the sound of the CD player racketing as she knocked.

"What?" The girl spat the word out, hostile, as always.

"I need to talk to you. Open the door." Julia had made it a rule that Courtney keep her door unlocked, in case of fire or some other emergency, but the girl stubbornly refused to listen to her.

"I'm busy."

"You'll be a lot less busy if I have to take an ax to this door, young lady. Open it now."

In a moment, the door opened a few inches, Courtney standing there in her usual pose of defiance. "What is it, Mother?" She stressed the last word.

"I'm picking you up after school tomorrow and taking you back to the office with me. You can help me there and do your homework. I'll wait for you at the end of the school driveway so you won't be embarrassed to have your friends see you talk to your mother or get in a car with her."

Courtney stared at her, mouth open. "You're kidding."

"No, I'm not. I'm tired of never knowing where you are or who you're with. And don't even think of ducking out on me. You won't like the consequences."

She turned away and the door slammed behind her. Another wonderful evening at home, she thought. She looked up to see Miranda holding a small tray.

"Someone needs to give that child the spanking of her life." Miranda walked with her down to the kitchen. She'd tactfully left Courtney and Julia alone during their discussion.

"Yes, well, I don't think I can take it on at her age. Although it's a good idea." Julia grimaced at the thought. "Anyway, I'll just have to find another solution."

"I made you some nice hot chocolate. You look like you could use it."

"I think my child-rearing skills have totally disappeared." Julia accepted the cup gratefully.

"You did a fine job with the twins," the woman reminded her.

"Yes, but at least they began life with the presence of a father," she pointed out.

Miranda snorted in disgust. "On their birth certificate. Maybe. But that man didn't have a spot in his heart for any of you except to trot you out on display when he needed to. Remember who you're talking to here."

"Charles tried his best," Julia protested. "He just…"

"Didn't know how to be a person," Miranda finished. "Whatever those kids got came from you. Look how great they turned out."

"Well, I've certainly lost my touch with Courtney."

"I'll tell you, she seems like a piece of her life is missing. I'm not smart enough to figure out what it is, though. All this thumbing her nose at everything? She's just trying to find where she belongs, because she's not one bit like those other two."

And wasn't that just the truth.

"Well, we'll see what happens tomorrow. I have to make a start somewhere."

Last night they'd celebrated Courtney's thirteenth birthday, although Julia wasn't sure it was much of a celebration. She'd chosen a restaurant she knew was Courtney's favorite, but no one could ignore the tension around the table. Her daughter saw the milestone as an open door to test the limits even further.

Julia couldn't understand what had gone wrong. Courtney had been such a sweet baby, an adorable toddler, a warm and funny child. It was always a pleasure doing things with her. Andy and Beth had fussed over her, too, and weekends were always filled with fun things for all four of them. Julia had done her best to be both mother and father to her children and they'd seemed to be flourishing.

She could mark the change in her daughter from the time her hormones kicked in at age twelve. The sunny disposition turned dark and suddenly she'd seemed at war with the world. Precocious and bright, she challenged everyone and everything. She believed rules were made to be broken and did so on a regular basis. Julia was at a loss what to do. If only she could find Luke. She wanted so desperately to tell him their beautiful daughter seemed bent on ruining her life, and beg him to help.

Despite the terms of the so-called bargain she'd made with Charles, she periodically made attempts to find Luke. She'd been such a weakling at the time, such a pushover. But the pressure of the situation and the physical and emotional strain of the pregnancy had robbed her of any ability to fight back. As time passed and her life changed, so did her resolve. Only it seemed to have come too late.

She continued with her attempts to locate him, despite Rod's dire warnings. Maybe if they were together they could find a way to counteract the plan Charles had set in motion. Fight for custody of the twins. Battle whatever campaign Rod waged against Luke. She'd asked Harry, who had connections everywhere, to put out feelers. She'd done searches on the Internet, found articles where his name was mentioned, always praising him for his innovations and guidance. But he seemed to be moving from place to place, company to company. Each time she was too late. He'd already left.

Claire suggested more than once she ask Harry to find a private investigator for her, but that was too overt a step for her to take. What if he was running from her? Didn't want to be found?

The last attempt she'd made was when the twins turned eighteen and custody would no longer be an issue. When Harry informed her he'd taken a position with a company headquartered in Europe she'd finally given up. Apparently, fate was telling her it was time to get on with her life. Only it wasn't giving her any advice on how to cope with her burgeoning wild child.

She'd stiffened her spine and smiled until her face hurt when Beth and Andy went off to college, both of them to the University of Texas at Austin, Beth to major in business and Andy in engineering. As much as she wanted to keep them close, she knew they needed to spread their wings. Courtney had still been the sweet-natured child they all loved, one both she and Miranda enjoyed. And the twins came home often enough to give her what she called her "twin fix." She had barely contained her excitement when, after graduation, they both took jobs in San Antonio. And while they were busy with their lives as newly-minted adults, they stopped by and called more than she could have expected.

At the worst moments, as Courtney's behavior escalated and her attitude turned more and more surly, Julia wished she liked to drink. Alcohol would certainly take the edge off at times like this. Handling a rebellious teenager, particularly as a single parent, was like riding on a roller coaster.

As she lay in bed later, Luke's face rose unbidden before her eyes. She ached with longing for him, the same yearning she'd unsuccessfully tried to bury for fourteen years. When Charles's illness and his demands had dragged on her too much, the memory of Luke had carried her through. In the long hours when Charles wallowed in self-pity, demanding her presence beside him every minute, she could close her eyes and remember the feel of Luke's hands on her body, his mouth on hers, the muskiness of his scent.

As she faced the disaster Courtney's life was turning out to be, she wished Luke was here to give her guidance. And help her with their daughter. Julia wondered if mental telepathy really worked. How lucky it would be if he got some of the signals she so desperately sent out.

* * * *

"I have to pick Courtney up after school today," Julia announced to Claire at the office. "I'm bringing her back here."

"In chains?" Claire asked with a sardonic smile.

"Not funny. I hope you don't mind but she's going to be doing her homework here every day. Maybe some filing if we need it. Something to keep her contained and off the streets until I take her home for dinner." She chewed her lip. "I can't just dump this on Miranda anymore."

"Try the police station. I understand they have pretty secure rooms there."

"This isn't funny." Julia blew out an exasperated breath. "I swear I don't know what I'm going to do with that child."

Claire poured coffee for herself, fixed a cup with hot water and a tea bag, brought both cups to the desk, and handed the tea to Julia. She sat down in the chair opposite her.

"I know you don't want to hear this, but you are exhausting yourself with Courtney. She's draining all your energy."

Julia closed her eyes for a moment. "I know, I know. I guess I was spoiled because Beth and Andy were so easy. And so was the kid until she turned twelve."

"Any luck getting ahold of Luke lately?"

Julia cradled the cup with her tea. She had confided the details of her search to her friend, who encouraged her to keep trying, but now she seemed to be at a dead end. "No. I haven't tried for a while. Ever since I heard he was in Europe."

"You need to check the Internet now and then. He'll pop up again."

"I wish. Maybe his steadying hand could make a big difference where Courtney is concerned." She bit her lip. "If he doesn't hate me for not letting him know about her."

"You tried, kiddo," Claire reminded her. "You made the effort."

"Too little, too late. I should have told him right away, just like you said. Maybe we could have fought Charles together."

"And maybe not." Claire took a swallow of coffee. "Maybe you were right at the time. Rod McGuire was on a tear then. Who knows what he would have done thinking he was repaying Charles."

"I guess." Julia sighed. "Anyway, he probably has a whole new life by now. Even if I could find him, I can't just disrupt his life by calling and saying, 'Hey Luke, guess what? We have a daughter, she's almost a juvenile delinquent, and I need you to help me straighten her out.'"

"I still think he'd want to know," Claire insisted. "There are ways he could participate without disrupting his life. And maybe if you told her the truth it would give her the answers she's looking for."

"I have a feeling it might make things worse. She'd blame me for not telling him right away. She'd hate me for keeping it a secret. So forget that."

"One more thing and then I'm finished. Don't shut your life off to the possibility of someone else. I know." She held up her hand when Julia started to interrupt her. "You worry about Rod's vendetta. But you need a man in your life to yank the reins on that child. The right man could give as good right back to him. And I can't imagine Andy and Beth would give more than a passing notice to those stupid letters. They know the kind of person you are. They love you. And they don't exactly have fond memories of their father."

Julia rolled her head to ease the tension in her neck. "I wish I hadn't been quite so vulnerable when Charles and Rod dropped their bombshells on me. If I'd had a spine of any kind I'd have told him to do his worst and figured out how to protect the children."

"We all wish we'd done a lot of things differently," Claire told her. "You were pregnant, stressed, barely surviving your marriage, and holding on with desperation for the divorce to be final. You were in no shape physically or emotionally to deal with that bastard."

Julia snorted. "Which one? Charles or Rod?"

"Glad to see you still have a sense of humor."

"For all the good it will do me. That was then and this is now. It would be bad enough to subject Luke to whatever Rod would do. I can't throw a stranger into the mix so let's leave that topic. Now let's do what we need to before I pick up Courtney and bring her here." Julia shook her head. "At least I can make sure she does her homework."

"All right, forget about men. For now. Let's get back to Courtney. I have an idea. Bring her to the office and she can work for me. I can use her three hours a day after school to file, enter stuff on the computer, and organize my project folders for me."

"We have a staff, for God's sake. What's left for her to do?"

"Plenty. Just leave it to me. Besides, I'm a lot tougher than you are. Let's see how she toes the line with me."

It was certainly an interesting experiment. When Julia picked up her daughter later that day, Courtney climbed into the car reluctantly and sulked all the way to the office. When Julia told her she was expected to work and what she'd be doing, her anger was hard to ignore.

"Are you planning to babysit me every day?" She made no effort to disguise her resentment. "What about my friends? I want to hang out with them after school. This sucks. And I don't want to work for you. You don't do anything but criticize me."

Julia flinched. "Courtney, if you made better choices about your friends and paid attention to house rules, this wouldn't be necessary. Anyway, technically you won't be working for me. You'll be working for Claire."

"Oh, great. The warden herself." Courtney slouched down in her seat. "I think she's a refugee from the Gestapo."

"Enough, Courtney." Julia was out of patience. "I'll expect you to conduct yourself courteously and professionally, and do what you're told. You might not like some of the alternatives."

"Oh? And what are they? Locking me in chains and throwing me bread and water?"

"Don't tempt me." Julia tightened her fingers on the steering wheel. "Try to remember under your pathetic layer of hostility you're actually a decent human being."

The afternoon went better than Julia expected. Claire was ready for Courtney as soon as they walked in. She showed her how to enter client information in the database and print reports. She also instructed her on how to organize client folders.

Julia watched sideways across the reception area through the slightly open door to Claire's office. It amazed her to see Courtney's annoyed posture change as she listened and tried to absorb the instructions. When she started to do her assigned work, she didn't look enthused, exactly, but there was more animation on her face than Julia had seen in a long time.

Maybe this would work. Maybe this would make a change in her attitude.

If it kept her away from the dregs of humanity she seemed to enjoy hanging out with, Julia would consider it a major accomplishment.

And she absolutely had to get the child some new clothes. Courtney had, for whatever reason, taken to wearing spandex bicycle shorts and oversized T-shirts as her normal style of dress. They were the clothes Julia bought her for hanging around the house or riding her bike, not for school and certainly not in an office where business was conducted. How had she even let her get away with wearing them to school? Because it was one more argument she didn't want to have?

Julia stared at her computer. Claire was right. The constant uphill battle kept her edgy and exhausted. What would Luke say if he could see how his daughter was turning out? Would he blame her? Would he help her?

They were getting ready to close up shop for the day when Claire hurried into Julia's office holding a fax.

"You aren't going to believe this." She stared at the paper in her hand, a stunned look on her face.

"Believe what?"

"I just got a call from someone at Connell Wilson. You know them, right?"

"Are you kidding?" Julia widened her eyes. "Who *doesn't* know about them? They're one of the biggest national manufacturers of sporting goods and apparel for college and professional sports. I read in the business journal they just gobbled up some smaller companies."

"Yes, well, it appears they've got something new going and we're invited to the party."

"What?" Julia dropped her pen. "I don't believe you. We're small potatoes compared to the agencies they use."

"Yeah, I was a little skeptical myself when the call came in, so I asked the guy to fax me the request in writing. Here it is." She held out the piece of paper she was holding.

Julia took it from her hand and skimmed the message. Connell Wilson, following some recent acquisitions, was changing its name and wanted a major advertising campaign to establish its new identity. Would Bright Ideas be interested in making a presentation?

"Major advertising campaign," Claire repeated, standing there in a daze.

"This just came out of the blue?" Julia asked. "No recommendation from someone?"

"No. Just the request. We got a follow-up phone call about ten minutes after they sent the fax."

"But why us? Connell Wilson is big league. Huge. And we're far from being close to major."

"Read what it says. They're aware of similar campaigns we've done before and they'd like to talk to us." She flopped down in one of the client chairs. "This is too weird, right?"

"Maybe they have our stuff on file." Julia was referring to the huge structured mailing Bright Ideas recently did in a prospecting, throw-everything-against-the-wall-and-see-what-sticks campaign.

Claire sat up straight. "If we get this account, it would mean really, really big bucks, Julia. I mean, we're actually fine. More than fine. We've got a nice portfolio of clients and they usually recommend us to others. But this is like representing the palace."

"Can we do something this huge?" Julia asked. "We might need to hire additional staff."

"Something to worry about later. Bright Ideas has come a long way since the Hot Ticket rollout, kiddo. Their campaign got us a lot of referrals and we've been humming ever since. This could be our biggest step up the ladder yet."

"You think?" Julia was the conservative one, Claire always the more adventurous of the two. They balanced each other out, allowing them to look at an opportunity like this from every angle.

"I do." Claire nodded. "If you agree we should go ahead, I'll call this guy back and get him to messenger over the information we'll need. Then I'll ask him when they want the presentation."

Julia fiddled with the pen she held. Maybe a challenge like this was just what she needed, something to take her mind off her personal problems. And Luke. "All right. Let's do it. Let me know when you have the info and we'll do some brainstorming for ideas."

Claire jumped up and hugged her. "Good for you. We need to stretch our wings. Besides, it means I can keep Courtney gainfully employed and under our thumb."

"Yeah, well, good luck with that." Julia couldn't hide her skepticism.

Driving home, however, she noticed a slight change in Courtney's demeanor. The girl actually engaged in conversation. She bristled when Julia mentioned the clothes thing, but at least agreed to think about it. To Julia, this was a major change, and she offered up silent prayers.

They ate the wonderful dinner Miranda made for them, but then Courtney went off to closet herself in her room.

"No telephone until your homework's done," Julia hollered after her.

The only reply was the usual slamming of the bedroom door. Julia swallowed a sigh. At least there'd been a brief interval of sanity.

"Drink this and relax." Miranda handed her a glass of wine. "That child needs a firm hand. You need to quit worrying because she has no father and make sure she's got a mother with gumption."

"Couldn't you wave a magic wand and change us into Cinderella?" Julia asked.

"Wouldn't that be something to hoot about? Meanwhile, you drink your wine and unwind. I can tell you got something big on your mind."

She did indeed. Later, discussing it with Beth on the phone, the full scope of the project—if they got it—suddenly hit her.

"You can do it, Mom." Beth's tone was matter-of-fact. "You've got the skills and the background. You'd just be promoting a beach instead of a sandbox. No big deal."

"Easy for you to say, my darling daughter. Everything comes so naturally to you."

"Yeah, yeah, that's me. The big star."

They both knew, however, the financial services agency where Beth interned for three summers had hired her right out of college. They considered her indispensable after little more than a year fulltime. Her natural talent for numbers and for reading business trends brought her a great deal of notice. She loved her work and her bosses loved her, already giving her one large bonus with another probable by the end of the year.

"How's Courtney?" Beth asked, changing the subject.

"Just as hostile as ever." Julia shook her head. "I swear I've never seen two sisters more unlike each other. You spoiled me, Bethie."

"Mom, she's thirteen and full of angst," Beth reminded her.

"There's a word." Julia groaned. "Angst. I'd like to take it out of the dictionary."

"Want her to come spend the weekend with me?" Beth lived in her own apartment in the northwest area of San Antonio, not far from work and away from the danger of city streets. It wasn't large, but she managed the cost herself, a big determining factor for her.

"I don't know. We'll see. She started a new job today working at the office."

"You think that's a good idea?" There was concern in Beth's voice. "She thinks you're too much of a guard dog as it is."

"She's working for Claire, so it's a little different."

Beth chuckled. "If anyone can whip her into shape, Claire can. I swear, Mom, how can someone so pretty be such a drill sergeant?"

"Wonder of wonders, Courtney didn't bitch about it. We actually had a decent if brief conversation, although now she's locked up tighter than a drum in her room again. I'm hoping this gives some order to her life. I'll do anything to get her away from those derelicts she insists on calling her friends."

"At least she doesn't have to put up with Grandma and Grandpa." Beth snorted. "I'd call it a blessing. Thank God we don't have to attend any of those stupid dinners anymore."

Until the twins went off to college, they had attended the obligatory monthly dinner with their grandparents, ever more reluctantly as they grew older. Charles's parents continued to deliberately and obviously ignore Courtney's existence. Julia tried confronting them about it once but Elise shut her down at once.

"She is not our blood."

While they said nothing either publicly or to the twins, as far as they were concerned, Julia and Courtney might as well not exist. It was a mixed blessing. She no longer had to endure punishing dinners and silent criticism, but the situation obviously made Courtney feel like some kind of pariah.

So when the twins went off grumbling each time, Julia always planned something special for Courtney. Something just for her. Fun things. Things that made her feel extraordinary. Still, her three offspring had always wondered why Courtney wasn't included.

And there was no way she could tell them.

"You're the lucky one," Beth had always pointed out to her sister.

Eventually Courtney simply stopped asking.

"Have you seen your grandparents lately?" Julia asked during one phone call.

"Grandfather called me at the office, of all things, and reminded me that I was ignoring my visits to them. Hell." She groaned. "I'd be happy if I never had to see them again, Mom, they are just thoroughly unpleasant people. Andy and I don't think they like us very much, but that's okay, because we don't like them. How did you ever put up with them? And how did you get them to leave you alone?"

That would be quite a story to tell her children.

"Never mind. How about this, I'm serious about the weekend. Why don't I pick Courtney up Friday from the office and she can stay with me 'til Sunday. We can hang out and watch chick flicks and play with my makeup. Maybe I can get her to tone hers down."

"Oh, honey, how wonderful, but I hate for you to give up your weekend."

"No problem, honest. Maybe it will give you and Claire time to brainstorm about the new account you're going after. I need a break, anyway. Too much going on."

"I love you. If you're going to do this, do you think you could take her shopping Saturday?" She hesitated to ask more but Beth had a better chance of making changes in Courtney's wardrobe. "I can't look at the awful spandex she's taken to anymore and she seems to be missing the fashion sense gene. She said she'd think about it, and I want to do it before she thinks too much. Use your credit card and give me the bill."

"Sure, Mom. No prob. Have the delinquent packed and ready when you take her to work Friday."

Julia hung up with a feeling of relief. She was truly blessed to have a daughter like Beth. She tried not to compare her with Courtney, but sometimes it was hard not to. She wished more than ever that Luke was there to give her words of wisdom.

Chapter 14

Although it was only make-work, the job at Bright Ideas did seem to give Courtney something to focus on besides her usual rebellion. Claire cautiously praised what she did and told Julia she thought this might work out after all.

"If we get the Connell Wilson account, we'll need every pair of hands we can get."

"By the way"—Julia paused in the doorway to her office—"did they send the stuff over for us to look at? And have they given us a date to meet with them?"

"Yes to both things. I asked Linda to make copies of everything for you so you can study up on the background and get an idea of what they might be looking for. And the appointment is for next Thursday."

Nine days away. Could they get ready in time? "Okay. I'll get on it right away. Are you up for a brainstorm session this weekend?"

"What about Courtney? Are you planning to chain her to her bed?" Claire grinned to take the sting out of her words.

"Actually, Beth has magnanimously invited Court to spend the weekend with her. She's picking her up here Friday."

"God, what a jewel she is. If I ever have kids, I'd want them to be just like her. Sure. The weekend sounds like a great idea. Let's do it at my place, though. Sometimes I can't think in the office."

"And by the way." Julia frowned. "How come the free weekend? You actually going to leave your hot husband alone? By himself?"

"Football weekend," Claire told her. "He and Charlie and Wes are going to College Station for the A&M game and are spending the night so they can pretend they're nineteen and party hearty."

Julia laughed. "Maybe next year they'll grow up."

Claire gave her a rueful grin. "Don't hold your breath. Anyway, it frees up Saturday and Sunday."

"All right. Let's do it at my place, though, so Miranda can feed us yummy stuff. I'll bring home whatever we'll need when we leave here

Friday night. You can show up bright and early Saturday so we can get started. I'm going to get one good night's sleep before we dive in."

* * * *

Courtney was actually pleased to go off with Beth for the weekend, even with a shopping trip on the agenda. Julia waved goodbye and said she'd see her Sunday afternoon. Claire arrived Saturday morning and by the time she left Sunday afternoon the structure of the plan was solid.

Courtney arrived home shortly after Claire left, sporting a new haircut, the smallest amount of makeup Julia ever remembered seeing her wear, and dressed in Gap jeans and a soft pink T-shirt. Julia swallowed a giggle and smiled her approval.

"Very nice. You look lovely, honey."

Courtney actually blushed. "Beth said if I'm going to work in your office, I might meet some cool people and I'd turn them off if I looked like the Queen of the Trailer Park."

Julia mouthed a thank you to Beth.

"Can I go upstairs now? I need to make some calls."

"Of course. And I love your new clothes."

Courtney picked up the stack of shopping bags she'd dropped on the floor, her duffel, and clumped up the stairs.

Julia turned to Beth. "I don't know how you did it, but thank you from the bottom of my heart."

"Well, it was a struggle, but she finally gave in. I think she actually enjoyed herself. And I liked having her with me. I should do this more often. It's good for both of us."

"Honey, you have a very busy life."

"Yeah, but I only have one sister. I need to keep remembering that." She gave her mother a quick hug and kiss. "Gotta go. Meeting some people for Chinese food. Call me and let me know how it goes. And about the new account, too," she added as she flew out the door.

Monday, the race to complete the Connell Wilson plan kicked into high gear. By the time Julia and Claire collapsed over sandwiches Wednesday evening, they were convinced the plan was a winner.

She arrived at the office early the next morning, determined not to forget any of her materials. Claire was already there, coffee in one hand, a folder in the other.

"If this doesn't do it, we don't deserve to get the job." Julia busied herself gathering what she needed.

"Don't jinx us," Claire told her. "We do deserve the job, and I think we'll knock their socks off."

Julia frowned. "You still don't know how our name got in the hopper?"

"Not a clue. I assume we'll find out today. Every one of the big shots will be sitting in on the meeting."

"Oh, great." Julia groaned. "Still with their grumpy morning faces on, I'll bet."

"Cheer up, sweetie. We'll wow them."

"Okay." She slipped the final folders inside her new, oversized Coach briefcase, a Christmas present to herself. Then she snuck a quick look at herself in the mirror in the tiny powder room in their office suite. A successful entrepreneur looked back at her.

Take that, Charles. Jackass.

"Julia, you look terrific. You'll knock 'em dead." Claire's voice was impatient. "Let's get it on."

"Coming, Mother," Julia grinned.

The Connell Wilson headquarters took up three floors of the Alamo Bank Building in downtown San Antonio. Both women were slightly on edge as they stepped off the elevator into a large reception area. An earnest young man in a sports jacket, waiting at the security desk, hurried to greet them and take them to sign in.

"Ms. Westbrook? Ms. Patterson?"

They both nodded.

"I'm Jeremy, an intern in the marketing department." He handed them two plastic ID badges. "You'll need to wear these while you're here, if you don't mind. Everyone's waiting for you in the boardroom, if you'll just follow me?"

He led them down a long carpeted corridor ending at two mahogany doors. Jeremy opened them to expose a sea of corporate faces gathered around a table nearly as long as the corridor.

Julia tried to catalog them quickly, knowing Claire did the same. There were at least fifteen people, some dressed in corporate attire, some in athletic gear. They were divided about half and half between male and female. Sometimes that was good, sometimes bad. Women often wanted to flex their muscle in front of their male counterparts, and men often needed to let the women know how much smarter they were.

Out of the corner of her eye, Julia glimpsed one person, a man in a navy sports jacket and grey slacks, standing at the coffee urn with his back turned. Something about him drew her attention, but then an older man in a dark grey suit came forward, distracting her.

"Thank you for coming." He shook their hands. "I'm Alan Wilson, CEO of Connell Wilson. I'll introduce everyone here but please don't think we expect you to remember their names."

"Oh, we'll manage." Claire answered, with her usual brashness.

"So *Hey You* will do just fine if you need to speak to someone." He smiled easily and Julia relaxed a bit. Maybe this wouldn't be so bad after all.

Wilson went around the table, identifying each person by name and position. Julia noticed Claire quietly turn on her pocket recorder so she could write everything down later.

"The gentleman hogging the coffee machine joined us only recently. We were lucky enough to steal him away from his previous position. We call him our senior whiz kid, and he's the real impetus for your invitation." The man turned and Julia nearly fainted. "Let me introduce our new corporate vice president, Luke Buchanan."

Julia felt as if a vacuum suddenly sucked every bit of breath out of her. Her body turned icy cold but her face felt hot, flushed. Her heart thundered and her pulse beat a jungle tattoo. For a desperate moment, she thought she might throw up. She curled her hands into fists to keep them from shaking, praying her legs would not collapse under her. Luke! She couldn't tear her eyes away from him. He still could ignite her with just his presence.

All the nights she'd lain in bed keeping his image close to her, remembering the feel of his hands on her body and the hot press of his mouth. The way he'd brought her to climax over and over again and made her feel wanted and desirable.

Not a day went by that she didn't regret the circumstance that forced her to walk away from him, full of despair that she'd never see him again.

She noted how well he'd aged, his body only slightly thicker, his dark brown hair attractively tinged with grey. His face showed a few more lines, and there was a new tension in his body. But he was still wonderful Luke, the man who would always own her heart.

I love you.

His words were permanently imprinted on her brain. On the bad, awful nights, she'd hugged them to her like a lifeline.

He came over to her now, hand outstretched. "Nice to see you again, Julia." His face was impassive but his eyes were speaking volumes to her.

"Nice to see you again, too, Luke." She didn't know where she found the voice to answer him. At the touch of his hand, her body went on full alert. Oh God, how could she do this?

Beside her, Claire did her level best to be unflappable, but Julia knew she was taking in every detail and nuance.

"Alan went along with my suggestion to give you a shot at this before we make a decision on an agency." His gaze was boring into her. "I explained what a good job you'd done for us at Hot Ticket and how well that turned out."

"Thank you." She was afraid she might faint. Her hand, when she retrieved it, tingled from his touch, and her whole body threatened to melt.

"Thanks for asking us in, Luke." Claire extended her hand. "Nice seeing you again after such a long time."

"You too, Claire." They exchanged grins.

Somehow, Julia pulled herself together and she and Claire set up the materials. Despite the shock that threatened to immobilize her, regardless of Claire's burning curiosity that was almost a living thing, they managed to put on a powerful presentation. Each person at the table asked specific questions. Claire recorded everything so they could get information later for whatever they couldn't answer now.

At noon, staff from the corporate kitchen delivered and served lunch at the boardroom table. Julia, like Claire, did her best to chat informally with as many people as possible. She noticed Luke carefully kept his distance, letting her do her thing.

At last it was over, and they began packing up their things to leave.

"I have to say I'm impressed," Alan Wilson told them. "I didn't know what to expect when Luke recommended you. We've pretty much stuck to the same two or three agencies for our work."

"We appreciate the opportunity," Claire said.

"Well, like everything else he's suggested since he came on board, your work is both interesting and exciting. Quite an innovative marketing plan."

"Thank you," Julia murmured.

"You came up with terrific suggestions for the product name change, too." He thought for a minute. "I'll need to go over this with my executive committee and digest your presentation. And of course, Luke will have the final say. But I think I can safely say you'll be getting a call for further discussion."

Tired and tense as she was, Julia still felt excitement surge through her. She and Claire managed to shake everyone's hand again, express their appreciation for their time, and make a graceful exit to the elevator.

"Wow!" Claire tried to high five her as they were waiting in the hall.

"Wow? We don't have the account yet."

"I'm not talking about the account, honey. I'm talking about that gorgeous man with the sexy voice. He just gets better looking with age. I can't believe you've stayed away from him all this time."

"Leaving everything else out," Julia told her, "I walked away from him. Didn't even call him for a long time. I thought for sure he'd hate me by now."

"Not even close."

The deep voice still sent shivers up her spine. Julia turned to find Luke standing almost directly behind her. She caught the familiar scent of his spicy aftershave and the memories it conjured up made her weak in the knees. She needed to get out of here. Now. But she couldn't make herself move.

"Excuse me?" Well that was a dumb response.

"I said, no, I don't hate you. Although I'd say we have some unfinished business." He looked at Claire. "I'm happy to see you again. Thanks again for jumping in for Julia to finish the Hot Ticket campaign when she was…ill." He turned his gaze to Julia. "I assume you're feeling better these days?"

"Yes." Her words came out in a whisper and she clutched her Coach bag in a death grip. "Much better."

"Good." His eyes held that same heated look she'd never forgotten, ratcheting up the beat of her pulse. "Then there's no reason you can't join me for a drink and dinner, is there? I'd like to have a chance to catch up on your life."

"Oh, I don't think…" No, no, no. Alone with Luke? Not possible.

"That's right. Don't think." Claire was firm, as if reading her mind. "You need a night out. And don't worry about the brat. I'll stop by the house and check on her and Miranda."

"The brat?" Luke raised his eyebrows.

"My daughter." Julia wet her lips. *Your daughter.* "I… I have a teenager."

"Oh." A strange look washed over his face. "I wasn't aware of any children other than the twins. Last time we saw each other I was under the impression…" He let his voice fade.

That she was close to being divorced. Yes, she had been. And now he'd found out she had another child. She knew exactly what he was thinking. That she'd gone from his bed to Charles's and everything that happened between them was a lie.

"I'm sorry." She dug deep for the courage to resist him. He was so close to her she couldn't breathe. "I don't think I can take the time for dinner, but thank you anyway."

"Just a simple meal?" he pressed. "For old time's sake?"

"Luke, this isn't a good idea." Butterflies awakened in her stomach and her palms began to sweat. No way could she be alone with him for an evening, only... She'd have to explain Courtney. Answer questions about the mess of her life. Tell Courtney and the twins. Explain why she'd waited all these years, kept it secret for so long. And then there was Rod. By now she might have the spine to stand up to him, but how could she let his rage spill over to Luke? Maybe affect this new position he had. How much influence did Rod and the firm actually have?

Oh, God, she was making herself crazy. But everything she felt for him burst through to the surface like a geyser erupting. She couldn't walk away from him again, no matter what.

She stood there, mind spinning and whirling, unable to make her feet move.

Luke watched her with questioning eyes then looked at Claire. "So it's all right with you if I capture your partner for a few hours?" He asked as if Julia had not said a word. "You can handle things for her?"

"Absolutely." Claire was already moving toward the elevator when Luke put a restraining hand on her arm.

"I think we forgot to give you a folder you'll need. Could we go back in the conference room for a minute?" To Julia he said, "I'll be right back."

They were back in seconds. Claire, grinning broadly, kissed Julia lightly on the cheek. "Don't hurry home. I'll clue Miranda in. You deserve a night out. And if Courtney makes a scene, I'll take her home with me and do the school delivery and pick up tomorrow." She stepped into the elevator and was gone.

"What? I'm... Wait. I don't..." But the elevator doors were already closed. Julia turned back to Luke, curious. "What did you forget?"

"Let's get my car." He ignored her question. "I know just the place to take you."

"Luke..."

But he was an unstoppable force, gentle yet firm as they took the next elevator down to the parking garage. She'd barely pulled in her scattered thoughts when they were in his car and pulling out onto the street. He made easy small talk as they drove to the restaurant. Julia, however, was so uptight she either babbled or said nothing at all. The electricity in the car sizzled and snapped around them and the sexual tension, raring back to life, was so thick she was sure she could touch it.

She gasped in surprise when they pulled up in front of Harry's House, a restaurant newly opened in an old Victorian home. Friends and clients raved about it, but it wasn't a place she'd been to yet. And nowhere she'd expected to see the inside of any time soon, since it had developed a reputation as a truly romantic rendezvous. Claire had waxed dreamily eloquent about it when Brad took her there for their anniversary. Although a couple of the rooms could accommodate parties as large as ten, it was mostly a place for lovers, for romance, for intimate dining. This wasn't a place for casual conversation.

Oh well, she thought. At least they wouldn't be out in the open for every set of prying eyes in San Antonio.

Julia could feel her heart race as Luke helped her from the car, eyes glittering.

"I believe this is our evening."

Chapter 15

Julia barely recollected entering Harry's House or Luke speaking to the host in quiet tones. Or climbing a winding flight of stairs and being ushered into a dining room for two, the table set with exquisite linen, china, and crystal. Her mind simply wouldn't function.

For fourteen years, Luke Buchanan had lived in her dreams and in her mind. Her heart. Memories of him were what kept her warm through the stressful time with Charles. She'd refused any anesthetic when Courtney was born for fear she would shout out his name in her delirium. And each time she looked at the perfect baby, visions of their nights together flashed across her mind. She'd never expected to see him again. Certainly not like this, a bombshell dropped at her feet waiting to explode.

He held her chair for her, waiting until she was comfortable before sitting down himself. Glancing around, she noticed a long couch and two comfortable chairs against one wall along with interesting Victorian accessories.

Luke grinned at her, noticing her eyes sweep the room. "They actually use that area for serving cocktails. Gives people a more relaxed atmosphere. Don't worry, Julia. I don't plan to ravish you on the couch."

"Oh. I didn't…"

"Yes. You did. But rest assured, for what I have in mind I need something far more comfortable." He reached across the table and took both of her hands in his. "Tonight I wanted someplace private to talk to you and this seemed the best idea at the time."

"It's fine." She trembled, still focused on the words 'what I have in mind.' As his hands touched hers, sparks shot through her, firing every nerve ending. God, fourteen years and he still affected her the same way.

A knock on the door preceded the waiter's entrance and his quiet request for their drink orders. He stood discreetly to one side, pen and pad poised.

"Canadian and Coke for me," Luke told him, "and amaretto on the rocks for the lady." He looked at Julia who nodded confirmation. "Make them doubles so you won't need to come back quite so soon. And one of those little platters of crackers and cheese."

The waiter bowed, his face a trained, impersonal mask, and left to get their drinks.

"You remembered." Her face heated.

"Of course." The deep timbre of his throat vibrated straight through her.

"But d-doubles?" she stammered.

"They last longer." Luke laughed. "Just sip slowly."

"It's a good thing you ordered some kind of food. I barely ate anything at lunch."

Another knock on the door and the waiter entered with their drinks and the cheese platter. Placing them carefully on the table, he bowed again and left the room.

"To you," Luke said, raising his glass in a toast.

Julia saw his eyes watching her intently. "Thank you. To you, too." She took a swallow of the smooth liqueur, hoping to still the trembling in her hands. She was so nervous she had to put her drink down on the table before she spilled it.

"You're still wearing the charm." He smiled. "You have no idea what that means to me."

Automatically she touched it. All these years it had been her only link to him, a talisman that gave her strength on her worst days. "I never take it off."

"I'm going to take that as a very good sign." Luke watched her with his hot, penetrating gaze. "I asked Claire if it would be a problem in case you didn't make it home tonight. She assured me it wasn't." He winked at her. "I think your friend enjoys a good fairy tale."

"Luke!" She felt the blood leave her face and shook her head. "No. I can't do that." She started to push back from the table. "I'm sorry. I shouldn't be here. This is a big mistake."

"A mistake?" His hand reached for hers, gripped it, and his eyes bored into hers. "I can't accept that."

"Please." She tried to pull her hand away. "You don't understand. Among other things, I have a daughter to think of. She'll ask more questions than I want to answer."

"Got it covered. Claire's definitely taking her out to eat—someplace she's hot to go to—and back to her house for the night. Apparently, this is some kind of special treat for your daughter. Claire said they'd have a girls' makeup night?" He looked at Julia for confirmation.

Julia bit her lip. "Courtney does idolize Claire lately. It's a big change in her attitude for which I am eternally grateful. So, yes, this will be extra special for her. B-But—"

"Julia." His voice held her as if glued in place. "Whatever it is, don't run away from it. We have so much unfinished business. Please. Just sit down."

She slowly lowered herself to the chair again, picked up her drink, then swallowed some of it. "Well." She took a moment to settle the butterflies. "Maybe Claire can pick up where Beth left off and keep it toned down from four layers to two."

"Sounds like she's going through typical teenage rebellion," he commented. "I faced similar challenges with my boys, only theirs didn't include makeup." He paused. "I was surprised to hear that you and your husband reconciled." His voice was even. Uninflected. But beneath it a wave of emotion was cresting.

"How did you know about that?" His comment took her by surprise. She could only imagine what he thought.

"Claire kept me pretty well informed." He gave her a serious look. "You were never out of my mind. Just because I didn't see you, didn't mean I wasn't thinking about you." He reached across the table to touch her hand again. "And you? Did you ever spare a thought for me?"

A thought? If he only knew all the nights she'd lain in bed aching for him.

"Charles was sick for a long time," she waffled. "When he was diagnosed with congestive heart failure and given only months to live, I felt I owed it to the children to give them a family structure for as long as possible."

"Even one that was a lie?" His words burned into her.

"I did what I needed to." She raised her eyes to his. "Can't you understand that?"

"And afterwards?" he pushed.

"Afterwards there were still the twins to raise. And then Courtney."

"Of course." He said it so tonelessly she couldn't stand it.

"I never forgot about you for one single minute," she blurted, then wished the words back. She was opening a door that needed to stay closed.

"Good. I was hoping that was the case." His voice was sharp with pain. "I went to sleep with your face in my mind every night."

Dangerous subject. Julia fiddled with a cracker and a slice of cheese. "How are your boys?"

"Changing the subject?" He took a healthy sip of his drink. "Okay. I'll play. For now. They're doing okay. Jared is twenty-five and Mark is thirty. Our relationships are still badly strained." He shook his head. "Just like I told you so long ago, their mother did a good job of painting me the bad guy there."

Julia didn't know what to say. It wasn't fair for him to shoulder all the blame, in a situation where he was the victim.

"Don't look so upset," he told her. "It's okay. I mean that."

"Do you see them?"

He fiddled with the silverware, occupying his hands as he chose his words with obvious care. "Now and then. They both live in Boston. Jared's a software specialist, has a great job, and is a dedicated ladies' man. Mark is a cop, married, with two children."

"So you're a grandpa." She grinned at him. "You don't look old enough. Do you at least get to see the grandchildren?"

"I fly into Boston about one weekend a month and do a fast family visit. I think that's as much as any of us can handle." He shook his head. "I kept a shaky marriage together for the sake of the kids, as they say in dime novels, and ended up somewhat estranged from them anyway. I guess I flunked parenthood big time."

An incredible sadness gripped Julia. For a brief moment, she was ready to tell him about Courtney, but she forced herself to hold back. She didn't know if he even wanted another child. What if it made him felt trapped, buried beneath an unwanted obligation? What if he hated her for keeping the secret for so many years? If he decided he never wanted to see her again, then telling him would be a big mistake.

"That must be some heavy thinking you're doing," Luke said, breaking her train of thought. "You're making your forehead look permanently wrinkled."

"A fast forward of my life in review." She nibbled her lower lip then blurted out, "Do you have a woman in your life? Wait." How did she even have the right to ask him that? "Forget I said that. It's none of my business."

"It's all of your business. And the answer is no. Who could ever replace you?" He paused. "And what about you, Julia? Anyone in your life?"

No one except you, she wanted to say but she just shook her head. "What have you been doing with yourself all this time?"

He shrugged. "Oh, moving here and there. Trying some different things."

Did she dare tell him she'd tried so many times to find him?

"But I know Bright Ideas has done very well." He grinned. "I've kept up with you, as you can tell."

The thought he'd followed her career warmed her. "Yes. It has."

They just sat and looked at each other a long moment. Then Luke reached across the table for her hand. "I don't want to discuss pleasantries, Julia. Am I interested in your life? Absolutely. But you know what I want right now?"

"What?" She whispered the word.

"To spend the night with you. That's what I want. Right now. Tonight."

Common sense told her to pull her hand back, pull *herself* back, tell him this was impossible and she needed to go home. How could she do this without telling him all her secrets first? What if he was angry? Outraged? Didn't understand her reasons for everything? Thought she should have tried harder to find him? But his touch still set her nerve endings dancing, bringing back erotic memories and fanning the banked flames of desire. Fourteen years and the intensity of her need for him ignited in only seconds.

"Say something, Julia." He grinned ruefully. "Even if it's just to tell me to go away."

"There are things… My life…" She wet her lips with her tongue. "Things you don't know."

"Whatever it is can wait. It's taken so long for us to get here again. Tell me you don't want me right now," he prodded. "Say it, we'll finish our drinks, and I'll drive you home."

"I can't do that," she whispered, as every bit of rational thought fled from her brain. "I have to be honest. I want your arms around me right now. I want you to hold me and never let me go."

"Julia..."

She wet her lips. "There are too many complications."

Luke stared at her for a long time. "Everyone's life is complicated. Right now, what's important is tonight. The rest we'll deal with later."

"Later." She repeated the word, hoping there would be a later.

He rose from his chair and she thought he was going to reach for her. Instead, he walked to the door and pressed a tiny button in the framing. Then he came to her and pulled her from her chair. Kissing her lightly, he reached for her coat.

"Let's get the check and get out of here. What I'm hungry for is something other than food."

Chapter 16

A light rain fell as Luke maneuvered carefully through the streets. Julia paid little attention to where they were going, wrapped heavily in her own thoughts. If this was a mistake, then so be it. She'd been a good and committed wife during the balance of Charles's illness, a condition that made him even more difficult to deal with. But she'd gritted her teeth and handled it with as much grace as she could muster. Andy and Beth had turned into amazing young adults. She continued to try her best with Courtney, although at the moment she felt like a terrible failure in that department.

But tonight was going to be for her. Whatever happened next would happen.

She roused herself from her reverie when they turned into the garage of a new all-suites hotel.

"My temporary home," he explained, helping her from the car and leading her to the elevator. "I haven't taken the time yet to look for something more permanent. Most of my time's been occupied with learning about the company and getting ready for this name change and a new product line."

They said little as the car ascended smoothly.

Her heart thudded with mixed anxiety and anticipation. Fourteen years had passed since she last felt Luke's hands on her body, his mouth on hers, his hard erection entering her and joining their bodies. The images took possession of her brain and buried any reasonable objections she could think of.

Luke put his arm around her and leaned his cheek against her hair, sensing her anxiety and offering her reassurance. Then the doors slid open and they walked silently down the thickly carpeted hall to a door Luke unlocked.

"A little ostentatious." He ushered her into a large suite furnished in what Julia could only call stark opulence.

"How nice." She spoke softly as she walked into the living room. "Certainly not your average hotel suite." A wall of windows opened to a spectacular view of downtown San Antonio. Couches in butter-soft leather were grouped for conversation, and against one wall, a fireplace was surrounded by an entertainment center.

"But no television." That surprised her since Luke was a huge sports fan. Where did he watch his games?

"In the bedroom and the guest room. Also in the den. I often work at home on the weekends."

"There's a den, too? And another bedroom?" She was amazed. The so-called suite was beyond any accommodation of this type she'd ever seen.

"The place was built for corporations requiring a residential facility available twenty-four seven." He waved his hand at the space. "A little much for me, but Connell Wilson has a permanent lease on it and at least it's comfortable.

"It's certainly luxurious." She was making idle conversation, hugging her coat to her chest, stalling to give her nerves time to settle.

"But not homelike," he told her in a quiet voice. "Right now I'm not too interested in discussing accommodations, though."

Standing behind her, he reached around and undid the buttons on her coat, slipping it off her shoulders. Almost casually, he turned her to face him. "God, Julia, I have missed you so much."

"I… I've missed you, too, Luke." God, had she.

He cupped her face with his hands, his eyes searching hers. "I have so much I want to say to you, so many questions to ask." He rubbed his thumb gently over her lower lip.

There went the butterfly wings in her stomach again. She knew where this was going and she was far from ready for that discussion. Maybe she'd never be ready.

"Can't we just enjoy tonight? Can't this be enough?" She didn't know if she was strong enough to take him into her life, to deal with the complexities of this relationship and the inevitable fallout, especially with Courtney hovering over everything like the Sword of Damocles.

"No, Julia. Not anymore." His face was inches from hers. "I let you walk out of my life once. I can't do it again. I want a lot more than this one night."

"You do?" She could hardly breathe.

"Yes. I want it all. But if one night is as much as you can give me right now, I'll start there." The tips of his fingers brushed her cheek.

Her skin tingled beneath the feathery caress and her heart now pounded so thunderously she thought it would burst from her chest. She trembled, as much from trepidation as from desire.

"I don't know what's wrong here, Julia," he persisted, his lips almost touching hers. "I only know that right now I have to have you, have to make up for the lost years."

His nearness was overpowering her, drowning her, making her forget about everything else. The rush of need and desire that consumed her melted her body.

"All right," she whispered. She'd worry about tomorrow later.

His mouth came down on hers, fierce and hard, claiming it. Claiming her. When she opened her lips for him he tangled his tongue with hers. And just like that the yesterdays began to fade away. She was transported back to the cabin in the snow, bathed in the heat of the fireplace. For a minute, she even thought she smelled the heady scent of pine.

"I love you." He spoke the words into her open mouth. "I never stopped."

She hesitated for just the briefest second, and then the words escaped from her mouth with a life of their own. "I love you, too, Luke." And she did. Body and soul. Why try to deny it?

He took a step back from her, his hands still holding her face. "I have a great bedroom," he said. "You ought to see it, you know."

"Of course." How could she say no when he looked at her like that?

He took her hand and led her to a door at one end of the living room. It opened into the largest bedroom Julia had ever seen. To one side was another wall of windows facing downtown, the lights of the city twinkling like a myriad of candles against the black night sky. Across from the bed, which looked large enough for a family of four, was a brick fireplace. Luke picked up a small remote control from the nightstand, pressed a button on it, and the fireplace leaped into flame.

"You have no idea how much you still turn me on." He began unfastening and removing her clothes, letting them drop one piece at a time, his gaze hungry on her as more and more of her was revealed.

"Luke?" She stilled his hand, suddenly both shy and nervous.

"Hmm?"

"I'm… I'm not a kid anymore." And her body showed every one of the past fourteen years, at least to her.

"Thank God. Neither am I." He chuckled. "Wait. Haven't we had this conversation before?"

She remembered their first time in the hotel, her nervousness then. "I'm…" She wasn't sure quite how to say it. "I don't look like I did last time we were together."

"Nor do I. But to me, you're more beautiful than ever." He stopped her when she tried to turn away from him. "No. Please let me look at you. Your image has been in my mind all these years."

He held her by the arms, his gaze roaming over her body, taking in every inch of the ripe, mature curves, the fullness of her breasts, the slight swell of her tummy. In his eyes, she could see he was awed by what he saw and it humbled her.

"You are more than I ever thought to ask for." His voice was not quite steady.

He ran the tip of a finger over the upper swell of her breasts, tracing the frothy lace of her bra. Thumbs brushed her nipples, igniting the fire smoldering in her veins.

Julia wet her lips nervously, suddenly self-conscious under his probing stare. She knew the changes in her body that marked the years. And she was not just older, she was long out of practice. For years, sex hadn't even been a factor in her life.

"I'm almost middle-aged, Luke." A blush of embarrassment crept up her cheeks. She tried hard to sound matter of fact. "Not the younger woman you took to bed so long ago. And I haven't... I mean, I didn't..."

God, she was making a mess out of this.

"Stop." Luke kissed her eyelids, her cheeks, the corners of her mouth. "You are exactly the woman I want." He chuckled. "And I understand sex is like riding a bicycle. You never forget."

In an instant, he was out of his own clothes. She looked at his body, aware that the years had been good to him. Grey spattered the crisp hair dusting his chest, but it was just as rich and tantalizing. He was thicker with age, but not heavier, and the thickness was more appealing than the younger, thinner Luke. And his erection. Oh, yes. There was definitely nothing wrong with that.

It rose, full and proud, from the nest of curls at his groin. It was still thick and swollen, still with the darkened head, the cock of a much younger man. Immediately her pussy responded, the scent of her musk so strong she could smell it herself.

He trailed his fingers over her arms, his lips tracing a path along her collarbone. He licked here and there, tasting, tasting. Every place he touched her sparked with need, with desire. He pressed close to her and the heated thickness of his cock branded itself against her flesh.

His mouth found hers again, feeding from it as he moved his hands to her bra, tossing it aside and taking the weight of her breasts in his warm palms. He brushed her nipples again with his thumbs, pressing lightly before rubbing gently back and forth. Desire exploded within her, hot and wild. She met his tongue with her own and followed him in the steps of the seductive dance.

His hands moved everywhere, touching her back, her waist, her hips, the curve of her ass. He slid his fingers into the scrap of silk that passed for a thong and sank them into the cleft in her buttocks. The tip of one finger found the tight ring of her anus. Julia tensed against the intrusion but Luke continued to kiss her as if he wanted nothing more than to keep his mouth fused to hers. On an exhalation of breath, she relaxed.

He'd taken her this way only the one time, but the memory of it always shot a bolt of lust through her. Wherever she was, whatever she was doing when she thought of it, her cream immediately soaked her panties and the walls of her pussy would quiver with need. As his finger circled the tight opening, she moaned and pressed herself against him.

"I need you in bed," he gasped, tearing his mouth from hers.

Releasing her for a moment, he deftly stripped back the covers. He followed her down, stretching out next to her, cradling her in one arm as he explored her with the other. He touched her reverently with his lean fingers, relearning every inch of her body.

Slowly he circled her nipples, feeling the tips harden at once and her breasts swell. He ran his hands over her skin, his cock flexing against her thigh as he touched each hot, secret place.

"You are so much better now." He murmured the words, his mouth at her ear, nipping the soft flesh of the lobe with his teeth. "You intoxicate me."

Julia lay with her eyes closed, reveling in the feel of his hands on her. She didn't know what she had expected. Maybe a paler, weaker version of the nights they'd once shared. But she could feel heat building in her with a greater intensity than she'd ever known. As Luke drifted his hand lower, she parted her thighs automatically, giving him greater access.

The years rolled away. The remembered feel of his hands on her, in her, came surging back. Her nerve endings were rioting, her hips thrusting against fingers touching her so intimately, rasping the inner wall of her sheath. With his thumb, he unerringly found the nub of her sex. Just the touch of the calloused skin sent rockets through her body.

She forgot to be self-conscious, forgot to be nervous, forgot everything except the sensations rocketing through her. Fourteen years of separation, of denial, made her frantic to feel him inside her.

With his fingers, he probed the slippery flesh of her cunt, brushing the bundle of nerves that was her swollen slit before slipping two fingers deep inside her. She clenched around them, trying to pull him in deeper, wanting that hot shaft rather than his educated fingers. And educated they were, scraping the sweet spot just so to bring a fresh flood of her cream and drawing tiny sounds of pleasure from her.

She slipped her hand down to close her fingers over his thick shaft, feeling the drop of fluid at the slit, rubbing it over the velvety flesh with her thumb.

"Your cunt is just as hot and tight and sweet as I remembered." His voice was rough with desire, his breath a heated breeze against her ear. "God, Julia. The minute I saw you again I wanted to lay you down and fuck you until neither of us could breathe."

The erotic words were like flames licking at her, driving her arousal higher and higher. When he moved his mouth to hers again, she nipped at his bottom lip and was rewarded by the flexing of his cock in her grip. More fluid seeped from the slit, and again she rubbed it over the smooth head. Luke groaned and moved his fingers faster in and out of her, his thumb busy at her clit.

"I'm sorry," he groaned. "I wanted to take longer. Make it last. The next one will be better, but right now I have to be inside you."

"Yes," she gasped. "Please."

When Luke rose over her, positioning himself at the entrance to her body, she opened her legs to embrace him. Slowly, she felt his shaft, like a thick rod, easing into her. Then he was seated to the hilt and they were joined. He filled her, stretched her, rubbing at every tiny nerve in the walls of her cunt. His hands slid beneath her ass and lifted her to him. They began moving together in a rhythm that the years hadn't washed away. Luke pulled her tighter to him, sweat beading his forehead, fighting to control himself as long as possible.

She met him stroke for stroke, lifting her hips, urging him deeper. She wrapped her legs around him to hold him in place, digging her heels into the small of his back and raking her nails over his skin.

"Open your eyes," he commanded. "Look at me."

When she did, what she saw in his nearly undid her. Lust. Fire. Passion. And love. The sheer emotion drove her up and up, carrying her to a plane of sensation that threatened to consume her. Deep inside her, that coil of desire unwound like a spring held too tight for too long. Julia felt Luke's muscles tighten, felt the tension growing, saw the muscles cord in his neck.

Then they were there, both of them, cresting at the peak. Luke drove into her hard, hammering her, and she flew, fracturing into tiny crystalline pieces. Rockets exploded around her, her pussy convulsing over and over. Inside her Luke came in powerful bursts as if he'd been saving it for so long. Her vaginal muscles gripped his cock, squeezed it, and milked it as she exploded around him. Their bodies slammed into each other, shaking with the force of their passion.

In the aftermath, they lay twined together, trying to drag air into their lungs. Luke remained inside her, connected to her, and she could feel his heart hammering against her ribs in cadence with her own. It was a long time before either of them spoke. He finally eased slowly from her body and padded to the bathroom. When he returned, he carried a warm washcloth that he used to clean her gently, bending now and then to place an open-mouthed kiss on her now ultra-sensitive clit. Finished, he tossed the washcloth on the carpet and climbed back into bed beside her. Sliding his arm beneath her, he cradled her against his body.

"I guess that answers the question of whether the spark is still there." His voice was tinged with amusement.

"No kidding." She smiled, drained and energized at the same time. "If it sparked any more, I think I'd be dead."

Luke raised himself on one elbow and leaned over her, placing the palm of his hand against her cheek and searching her eyes. "Here's a question that still needs answering, though," he said. "Where do we go from here?"

Chapter 17

Julia closed her eyes. "That is definitely the question of the night."

"More for you than me," Luke told her. "I know what I want and there's nothing holding me back. But I know you have obligations you need to consider." He rolled to the side and off the bed. "Don't say a word yet. I'll be right back."

He returned carrying a bottle of cognac and two brandy snifters. "Remy Martin. The night calls for something special." He poured a drink for each of them, handed her a glass, and raised his own in a toast. "To you, my wonderful, special Julia. And to our future?"

It was a question more than a statement, and Julia wasn't sure at the moment how she wanted to answer it. She'd never expected Luke to walk back into her life again. So much had happened since the last time they were together, her life turned upside down. Now, unexpectedly, here he was in the flesh. More than anything, she wanted to shut out the rest of the world and cocoon herself with him, but that wasn't possible. If they were to go forward, she needed to find a way to introduce him into her life. To her children. And most of all, to Courtney.

Hello, children. Meet the love of my life. I had an affair with him fourteen years ago and oh, Courtney, by the way, he's your father. Only he just found out about it.

She didn't even know if he'd want the responsibility of raising another child. His sons were grown, his responsibilities minimal, his life belonging only to him. A rebellious teenager wasn't exactly an "I love you" present to drop into that smoothly sailing boat.

There was also the nastiness of Rod McGuire to face. With the passage of time, she felt less and less threatened by him. But the choice had to be Luke's. At least he'd have all the facts. All she needed to do was find the courage to tell him everything.

Walking away wasn't an option, either. If she'd never seen him again, maybe. Especially after her efforts to find him yielded nothing, she'd accepted the fact he would never be in her life again. But now he was here, wanting them to be together again. To be working with him on a project, seeing him, being close to him, and not be with him was impossible. She needed to make some hard decisions. She groaned softly.

"Are you okay?" Luke asked, concern in his voice.

"Yes." She smiled at him. "More than." She clinked her snifter against his and said, with her heart in her mouth, "To the future."

"Tell me what's going on with you?" Luke leaned back against the pillows.

God, where to begin. "I guess my life's pretty ordinary. The twins graduated college and are gainfully employed, thank heavens. And doing well, I might add." She couldn't help the touch of pride in her voice. "We see each other as often as possible, but we have busy lives."

"They're still in the area?"

"Oh, yes. I've been lucky that way." She sipped at the brandy. "And the business has done extremely well. I feel good about that."

"I know." He looked at her with those dark, dangerous eyes. "Julia, you haven't been out of my thoughts for a single minute since that last time together. I see your face in my mind the last thing at night and first thing in the morning." A muscle twitched in his jaw. "I ran, you know."

She frowned. "Ran?"

"When you wouldn't take my calls, wouldn't talk to me, I had to leave all the places we'd been together. Fortunately, I seem to have a skill that's marketable. It seems a lot of companies are looking for people like me."

"Where did you go?"

"Everywhere. Different states. Even a stint in Europe for a while. But I couldn't outrun my memories or my feelings. When Connell Wilson reached out to me I saw this as kind of an omen and I jumped."

So that was why she couldn't find him. Her throat tightened and her hands began to tremble. She clutched the brandy snifter to still them.

"If you tell me you haven't thought of me at all, my heart will be broken."

He said it lightly, but she knew what he wanted to hear.

She swallowed hard. If he only knew. "Of course I've thought of you, Luke. Did you think I wouldn't?"

He bent his head to hers and kissed her, a kiss full of meaning she wasn't sure she was ready for. His tongue dusted across her lips and when she opened for him, he plunged inside as if about to swallow her whole. Instant fire blazed through her, waking up the tiny nerves in the walls of her pussy, nerves she'd thought a moment ago were sleeping after the crashing orgasm. The familiar flutter in her vaginal walls was an erotic signal that she wanted Luke badly. Again. And so quickly.

Leaning to the side, she placed the brandy snifter carefully on the nightstand. Then she reached her hand down, trailing her fingers across his stomach until they found his cock and gripped it lightly. Luke swallowed a moan, and clamped his hand on her wrist.

"Give me a minute," he huffed. "Okay? Remember we aren't teenagers."

Julia laughed with delight, forgetting everything in this moment of voluptuous bliss, at the knowledge that he could respond to her so fast.

"What about your younger daughter?" Luke changed the subject abruptly, his fingers still holding her wrist. "The one Claire has with her tonight?"

"Courtney." His daughter.

"Tell me about her. What's she like?"

Where to begin.

"She's a typical teenager, I'm afraid. Full of anger and rebellion. I'd either forgotten what the teen years are like or Courtney's taking it to greater extremes than Beth or Andy."

"Teenagers can be pistols," he agreed. "I've heard girls are much worse than boys, although as you can understand, I've only had occasional exposure to it."

"Only because the pitfalls for them are so much more complex."

"You have your hands full," he mused.

"That's an understatement." She pressed closer to him. "Some days I'd like to take a pill and wake up when she's married with a family of her own."

"I'm sure it's been hard for her growing up without a father. And for you, having to be both parents to her." Luke's tone carried a mixture of concern and latent resentment. And why shouldn't it? She'd led him to believe her life was about to be her own, that she was finally finding herself. Then, like slamming a door, she'd walked away from him without a word.

"You're right." Julia lifted her hand from his erection and tangled her fingers through the crisp curls surrounding it. "I felt stretched so thin all those years. Maybe I just didn't give her what she needed and this is payback."

"No." Luke shook his head. "That's not what I meant. I can't see you as anything but a good mother, Julia. But kids react differently to stressful situations. That's as much as I'm saying."

"Well, this too shall pass." She ran her hands over the familiar lines of his body. "But I think I'm through talking for now."

Luke pulled her into his arms, holding her close to him as he explored her with his hands. He cupped each breast in turn, lightly kneading the flesh, bending his head to take each nipple into his mouth. He took tiny nips, soothed with his tongue, then nipped again. The dual sensations of pain and pleasure sent her pulse rocketing again and the insistent throb in her cunt vibrating through her body.

She reached for his cock again, gripping it firmly this time and sliding her hand up and down, feeling the hot, rigid shaft beneath the soft skin covering it, and the thrum of the blood pulsing through its veins. Luke moaned against her flesh as he continued to work magic on her nipples with his mouth. The harder he sucked, the more she pumped, feeling him flex in her fingers.

His tongue traced a wet line between her breasts down to her navel, licking the tiny whorls of flesh. Julia tightened her fingers around him, then slipped her hand between his thighs to cup his sac. The fine hair covering the skin was baby-soft to her touch and she feathered her fingers back and forth over its surface. She was rewarded with the hot press of the swollen cock against her thigh and the dampness that was the tiny pearlescent drop seeping from the slit. She wanted to concentrate on giving him pleasure, but he nudged her thighs apart and cupped her mound with his hand, pressing his thumb against her clit, and concentration fled.

"You're soaking wet again." He easily slid two fingers inside her and lazily pumped them. "Let's do this."

He slid his fingers out and flipped her over to her stomach, one hand beneath her working her clit, the other gathering her cream, and spreading her pussy wide, around her opening, and on to the tight muscle of her anus. Julia gasped and flinched at the expected intrusion, but Luke simply continued rubbing and coaxing, gathering more and more of her liquid to lubricate her.

"Relax." His voice was rough with anticipated pleasure. "You liked it when we did this before, Julia. Remember?" He shifted so he could place his mouth at her ear again. "Remember how hot it made you? You came like a maniac."

Julia shivered. Every response came roaring back and her body became one throbbing pulse of insistent need. Everything fell away except her and Luke, wrapped in a black velvet cloak of sensuality. And while he rubbed and stroked, he licked her ear, trailed his mouth down her neck, grazed his teeth along her shoulder. Scattered kisses down her spine. With each touch, each caress, she became more aroused. Her body more open to him.

"Next time," he whispered. "Next time I'll be prepared and I'll take you again here. Count on it."

He moved then, pulling her to her knees. She felt hot, wet kisses on the cheeks of her ass and warm breath blowing over them and she shivered with anticipation. Pillows were plumped beneath her stomach. He stroked his fingers the length of her spine before positioning his cock at the opening of her cunt.

"Take a deep breath." His voice was rich and thick like melted chocolate.

One strong thrust and he was completely inside her, muscles clenching around his cock. Luke's hands were on her hips now, steadying her, guiding her, his voice murmuring, rolling over her like the slow sweep of thick molasses.

Now he moved, pumping steadily in and out of her, the friction stimulating every nerve, sensations cascading through her one after the other, stealing her breath. Her skin felt icy hot while blood rushed hotly in her veins and her heart raced madly. This was where she belonged. Right here. With him. How had she lived without this all this time? Without this feeling of being one with him? Of giving herself to him so completely? She clamped down on the thickness of him, relishing in the hot, solid feel of him. Caught his rhythm and rocked her hips with him, taking him as deep as she could. He tightened his fingers on her hips and a low growl rumbled up from his throat. She was rising, rising, rising, the black velvet swirling, the sound of flesh on flesh a punctuation to their accelerated rhythm.

She grasped the bedding as her orgasm climbed within her, seeking its release. *Yes*, she wanted to shout. *I love you, Luke. Love you, love you, love you.* In a moment she exploded, shaking with the force of her climax. Luke shouted her name and emptied himself into her in thick, hot spurts. They fell over the cliff together, spiraling and spinning until they were finally spent.

And everything else was forgotten.

Chapter 18

"I noticed how neatly you avoided my question last night."

They were in the kitchen. Julia sat at the raised counter, drinking coffee, and thinking about how pleasantly sore she was in so many places. Luke buttered toast for them.

"What question was that?" she asked carefully.

"Don't play games, Julia." He looked up, his eyes dark. "The one about where we go from here."

He wouldn't be put off. She knew that. And in her heart she didn't want him to be. Not after last night. She'd dipped her toe into the shallow end of the pool again and immediately found herself over her head. A good reason why she should have gone home.

There were just so many problems to work out, problems she couldn't share with him. How would Andy and Beth react to a new man in her life? What about Courtney, who seemed thrown for a loop by everything these days? And who bore the stamp of Luke with her eyes and her full mouth, both a dead giveaway. One look at her and it would be over.

And then of course there was Mr. Nasty, Rod McGuire. She'd about come to the conclusion, with Claire's prompting, that she could face him down. But at what cost to Luke? He was here, in Rod's town, in a new position. Could Rod really screw that up for him? She knew what Claire would say—*It's Luke's choice. You have to let him make it.* And what if Rod decided to confront Andy and Beth before she had a chance to tell them in her own words? But now, sitting here with Luke, she recalled the last time she'd seen Rod.

"I'm still watching you, Julia." They'd happened to find themselves at the same art show one time and he made it a point to tell her.

"Charles is long gone and the twins are adults," she'd told him, jutting out her chin. "They're earning their own money and so am I. You can shut off the financial spigot any time you want."

"Cocky, aren't you." His eyes glittered with dislike. "I promised Charles you'd never have peace after what you put him through." His voice was harsh, like metal grating on metal. "I intend to keep my word."

"To what end?" She'd been proud of herself, not giving any indication of how much he rattled her.

"To carry out the wishes of a dying man. A man you destroyed. You weren't worth half of him."

"You can do what you want." She was disgusted with the whole thing and tired of his games. "My 'situation,' as you call it, isn't so unusual or scandalous anymore, Rod. Do whatever you want. We'll survive."

He'd eyed her from head to toe. "You took your moment of happiness, Julia, for what it was worth. That's as much as you'll ever get."

But when he'd walked away from her, instead of the usual sick feeling a confrontation left her with, she'd felt strangely freed. Instead of wilting, she'd faced him down. That was the first real moment she'd had hope for herself. And for Luke, if fate every brought them together again. But again, that meant telling him everything, in a way that he'd understand. Trying to explain how difficult her position had been, that she'd been threatened on so many fronts and at the time didn't have the strength to stand up for herself. At least she could tell him she'd tried to find him, if that would help.

"I didn't think that was such a hard question," Luke said testily when she was silent for so long. He handed her a plate of toast. "Did I mistake last night for something else?"

"No." She was emphatic. Despite the devil waiting to destroy her, there was no question about what last night was. "You didn't make a mistake at all." She picked up a piece of toast, nibbling at it for something to do. "I just have to figure out how to do this."

"Are you worried about your kids?" he asked, his shrewd eyes on her. "I'd think they'd be glad for you to have a little happiness after so long."

"For one thing, I've never brought another man into the house, or even dated one," she told him. "This would be a whole new experience for them. Exactly how do I explain you to them? Hi kids, here's the man I slept with fourteen years ago and gave my heart to?"

"Did you?" he asked, his voice low. "Give your heart to me?"

"Yes," she whispered, and in an instant, his arms were around her and he was kissing her forehead.

"Then we'll work this out." He sat down on the bar stool next to her. "This doesn't have to be complicated, you know. I'm someone you did business with a long time ago. Now I find myself in the same city as you, I asked you to bid on our account and we went to dinner to renew our acquaintance. What's wrong with that?"

And when he got a look at Courtney for the first time, what then? She needed time to figure this out. To plan how she would tell him everything. She didn't even want to think how enraged he would be when she told him about Rod. And as Claire had pointed out so many times, rightfully so. What a stupid idiot she'd been.

"Julia." He took one of her hands in his. "Beth and Andy are out on their own. They're young adults. I can't see them as a problem."

"Maybe. But Courtney is another matter altogether." Especially once he got a good look at her.

"Let's try this." He brushed his knuckles against her cheek. "Go home. Change clothes. Go to work. I'll call you at your office on Monday and ask you out to dinner for next Friday night. That puts enough space between last night and our next…date. How's that?"

"You make it sound so easy." She gave him a tremulous smile. If only.

"It *will* be easy. This is our dance but you have to let me lead. Okay?"

"Please give me a little space to think about this," she begged.

For a moment, his face tightened with suppressed emotion. Then he forced a smile. "All right." He kissed her again, this time molding his mouth to hers, his tongue hot and searching. When he sat back he said, "You've got the weekend to mull it over. But I'm giving you fair warning. I'm not letting you get away this time." He brushed his knuckles lightly over her cheek. "It's still there, Julia. We're both single adults. I want to spend the rest of my life with you and I'm going to find a way to make it happen."

Her heart skipped and stuttered. "Oh, Luke. If only that could happen."

He hugged her, hard. "It could, if you'd just say yes."

She shook her head. It wasn't that simple. "There are…complications." Suddenly she needed to get away. Catch her breath. Think without his mesmerizing presence surrounding her. "I have to go, Luke. I'll catch a cab." She picked up her purse and suit jacket.

"Julia, wait. What's wrong?" He reached for her but she eluded him, nearly racing for the door.

"Please. Just…I need to leave."

With that, she shot out the door and raced down the hall to the elevator. He followed her into the hall, hurrying after her. Grabbing her arm, he managed to pull her to a stop.

"Julia, we're still having dinner next Friday night. If you don't call me with a time and place, I'm showing up on your doorstep, so you'd better be ready."

"Luke, listen…"

He gripped both arms, his eyes boring into hers like twin lasers. "Whatever the problem is, we'll fix it. But there's no way I'm letting you walk out of my life a second time. Count on it."

Oh, if only that could be true.

"Friday night," he repeated, his words underscored with determination.

The last thing she saw as the elevator doors closed with Luke in the hallway, the expression on his face a combination of love and resolution.

Please let it be all right. Please.

* * * *

Miranda started to ask her a question when she walked into the house. One look at Julia's face and she just said, "We're having chicken for dinner," and walked back into the kitchen.

In the shower, every moment of the previous night replayed itself in Julia's mind. Her body stirred just remembering the touch of Luke's hands, the passion of his kisses, the incredible sense of him inside her, filling her. Over the past fourteen years, the magic had only increased. She could no more have walked away at the Connell Wilson offices than she could have jumped out a window. The tug, the lure, were still as strong.

At least she'd avoided a showdown with Rod for the moment. Harry's House had been an excellent choice of restaurants with its private, secluded rooms. But if she continued to see Luke she knew it would happen sooner rather than later. One thing at a time, she told herself. She turned off the shower and tried to make her brain work as she dried herself off. She knew what she needed to do for things to go forward with Luke and for that she had to have a plan.

As sure as she knew her name, she was certain he would not be put off. His intentions were crystal clear. He was not a man deterred by flimsy excuses. And once he got a good look at Courtney, he'd have even more questions and would be even more determined. Their daughter had Luke's dark brown eyes and his distinctive eyebrows. She wondered what other physical traits of the Buchanan family her daughter also carried. She could just imagine the shock when he saw the daughter he didn't even know he had.

She popped two acetaminophen to dull the headache bullying its way up from behind her eyes. Then she dressed quickly, brushed her hair, and made do with blush and lip gloss for makeup. No clients today so she didn't need a full-court press. She just needed to get herself together before facing Claire.

Claire!

Now there was one person she could barely keep anything from. The woman would take one look at her and pry everything out of her. She swallowed a strangled laugh as she imagined Claire marching into Charles's hospital room and, heart attack or not, giving him a scathing piece of her mind. Well, she could use some of that brashness now to help her stiffen her spine.

"See you later," she called to Miranda as she hurried out to her car.

* * * *

"Well?" Claire was on the phone but hung up as soon as Julia walked into the office.

"Well, what?" Julia deliberately kept her face blank.

"Come on, give." Claire grinned. "Was it wonderful?"

Julia dropped into the chair in front of Claire's desk, ran her fingers through her hair, and leaned her head back. "Yes. It was beyond wonderful."

Claire leaned forward. "Then what's the problem? Why do you look so stressed? I thought you'd tell me you'd died and gone to heaven."

"Almost." She closed her eyes, willing herself under control.

"What's that supposed to mean? My God, Charles is long out of the picture, you've lived like a nun since his death, and Andy and Beth are out on their own. There might even be hope for Courtney. Why isn't it time for Julia?"

"I don't want to discuss it right now, okay?" Julia sat up, rotating her neck to relieve the tension.

"No, not okay. If I weren't married and that man walked back into my life, I'd chain him to the bed. God, Julia. What is wrong with you?"

More than I can tell you, she wanted to say. She'd have to lay everything out for Luke before they could move forward and all that was still tumbling around in her brain.

"There are just…complications." The same excuse she'd used with Luke

"Honey, I know the whole story, remember? There's nothing that can't be uncomplicated."

"Claire," she began.

"Julia." Claire's voice softened. "Please tell me you aren't giving Charles the power to reach out from the grave and ruin your life."

Julia shook her head. "It's not that, I promise you. I'm just so afraid of what will happen if—when—Luke finds out about Courtney. Will he hate me for not tracking him down?"

"You tried," Claire pointed out.

"I could have tried harder," she protested.

"Give Luke some credit, okay? He still loves you. A lot. Will this be a challenge? Of course. But I have faith the two of you can weather it."

"How was Courtney?" Julia segued into a new topic.

"Okay, change the subject." Claire sighed. "But just for now. Courtney was fine. She behaved politely, showed me what Beth told her about makeup, and actually looked decent when I dropped her off at school today."

"Thank you so much. It was wonderful of you to do that."

"If I'm so wonderful, then pay attention to what I'm telling you."

"I will. Soon," she hedged and stood up. "I want to check my messages and then we can debrief yesterday's presentation, okay?"

Claire simply sat there, studying her for a long time before she spoke. "Fine. But I'm not through taking to you about this. You've got something very good here. I won't let you lose it again because you're afraid. It's time to put those fears aside and grab on to the life you've missed out on all these years."

* * * *

Luke closed the door to his office, telling Ellen, his secretary, he didn't want to be disturbed for a while. He had a meeting in an hour and he needed to straighten out his head before he got to it.

What the hell had been wrong with Julia this morning? Last night he'd thought what they felt for each other had slammed back at them stronger than ever. Missing her and wanting her for so long, and finally he could touch her again and hold her in his arms. When his lips touched hers, the electricity between them could have lit up the room. Maybe even had.

He could almost taste that kiss now, thinking about it. So many years, so much misery since he'd left her at the airport that snowy day. He'd called and called to talk to her, but she never took his calls and never returned them. Claire was always his lifeline, keeping him informed. But even she couldn't tell him why Julia wouldn't at least speak to him or what was happening that was so wrong.

He'd known there was something, just by her tone of voice. But it was hard to fight what he didn't know. For one impulsive moment, he'd been tempted to get on a plane, fly to San Antonio, and confront Julia; but he was afraid he'd only worsen whatever the hell was going on.

He'd have certainly understood if Charles's heart attack had created problems for her. He was, after all, still the father of her children.

Jealousy stabbed at him. *He* wanted to be the father of her children, but the opportunity for that was long past. Now he'd settle for just being her husband. That is, if he could ever get her to realize what they had went far beyond the little time they'd spent together. If he could just get her to talk to him. One minute this morning she'd been fine, then an invisible door had suddenly closed.

Yesterday he'd sensed an ally in Claire. He'd have to explore that possibility. He'd have to do something because Julia was well and truly spooked. Feeling despair settle over him, he turned and opened the folder for his meeting.

* * * *

Julia managed to avoid the confrontation with Claire for the moment by pleading a headache at the end of the day. And that was no cheap lie. But she knew her friend wouldn't be put off much longer.

She'd come home from the office, made a pretense of eating with Courtney, then gone to her room, put on her favorite robe, and lay down on the bed. She needed to think but her head still hurt from the day's tension.

"Mom?" There was a soft tap on the bedroom door.

"Yes?" Julia roused herself.

"Hi." The door swung open and Beth hurried over to hug her. "Are you okay? I called earlier and Miranda said you didn't seem yourself. I thought I'd stop by and check it out for myself." She looked at her mother carefully, searching for telltale signs of whatever was wrong.

"I'm fine, sweetie. Truly. But I'm glad you came over. You know I always love seeing you."

"You don't look so fine." Beth eyed her mother critically. "Are you coming down with something? You don't take half enough care of yourself."

She took one of Beth's hands in both of hers. "I'm fine. Truly."

Beth narrowed her eyes. "Is it Courtney?" She smiled, flashing a dimple. "Do I need to take her over my knee again?"

"Courtney is still…Courtney. But at least thanks to you she's dressing better and doesn't look like she's wearing an entire makeup counter when she goes out." She shook her head. "Where do thirteen-year-old girls get their ideas, anyway? You were never like that."

Beth laughed. "I was the perfect child, remember?" She hugged Julia. "I'm calling you Monday. If I don't like the way you sound, I'm taking you out to dinner for some Mom therapy."

Monday was apparently the day everyone was going to call her.

"Mom?" Beth's voice held an edge of concern. "What's wrong? You just turned white as a sheet. Okay. That does it. Monday for sure I'm calling the doctor and making an appointment for you."

"No, don't. Please." Julia let out a long, slow breath. "I'm fine. Just tired. You're right. I need to eat better and get more sleep." She forced a smile. "And I promise to do that."

"You know, Mom, it wouldn't kill you to go out on a date now and then."

"Date?" She wanted to laugh hysterically. "Honey, I'm doing just fine. I have the business and Claire and you guys."

Beth frowned. "But—"

Julia reached out her fingers and pressed them to Beth's lips. "It's okay, baby. I'm fine. I'll do a better job of eating and sleeping. I promise."

If only, she thought, everything else was that simple.

"Anyway, it's Friday night." She made herself dredge up a smile. "What are you doing at your mother's on a Friday night? I can't believe that's what your social life is reduced to."

Beth laughed. "Actually, I'm meeting some friends at *La Marguerita* but not until much later. They went to a movie first but I'd already seen it." She hugged her mother. "I'm going now, but I'm keeping my eye on you."

Julia could only hope her daughter wouldn't be looking too closely.

Chapter 19

The weekend dragged endlessly. Julia's sleep was disturbed by dreams of Luke, erotic dreams that left her waking in a sweat, panting, her arousal wetting her thighs and her breasts aching for the touch of his hands or his mouth. But the sexual haze was later disrupted by one argument after another with Courtney. Saturday morning she was at her best. Or worst.

"Why can't I go to the party?" The teenager faced her in the kitchen, irritation sparking from her.

"We've been over this." Julia did her best to keep her voice level and calm, even as her stomach cramped and acid burned through her. "Those kids are older than you are and not the right group for you to be hanging out with. Anyway, you're just a novelty to them."

"They *like* me," Courtney insisted. "They wouldn't ask me if they didn't." She clenched her hands into fists. "Don't you think people can like me?"

"Courtney." Julia stretched out a hand to her daughter, only to have the girl turn away from her. "Of course I think people can like you. I know they do, as a matter of fact. But you aren't old enough yet to have the judgment to know when to say no to things that can harm you. I'm just looking out for your best interests. Your welfare."

"You're just jealous," Courtney sneered, her tone hateful. "Just because you don't have any friends, you don't want me to have them."

"Honey, that's not true. I *do* want you to have friends. Just the right ones. When you spend time with this group, your grades go straight into the toilet and you start dressing like some kind of freak."

"You hate me," Courtney spat out. "Admit it. You wish you'd never had me."

"Oh, sweetheart." Julia reached for her daughter again. "That is so not true."

"Yes. It is. And Grandma and Grandpa Patterson feel the same way. They never come to see me or ask about me. All those times they came to take Andy and Beth? I never got to go with them. There must be something terrible about me."

Oh, my God!

"Courtney, no. You're getting this wrong."

But Courtney whirled away, storming up the stairs. "Just leave me alone."

She slammed the door to her room, leaving Julia staring after her, fear stabbing at her heart. Was that what Courtney thought underneath it all? That Julia wished she'd never been born? How on earth had they arrived at this point? She'd tried to do her best to make her feel loved and wanted. To counteract the attitude of the elder Pattersons. To give her daughter a sense of security. Apparently she'd failed miserably and so much had festered inside Courtney for a long time. How had she missed all of that?

And was Courtney right that she, Julia, was without friends? There was Claire. Of course. But who else did she ever let into her life? No one in Charles's circle had ever given her the time of day, including his parents. Somehow, it was always easier after the mess she'd made of her life to focus on the kids, Claire, and the business. Was it coming back to haunt her now? And what the hell could she do? If she laid it all out for Luke, would he understand and want to help?

Sunday, she coaxed Courtney into lunch on the Riverwalk, the drive downtown filled with a sullen silence. By the time they'd finished lunch, though, and Julia tempted her with a shopping trip to some of the boutiques that lined the waterway, the atmosphere lightened a little.

But not much.

Sunday night, Courtney closeted herself in her room again and when she hurried to catch the school bus Monday morning, it was without a word of goodbye.

Julia was left with an aching, uneasy feeling and anger at the unfairness of life. She couldn't seem to find answers to problems that looked insurmountable. She almost dreaded going to the office Monday morning. When she walked in, she found Claire already there, waiting for her with questions in her eyes.

"You're not getting away from me this time," she warned.

But before they could get into anything, the phone rang and Margot, the receptionist, told Julia that a Mr. Buchanan was on the line for her.

"Take it," Claire insisted. "Right now. And then we're going to talk. Margot, tell Mr. Buchanan Julia will be right with him, then bring her a cup of tea."

Julia stowed her purse in her office and nodded at Margot who set a filled mug on her desk. Then she picked up the phone, her hand trembling slightly.

"Hello?"

"Good morning."

The deep timbre and molasses-thick warmth of his voice sent shivers along her spine and made her pulse throb. Images of Thursday night flashed through her mind like a video rerun, only with these images came sensations and responses. Julia drew in a deep breath to steady herself and slowly released it. She could do this. Somehow.

"Good morning." She couldn't help smiling. "Did you have a good weekend?"

"It would have been much better with you." There was no mistaking the intimacy of the tone.

"Luke…"

"We'll get back to that in a minute. Business first."

Julia wasn't sure if she waited eagerly or with dread for his announcement. "You've made a decision already?"

"At this morning's executive staff meeting, after everyone took the weekend to review everything. The contract is yours. The selection of Bright Ideas for the campaign was unanimous. My secretary's going to call your office later to set up a planning meeting."

Yes!

For one exhilarating moment, she forgot her personal issues in the thrill of success. This would lift the agency to a whole new category. She wanted to punch the air in a gesture of victory. Then reality returned. Everything else aside, she'd now be working closely with Luke Buchanan. Keeping him out of her life—and her heart—was going to be next to impossible.

"Julia?" Luke's voice held a mixture of curiosity and amusement. "You still there?"

She forced herself back to earth. "Yes. Yes, I am. I can tell you that we're thrilled you've chosen us and assure you we will work hard to implement a successful campaign."

"I know you will. So does everyone else. My secretary is faxing over the contracts as we speak." He paused, and when he spoke again there was a different tenor to his voice. "On another note, I don't want you to forget about Friday night."

"Friday night." She repeated the words, suddenly stiff and edgy.

"Dinner. Remember? Name the place or I'll be at your door."

"Luke, listen…"

"No." She felt the authority in the word humming through the connection. "We *will* be having dinner, Julia. The location and manner of meeting is up to you. I'll call you Thursday afternoon or Friday morning."

Another pause. "Just keep remembering that I love you. That I never stopped." Then he broke the connection.

She held on to those words with desperation.

"Time to celebrate." She looked up and saw Claire standing in the doorway, holding a stack of papers in her hand, her eyes alight with excitement. She waved the papers in the air. "Contracts just came in."

For a brief moment, Julia remembered when the Hot Ticket contracts were faxed to them. The scene was almost the same. Who had known what that would set in motion? She tamped down her anxiety and grinned back at Claire. She owed it to her partner and friend to celebrate this huge break for them.

"That was fast. I just got off the phone with Luke, getting the official word. He said they made the decision this morning."

"And of course he wanted to tell you himself." Claire grinned. "And so?"

Julia tried to keep her features carefully arranged. "And so what?"

"God, Julia." Claire dropped into the big client chair opposite the desk. "Anyone with half an eye could see the man is still head over heels in love with you. I'm surprised the conference room didn't go up in flames when we were doing our presentation."

Julia's eyes dropped, staring at her hands. "I hardly think that's true."

"I think it's time we had that talk, honey," Claire insisted. "Really."

"Give it a rest, Claire. Nothing's going to happen."

"I know you didn't come home Thursday night and you haven't said a word about what happened. And you got a strange look on your face when you hung up the phone. So give." She stacked the papers on the desk. "We have a huge contract here, sweetie. This will more than put us on the map. You owe it to the business to let me know what's happening."

Julia leaned back in her chair and closed her eyes for a moment. "He wants us to have dinner Friday night."

"What? But that's wonderful. Oh, honey, I'm so glad for you. You deserve some happiness."

Julia opened her eyes and looked at her friend. "You know that's not possible. I can be professional and do the work on the account, but there can never be anything personal between Luke and me. Never again."

"Julia, we've talked about the stupid situation with Rod McGuire. I thought we got past that, all that stupid manipulation from the grave."

"It's not that." She chewed her bottom lip. "Well, maybe a little. He might decide to block the twins' trust funds. He is, after all, the executor."

"Julia." Claire gave her a hard look. "Those kids don't give a damn about those trust funds and you know it. So what's this really all about?"

"I just don't know how he'll react when I tell him everything. He'll be upset that I didn't tell him from the beginning. Maybe angry that I didn't trust him enough to help me handle the situation. And he'd probably be right."

"Sweetie, you were pregnant, sick, and faced with enormous pressure. I think he'll give you a break on that."

"And even though I got in Rod's face that one time, he could still try to make trouble for Luke."

Claire set the fax sheets down on the desk. "Rod McGuire is nothing but a big bully. So he owed Charles a huge personal debt. Fine. That doesn't give him license to ruin your life or Luke's." A corner of her mouth tipped up in a smile. "Luke is a big boy, and every bit as powerful in his own right. I'll bet he could give Rod McGuire a run for his money any day of the week. He's not without resources. He can handle it."

"I hear you, but—" God, she seemed to be stuck in place. What was the matter with her?

"You need to trust Luke on this. That's my final word. At least for the moment." Claire rose and shoved the stack of papers at Julia. "Look these over, make a note of any questions you have and we'll go over them at lunch. That good with you?"

"Yes. Fine."

"And Julia? You've lived in the worst kind of purgatory for fourteen years. It's time to unlock the jail cell."

The week alternately sped up and crawled by. Julia and Claire finalized the Connell Wilson contract and made plans to meet with Luke and two others the following Monday to get into the specifics of the campaign. The rest of the week they spent making sure other clients would be taken care of during the time they were immersed in the first monster campaign of their career, and fleshing out the campaign itself.

Courtney was still doing well at the office, but the anger and resentment continued to bubble just beneath the surface. At home every tone of voice, every angle of body underscored it.

"Does she ever say anything to you?" Julia asked Beth one night on the phone.

"About what, Mom?"

"You know, whatever's bothering her."

"Mom, everything's bothering her right now." Beth laughed. "She's thirteen."

"No. I think there's something going on with her besides normal teenage stuff. I just wish I knew what it was."

Every day she braced herself for Luke's call, but her phone remained strangely silent where he was concerned. And that made her even edgier. In her nightmares, he showed up at her house unannounced, took one look at Courtney and exploded with righteous anger. She was jumpy and edgy, snapping Claire's head off, then apologizing for it. Claire just watched her carefully and said nothing.

Thursday afternoon Beth called.

"I'm taking Courtney for the weekend again," she told her mother. "I'm calling her tonight so she can pack a bag. Tomorrow I can cut out early, so I'll pick her up right from school. That will give you some relief and maybe I can get her to open up a little to me. If it's more than teenage angst, we need to know."

"Honey, did Claire put you up to this?" Julia's stomach clenched at visions of Claire spilling everything to Beth and enlisting her to clear the decks for Friday evening.

"Nope. I have no special plans and I thought it would do both of you some good to have some breathing room. Especially after our last conversation." Silence hummed along the connection. "Why? Is something special going on?"

"No." Julia nearly shouted the word, then swallowed and dialed it back. "Nothing at all. But maybe I'll have dinner with some...friends."

"Mom." Beth's voice was chiding. "I'll say this again. You should find yourself a hunk and go out on a date. You're practically a nun."

"Beth!" Julia's hand twitched on the phone, because her daughter was so close to what had worried her every day during the week.

"I mean it. Dad's been gone for years and Andy and I are good to go. It's just you and the hormonal teenager." She paused. "It might do her some good to see you with some male company."

"Are you sure you haven't been talking to Claire?"

"Uh uh. But if she's singing the same song, good for her. It means you have to listen. Bye. Gotta run."

Julia was still holding the phone when it rang again, the sound making her jump.

"You have a call holding for you, Mrs. Patterson." Margot, their receptionist, refused to call them by their first names, even though she'd been with them for five years now. It always made both Claire and Julia smile.

"Okay. Put it through." She was flipping through the stack of messages Margot brought in a few minutes before when, paying little attention, the voice at her ear jerked her upright.

"So. We're on for tomorrow night, right?"

Julia swore the deep timbre of Luke's voice vibrated through the connection. It certainly pulsed through her. She nearly dropped the receiver. For a long moment, she couldn't make her mouth work to say anything.

"Julia? You there?"

"Uh...um...yes." She exhaled slowly. In for a penny, she thought. "Hi." Wow. Didn't she just sound like an idiot? Her palms were sweating and her heart thudded against her ribs.

"Tomorrow night," he prompted.

"Yes. Tomorrow night." Suddenly she was tired of making excuses, to herself as well as Claire. She was an adult. It was time to tell Luke everything and pray he'd understand. She thought for a moment. "There's a great little restaurant just at the north edge of the city that I've been dying to try." She gave him the name and location. "Sound good to you? I can meet you there."

"Julia." He spoke in a quiet voice. "I thought maybe we'd go to someplace on the Riverwalk. Are you trying to hide me away?"

"N-No. Not at all. I...just like to be...away from people. I'm with them all week."

More silence.

"All right. I'll take you at your word. This time. Is there some reason why I can't pick you up at the house?"

If he only knew.

"I just think it would be better if we met there." Until she could lay everything out for him and deal with his reaction.

"All right." Then he added, "This time. Is eight o'clock good for you?"

"That'll be fine. See you then." She hung up before her discipline broke down and she blurted everything out to him.

Something caught her eye and she looked up to see Claire leaning in the doorway.

"Please tell me you're going out with him again."

Julia shrugged. "I guess. Beth is taking Courtney and Luke threatened to show up on my doorstep if I didn't."

"Are you going to tell him everything?"

She pushed her chair back from her desk. "After."

"After what?"

"After we spend the night together without all that crap interfering."

Claire laughed. "At least you're calling it crap. That's a start."

* * * *

By the next day, Julia was a nervous wreck. It had taken every bit of personal discipline to get through the week dealing with Courtney at home and the Connell Wilson contract at work, not to mention overseeing the projects for other clients. She'd called Luke at his office that morning, hands trembling as she punched in his private number.

"I hope this isn't a call trying to cancel tonight," were his first words.

As usual, the deep voice rumbled across the connection and sent shivers skittering along her spine.

"No. Not at all." She wet her lips. "I realized I forgot to tell you this place is casual. In case you wanted to stop at home and change first, I mean."

"Julia." She could almost see the half-smile on his face. "What I wear isn't as important as who I'll be with. But thanks for the heads-up." He paused. "Eight o'clock, right?"

"Yes. If that's okay. It'll give me a chance to go home myself and change."

"See you then."

He clicked off and she sat there holding the receiver for a long moment. A sound made her look up to see Claire standing in the doorway.

"I'm going to charge you with lurking," Julia said, half teasing. "You're always hanging out in my doorway."

"It's the only way I find anything out." Claire laughed. She walked in and sat down in one of the client chairs. "Don't screw this up, Julia. You've done penance long enough and for what? Give yourself a break. Luke's a good man. Hang on to him."

"I know, I know."

"I hope so. I really do. It's time. If Luke's living and working in San Antonio now, you can't hide Courtney away forever."

"I hear you." She exhaled a long breath.

"All right." Claire stood up. "I'll be crossing all my fingers for you."

Julia finished her work with Claire's words echoing in her head and closed up for the day. At home, she showered, dressed, and applied her makeup, the words repeating over and over like a mantra. Images slammed into her of Luke unexpectedly meeting Courtney and the shock on his face. Of Andy and Beth looking at her as if they'd never seen her.

Of Rod Maguire as he was each time she ran into him, intense dislike blazing in his eyes.

She sprayed herself with perfume, applied lip gloss, and stared at herself in the mirror. Who was she, anyway? Who was the real Julia Patterson? Mother? Widow? Business executive?

Lover?

Had she been so busy finding herself that she'd again lost the real Julia?

She had a chance with Luke again. Did she have the courage to reach out and grab it with both hands?

She checked her watch. No time for mind-bending ruminating now. She wanted tonight just for the two of them. Tomorrow, at breakfast, maybe in a restaurant where he'd have to keep his outrage under control, she'd tell him everything.

* * * *

Mardi's was a fairly new, upscale casual restaurant that Claire raved about all the time.

"Great steaks and great drinks," she'd enthused. "And as many people in jeans as anything else."

The restaurant, on the far north side of the city, was filled on Friday night. Thick carpet muted footfalls and dark paneling halfway up the walls absorbed sound, softening the buzz of conversation. Waiters and waitresses moved deftly among the tables balancing large trays, and glasses clinked as people kept the bartender busy.

Eyes scanning the room for Luke, Julia gave her name to the hostess and tried to still her nervousness.

The woman smiled at her. "Right this way, please."

She led Julia to a table in the far corner, almost tucked out of sight from the rest of the room. Luke rose to meet her as she approached. He reached for her hand and squeezed it gently, then held her chair for her.

"How much did it cost you to get this much privacy in a public room?" she teased.

"I'd have paid any price to make you comfortable." He smiled. "Crowds seem to make you nervous, so I figured this was a good compromise." He looked across the table at her. "Or is it me you're afraid of, Julia?"

She was saved from an immediate answer by the arrival of their waiter with her drink.

"Been watching for you," he told her. "The gentleman ordered and said to bring it as soon as you got here."

The aroma and color told her it was her favorite amaretto. She smiled her thanks, picked up the glass, and sipped, hoping the liqueur would settle her nerves.

"Okay, then." The waiter placed menus in front of them. "I'll give you some time to decide on your choices." He melted away into the crowd.

"I hope it was okay for me to order for you?" Luke was studying her with eyes that saw far too much.

"Absolutely. Thank you." She sipped again, then carefully placed the glass on the table.

She drank him in with her eyes. She hadn't seen him for a week but it seemed more like a year. He wore a long-sleeved sports shirt, but the sleeves were rolled back to reveal the soft dark hair on his arms. Heat surged through her and she squeezed her legs at the throbbing in her cunt that just his presence seemed to ignite. His slow, sexy smile did nothing to calm her racing pulse or ease the sudden need that gripped her. The other night was proof in fourteen years her overwhelming desire apparently hadn't cooled one bit.

Luke reached across the table and took the fingers of one hand. "I see such heavy thoughts weighing down your mind. How about if we just have drinks, dinner, and a nice evening and take it from there?"

The touch of his hand sent familiar sparks shooting through her. "That's exactly what I'd like."

"And it will be. No protests, no arguments. Okay? Sound good to you?"

She couldn't help smiling at him. It seemed even the most insurmountable problems didn't quench her desire for him.

The conversation got easier after that. Luke talked about his life during the intervening years, his continued uneven relationship with his sons, his progress through the industry to reach his position at Connell Wilson. The food was as good as Claire had promised, the atmosphere relaxing. Little by little, Julia felt her nerves and muscles relaxing and the tension easing from her neck.

Luke pushed his plate away at last and leaned forward on his elbows. "I have to admit, the fact you live here was a factor in my taking the job."

"Luke," she began.

"Don't say it, okay." He picked up the fresh drink the waiter brought and took a healthy swallow. "I don't know what happened all those years ago that you broke it off so suddenly. Not even a phone call. I tried running away from it and that didn't work so I'm not going to stop until I find out. Until I get answers. Until I can push aside whatever obstacles you think will keep us apart now." He set his glass down and leaned forward. "I love you. That hasn't changed. You told me you love me. So what we have to do next is find a solution to whatever problem has got you stuck."

"I know, I know." She fiddled with her dessert fork. "It's just… There's so much I don't know how to tell you."

His voiced wrapped around her like a warm blanket. "How about if we take it one thing at a time? For right now, let's just take tonight." His gaze caressed her face. "How late can you stay out?"

She could lie to him and tell him she needed to be home, but Julia wanted this night as much as he did. If she finally blurted out the truth, this might be the last time they were together.

"I'm good until noon tomorrow."

He visibly relaxed. "Good. Then how about coming home with me? If you promise not to change your mind, you can follow me in your car and park in one of the guest spots."

Julia took a last sip of her drink and looked across at him. "All right. And I won't change my mind."

Although on the drive across town, she was tempted to several times. But the need to be with him overrode everything else. She followed Luke into the underground parking and into the parking place he indicated. Taking a deep breath, she got out of her car and let him lead her to the elevator.

Chapter 20

"Nothing for me, thanks." She shook her head when he offered her a drink. She'd had wine with dinner and her senses were already on high alert, her brain a little fuzzy, except for registering the man standing in front of her in his big bedroom. They faced each other, inches apart, the heat crackling between them filling the room.

Luke took a step closer, placed his palms on her cheeks, and proceeded to seduce her with his mouth. His lips whispered back and forth against hers. It was nothing more than the merest touch of mouth on mouth, but it cloaked her in the voluptuous feeling of black velvet. She wrapped her fingers around his wrists, not to push him away but to hold him in place. Every nerve in her body seemed centered on her lips, the throbbing in her cunt a metronomic beat in time with the movement of his mouth.

She was so wet she could feel moisture on the inside of her thighs. What was it about Luke Buchanan where just a touch carried her to a plane of sexual arousal demanding more? Much more. Breathing in through her nose, she inhaled the wonderful scent of him, the scent that was pure Luke.

Almost tentatively, he traced the seam of her lips with his tongue, a back and forth motion demanding she part for him. When she did, the sweep of that tongue was light and graceful, no longer demanding but seductive. It flicked and danced, tasting first here, then there, leaving tiny bonfires every place it touched. Automatically, she tried to suck him deeper into her mouth, but he was too quick for her, following his own choreographed path. When she met his tongue with her own he nipped at it lightly with his teeth, and the throbbing in her pussy, the ache in her breasts, grew even more intense.

She wanted to cry out in protest when he lifted his mouth from hers, but in a moment she felt him working his hot lips in slow motion along her jawline and beneath her ear. He paused to bite gently on the soft lobe, sending shivers skating over her skin. Julia moaned, a tiny little sound vibrating at the back of her throat and increasing when he trailed his mouth down her neck. He slid one hand back to the collar of her sweater, giving himself access to the erogenous zone where her neck and shoulder joined. She tightened her fingers on his wrists, balancing herself as the floor seemed to fade away beneath her feet, leaving her floating in space.

Luke spent long moments paying homage to her neck, moving his mouth to the hollow of her throat where her pulse pounded erratically. Then at last—at last!—he shifted his hands to tug at the bottom of the sweater and broke contact with her long enough to pull it over her head and toss it to the side.

Now she flew into a frenzy for intimate contact. Her fingers trembled as she fumbled with the buttons on his shirt, finally pulling it open, buttons flying to the floor. She pushed it down his arms and he obligingly shrugged the rest of the way out of it. Frantic with the need to touch him without the barrier of clothing, she ran her hands over his thick pelt of soft hair. A sound of raw need rumbled up from his throat when she raked her fingernails over his flat nipples.

He trailed kisses from her throat down between the valley of her breasts and tweaked her nipples through the flimsy silk of her bra. His tongue was a sensual weapon he drew lazily across the upper swell of her breasts before moving his head to pull one distended nipple into his mouth, fabric and all. Julia sucked in her breath, squeezing her thighs together in an effort to contain her growing need, but it surged through her with the speed and force of a lightning bolt.

Somehow, her bra disappeared and she was skin to skin with Luke, her sensitized breasts pressed against the wall of his chest, the fine mat of hair abrading her nipples like tiny branding irons. She was hot all over, her skin too tight, her body soft and pliant and somehow not even her own any more. And still Luke continued his slow, seductive torment, tasting here, nibbling there.

"Oh, please," she breathed, a small sound of satisfaction bubbling from her as his fingers moved over the button and zipper of her slacks.

Moving the material out of the way, he slid a hand inside her panties and cupped one cheek of her ass with his long, hot fingers. Her blood raced at the contact, muscles quivered and the scent of her musk drifted up to her nostrils. When he glided his warm palms over the surface of her cheeks, more nerves sparked and sizzled, fed by the continued assault of his mouth on her breasts. That talented, clever, seductive mouth was everywhere, sliding over every surface of her skin, while he continued to stroke her buttocks. When he slipped his fingers into the hot cleft between the cheeks she gasped, a jab of lust spearing her. She remembered the erotic burn of his cock inside her there and wanted it—*craved it*—again. She surged into his touch and felt the curve of his smile against her skin.

She trembled, wanting him everywhere in and out of her body, yet still he took his time, touching, caressing, licking, nipping, until she was half out of her mind. Her hunger for him was so strong it threatened to engulf her. She pressed herself against his body, smiling at the thick feel of his hard cock, evidence of his arousal. She slipped one hand between them and closed her fingers around his shaft, fabric and all. His strangled moan was her reward.

Lifting his head, he brushed his mouth over hers again. Against her lips, he whispered, "I'm going to fuck you, Julia. In more ways than you can imagine. And when I'm through, the last thing you'll think about is walking away from me."

He broke their contact long enough to rid them of the rest of their clothes and rip the covers back on the bed. Then she was lying on the cool crisp sheets, her legs over his shoulders, him lapping with unabashed desire at her slit. He licked her labia with deliberate strokes and probed at the entrance of her pussy. With strong yet gentle fingers, he opened her outer lips to his invasion, and ate her like a starving man. The flick of his tongue was like an electric torch wherever he touched her, blazing through her bloodstream. Julia fisted her hands in the sheet, anchoring herself as he worked her, touching every inch of her slick tunnel. Soft ragged sounds of pleasure drifted on the air and she realized they were hers, signs of the ragged edge on which her body was perched.

When he found her clit with his thumb and rubbed it gently, she was done. The orgasm ripped through her like a cyclone, shaking her until she thought her bones would disintegrate. He stroked and sucked, keeping her in an erotic whirlpool, body convulsing, until the spasms weakened into aftershocks. But instead of taking her down gently, waiting until the throbbing faded, he rose to his knees, positioned his cock against her still throbbing flesh, and entered her with one stunning thrust of his hips. In an instant, she felt desire growing again. The hot spiral of need burned low in her belly, unwinding and rippling through her.

His movements were steady but hard, each forward thrust bumping the head of his cock against the mouth of her womb. She scrabbled to hold him with her hands, raking her nails across his back. He pounded her with a steady rhythm and strength a younger man would have been proud of. He rode her, pushed her, until the next climax grabbed her like a fist and she quaked with the incredible power of it. The walls of her pussy clenched around his hot erection, gripping it as her climax roared through her.

When she lay there sweaty and panting, head tossed back against the pillow, it suddenly occurred to her Luke held back on his own release. She could only imagine the kind of control it took. She opened her eyes and looked at him.

"You didn't—"

"No." He smiled, and reached for something on the nightstand. "But I'm going to now. Tonight I'm prepared."

He flipped her over to her stomach and pulled her to her knees, bracing her with pillows beneath her stomach. He touched his lips lightly to each curve of her ass. Her body hummed in response but she tensed slightly when she felt something cool and smooth at her rear entrance.

"Gel," he whispered. "So I don't hurt you. Relax and let me get you ready."

Using one lean finger, he rubbed the lube into the tissues around that opening before easing inside. The coolness of the gel radiated out to her inner tissues. She closed her eyes and leaned into the pillows as he added a second finger to the first, more lube, more stroking. Despite the coolness of the gel, the sensation spreading through her body was fiery hot. Her body wanted him, softened for him, eagerly accepted the fingers as he worked the lube into her hot channel.

In a voice ragged with his own hunger and need, he whispered, "Breathe, Julia. Breathe deep."

She didn't need him to tell her. She still remembered the feel of him there. She arched her back to thrust her buttocks out at him, pulled in a breath, and readied herself for his penetration. When it came, the familiar mixture of ice and heat fractured through her. Her blood drummed in her ears and her heartbeat sped up. Luke gripped the soft skin of her ass and he began the ride.

In and out. Deeper, deeper. Harder, harder. And incredibly her body responded again. She matched his tempo, rocking with him, until she felt him spurting inside her and one more orgasm overtook her. She hadn't thought her body could stand another onslaught, but Luke managed to drag it out of her, this one more powerful than the others. Nothing existed except the two of them and this incredible connection, the erotic sensations racing through her, the climax that shook her with the force of an earthquake.

"I'm dead," she murmured, when he finally let her collapse, the sounds of ragged breathing punctuating the air.

"No, just satisfied." She heard the smile in his voice as he eased himself from her body. Rolling to the side, he skimmed a kiss over her face. "Come on. Shower."

"Nooo," she whined, so limp she wondered if she'd ever be able to move again. "I promise you I can't get up. Go 'way."

He laughed, the throaty delicious sound she loved. "I'll help. I want to make sure to clean you up and ease those sore muscles. You'll sleep better, I promise."

"I'll sleep in the shower," she protested.

But he dragged her unwilling body from the bed into the huge shower, adjusted the spray so it was almost a fine mist, and bathed her like a baby, kissing her now and then.

Finally he crawled into bed with her, pulled her up against him, and she fell asleep, hoping tomorrow wouldn't come crashing down on her head.

* * * *

"We're going out to brunch," Luke announced when he brought her coffee in bed. "I'd cook, but you wore me out."

"Oh?" She sipped at the hot liquid. "Exactly who did the wearing out?"

"No matter. We're still going out to eat before you disappear for the day."

Julia set the coffee mug on the nightstand. It was time to talk. For a moment, she thought she should do it here. But then, if he got angry, at least in public he'd have to use some sort of control, enough for her to make a quick exit. "All right."

"Wow." He grinned. "I was all prepared for an argument. " He leaned down and gave her one of those feathery kisses on her cheek. "We have a lot to talk about and I always plead my case best on a full stomach.

"All right." She blew out a breath. "But let's take both cars so I can leave from the restaurant." Make a quick escape if she needed to.

"I'd argue with you but I'm sure I'd lose, so okay. Let's do it. I found a place that serves the best all-day restaurant breakfast I've eaten in ages."

He took her to Paul's Pancakes, another place Claire had raved about. And she discovered she was extremely hungry. She took a deep breath, let it out slowly, and got out of the car.

Luke linked his fingers through hers. "I meant it about needing to talk, Julia. Whatever problems you think you've got, whatever happened all those years ago, we'll face it all together. I'm not an unreasonable man. Or a weak one. I can face anything with you."

"You may be asking for more than you know," she warned.

He opened the restaurant door for her. "I can handle it."

"We'll see."

He held her hand until they were seated in a booth against the window wall, releasing it only with obvious reluctance. "I'm afraid if I let you go, you might disappear."

Julia picked up the coffee the waitress brought to give herself something to do with her hands. "When we have our 'talk,' you might wish you had."

"Does this mean you're finally going to lay everything out on the table? Tell me what's so terrible it's kept us apart?"

She placed the cup slowly back in the saucer, careful not to slosh any of the hot liquid, and tried to decide where to begin. But then two people walked into the restaurant and she froze. Beth and Courtney were laughing at something, giggling as if they were both thirteen. Julia felt the blood drain from her face. Of all the places Beth could have taken her sister, why did it have to be here? The very thing she'd fought so hard to prevent, the knowledge she'd sacrificed her life to keep hidden, was going to come out and in a way she couldn't control.

"Julia?" She heard the concern in Luke's voice. "What's wrong? You look like you're about to pass out."

"Oh, God." She bent her head low over her coffee cup, hoping her daughters would take a booth at the far side of the restaurant.

"What?" He reached across the table and closed his fingers around her wrist. "What's going on here?"

"I-I…"

But she never got the chance to get any more words out.

"Mom?" Beth was suddenly beside them, astonishment plain on her face. "Mom, what are you doing here?"

"Why are you here with a man?" Courtney's tone was harsh and defensive. "On a Saturday? Who is he?"

Julia finally found her voice. "Beth, Courtney. I'd like you to meet…a friend of mine. Luke Buchanan."

She twisted her hands together in her lap to keep them from trembling and looked across the table at Luke. He stared at Courtney with an expression of half shock and half anger, his face taut, a muscle twitching in his jaw.

"Um, Luke? These are my daughters, Beth and Courtney." Oh God, everything was going to hell in a handbasket.

The girls and Luke just continued staring at each other, no one saying a word.

"Hello." Beth's voice held the strangest sound.

Courtney said nothing.

"Mr. Buchanan is with Connell Wilson." Julia tried to make her voice as bright as possible. "A new client. We were just discussing the new campaign Bright Ideas is rolling out for them."

Luke couldn't seem to drag his eyes away from Courtney. "Hello, girls. Nice to meet you."

An uncomfortable silence draped itself over them.

"Well, we're just going to have some breakfast," Beth interjected as the silence dragged on. "I've been raving about the peach pancakes."

Courtney turned away. "Let's eat. I'm hungry."

"Mom?" Beth turned back to her. "Are you going home from here? I'll see you there."

"Yes. Fine, honey. Enjoy your meal."

Luke's gaze followed them as they walked away and slid into a corner booth. When he turned to Julia, the look in his eyes made her want to crawl under the table.

"Exactly how old is Courtney?"

Julia wet her lips with her tongue and wished she could transport herself to another planet.

"Julia?" Luke's voice was insistent. "Did you hear me? How old is your daughter?"

"Th-Thirteen."

"Interesting. Were you ever planning to tell me, or were you just going to shut me out of her life forever?"

"How did—"

"There's no way you could know this, but she looks exactly like my mother did at that age." The rage in his voice was barely controlled, but underneath it was a lot of pain.

Nausea rose up in her throat. "I'm so sorry," she whispered, unable to look at him anymore.

"Sorry doesn't begin to cut it." He shoved away his coffee cup. "Look, I don't intend to make a scene in public so we're going to get up and walk out of here quietly. Wave to your daughters. Then we're going back to my place, where you're going to give me some answers."

But all her good intentions, her carefully crafted courage fled in the face of his all-consuming anger. "I can't." She could barely speak. "Not now. Not now."

She grabbed her purse and pushed herself out of the booth. Luke dropped some bills on the table and followed her but she managed to stay ahead of him. By the time he ran out of the restaurant, she was already pulling out of the parking lot, praying he didn't follow her back to the house.

* * * *

"Who is he?" Courtney demanded.

She and Beth walked in the door loaded for bear, each in her own way, Courtney ferocious and angry, Beth confused and uncertain.

"He's a…client," Julia said, waiting for the tea to brew. Soothing tea, her answer to everything.

"Baloney. You're lying to me. Something else is going on. You were so nervous I thought you were going to throw up." Courtney's smile was anything but pleasant. "You sounded like me when I'm trying to get away with something.

"Courtney's right." Beth frowned. "We've never seen you with a man all these years. Besides, I don't ever remember you having breakfast on a Saturday with a client. Not once. And he didn't look at you like he was a client. So what gives? And why is he such a big secret?"

Julia stirred sweetener into her tea with an unsteady motion, carried it to the kitchen table, and placed it carefully in front of her as she sat down. How to do this? Where to start? Well, Claire had warned her and she'd waited too long to listen.

"Courtney, I'd like to talk to Beth alone for a few minutes, if you don't mind?"

What Julia called her daughter's black look descended on her face. "What's so weird you can't tell *me*? Some dark, terrible secret only Beth is old enough to know?" She folded her arms defiantly across her chest and refused to move.

Beth looked at her mother, then back at Courtney. "Go on upstairs, kiddo. I promise whatever it is, either I'll tell you or Mom will. Go on."

"No." Courtney glowered. The only word for it. "I'm not moving. I have as much right as you to get some answers."

Beth wrapped an arm around her sister's stiff body. "You absolutely do. But can you just give Mom and me a few minutes? You have my word I'll make sure you know everything."

"So why can't I know it now?" Courtney whined. "I'm not a baby anymore."

"No, you're not. And because you are turning into a mature young lady, a sister I'm proud of, you're going to do this one thing for me. Right?"

Finally, Courtney uncrossed her arms. "Fine. Fine, fine, fine." She stomped out of the room.

Julia flinched.

Beth sat down in the chair next to her. "Okay, truth or consequences, Mom. I'm over twenty-one, on my own, and whether you want to hear it or not, I've had sex already."

Julia looked at her with a pained expression. "I can't say I'm surprised but you didn't actually have to tell me."

Beth put her hand on her mother's arm. "I'm telling you only because it gave me the experience to know immediately the atmosphere between you and Luke Buchanan was definitely not of a business nature. I don't want any details, and to tell you the truth, I'm glad to find out my mother might be finally coming out of the deep freeze." She smiled. "You've kept yourself in a very unhealthy place since Dad passed away. It's time to move forward."

"Would that be so bad if I did?" Julia asked anxiously. "Does it bother you?"

"No." Beth shook her head. "What bothers me first is you think you have to hide it for some unknown reason."

Julia started to answer her but Beth held up a hand.

"Not finished here. I'm going to stick my neck out and guess the reason you're scrunched up in a ball is the fact my sister bears a striking resemblance to the man you were with. Am I right?"

Julia felt a pressure on her chest so great she thought her heart would stop beating. She lifted her cup with shaking hands, nearly spilling the tea, and took a sip, trying to give herself time to organize her thoughts. She opened her mouth to answer Beth but nothing would come out. Everything she wanted to say stuck in her throat, and even her favorite tea couldn't loosen the log jam.

"Mom? Please answer me. You're scaring me."

Julia looked at her daughter, concern in her eyes and a hint of panic. Her inner voice was shouting to her to get on with it. That it was way past time. She took another sip of the tea and dredged up some measure of calm.

"I have a story to tell you, Bethie. It's complex and there are parts of it you aren't going to like at all. I just want you to remember no matter what I say and no matter what happened, your father loved you very much. And I have always loved you. Each of you. My children have always come first with me."

"I know, Mom. You're a great mother." Beth leaned forward. "And nothing's ever going to change how much we love you, okay? So whatever it is, just…say it. Unless you murdered someone, I don't think there's anything we can't get through." Her lips curved in a weak smile. "And depending on who it is, maybe we could even handle murder."

"Hold on to that thought, will you? Let me fix myself another cup of tea first, and then I'll tell you everything. And you have to promise not to say anything until I'm finished. After that I'll answer whatever questions you ask."

It took her two more cups of tea and a glass of wine to get the entire story out, the pain as she dredged it up consuming her. She spared herself nothing, doing her best to paint herself as the villain in the breakup of her marriage, to leave her children a good memory of their father.

Beth sat quietly, getting up only once to fix a cup of coffee from the new Keurig machine, and then to pour some wine for herself. When Julia was finished, an eerie quiet spread through the kitchen, almost as if someone had died.

"I know I can't expect you to understand," Julia began, but Beth interrupted her.

"Now there's where you're wrong." She got up from her chair and went to stand at the sink, looking out the window to the view in the huge back yard. "Andy and I were just little kids when Daddy passed away, but even little kids know when their father can't connect with them, when he thinks they're a nuisance. When he…doesn't know how to love. We've talked about it a lot over the years and wanted to ask you if there was something we'd done wrong, but you seemed intent on putting him on a pedestal and we were afraid to say anything."

"Oh, sweetheart, no." Julia went to stand by her daughter. "You and your brother were—and are—terrific kids. The best. I just wanted you to have memories to cherish."

Beth made a sound half snort and half cry. "You have no idea what our memories of him are. We always hoped after he died you'd meet someone who could really love all of us."

"Beth…"

"I'm not through. We have friends whose parents got divorced, or in a couple of cases one parent died. They always seemed to move on, have full, rich lives. Meet other people. Find good relationships. We never knew why you chose not to do this." She turned to face Julia. "If you and Daddy were practically divorced when you met Mr. Buchanan, why did you walk away from him? And if you felt you owed it to Daddy to nurse him those last few months, why didn't you call him after…after the funeral?"

Pain lanced through Julia. Why, indeed.

"There were…reasons," was the only thing she could find to say.

Beth shook her head. "Not good enough. If there were reasons, tell me about them. Tell *us*. Didn't you think Courtney deserved to know who her real father was? Maybe to have him as an influence in her life when she was growing up?"

"Yes, didn't you?"

The words were almost a shout. Julia and Beth turned to see Courtney standing at the entrance to the kitchen, the expression on her face an emotional cocktail of so much pain, Julia rushed to her to put her arms around her.

"You heard?"

"Of course I heard. I sat on the stairs listening. How else am I supposed to find out anything?" She pushed her mother away. "Don't. Don't touch me. How could you? How could you never tell me there was a father somewhere who might have loved me? Wanted to be with me? Just… wanted me?"

"Courtney. Honey." Julia tried to reach for her again but the girl stepped away.

"Stay away from me. My whole life has been a lie. I thought my grandparents—no, *Charles's* parents—hated me because of something I'd done. But it wasn't me. It was you. They hated *you*, and punished me because of it."

Beth rushed to her sister, grabbed one of her hands. "Trust me, Court. You would never have wanted to suffer through those damned visits the way Andy and I did. It was worse than the tortures of the damned." She brushed a stray hair form her face. "Thank God we finally reached a point where we all agreed it could stop."

"But I had no one," Courtney cried. "No one at all."

"Ssh, ssh." Beth tried to hug her. "There's always been Andy and me. And Mom. Look at her, kiddo. See how much she's hurting? She loves you more than you can imagine."

"No." Courtney wrenched herself away. "She only loves herself. And her secrets. So many secrets." She ran from the room. In a moment, they heard the slam of her bedroom door.

Julia looked at Beth. "Well, that went well. Not." She felt as if she were crumbling into a million pieces.

"Are you going to tell me the last of the deep dark secrets? The reason for all of this?"

"If you promise not to hate me." God, she sounded sop pitiful.

Beth hugged her. "We could never hate you, don't you know that?" She took her mother's hand. "Now give."

It took every ounce of courage Julia could dredge up to spit out the shameful story. If Beth had ever had any love for her father, Julia was sure this would kill it completely as the litany of events unfolded. Julia stared down at her lap while she spelled out the terms Charles had imposed, afraid to look at her child, afraid of what she'd see in her face.

"Is that all of it?" Beth asked when she finished.

"Yes. Every bit. My only excuse is that I was trying to protect everyone. I was in a very vulnerable place and didn't have the strength to fight. I've had a lot of years to regret it."

"Okay."

Julia finally looked up at her daughter and was stunned at the fury in her eyes. "Please don't hate me. Bethie. I—"

"Hate you? Oh, God." She reached out to give her mother a hug. "How could I hate you? If I hate anyone it's that bastard you married—I refuse to call him our father—and that smug son of a bitch Rod McGuire. How could they do that to you? To us? To Courtney?"

"Those letters—"

"Are nothing more than pieces of paper. Don't you think we know how much you love us? Besides, you aren't the first person caught in a situation like this and won't be the last. I'm just sorry you had to waste so many years with Mr. Buchanan." She made a rude noise. "I guarantee you he'd have been a lot nicer to us than our so-called father."

"I'm so sorry." Julia fought back tears. "If it's any consolation, I had already made up my mind to tell him. This morning at breakfast. And then to talk to all of you, but Courtney first. I want you to believe that."

"Mom. Oh, Mom." Beth tugged her from her chair and pulled her into a hug. "Of course I do. I told you. We love you. And together we'll figure a way to sort this all out."

"Luke probably hates me now," she whispered. "I deserve it."

"I promise you he doesn't. He might be upset. Even a little angry. But hate you? Not from the way he looked at you."

"But I'm going to make this right," Julia promised, her voice stronger. "For everyone. Somehow. In fact—"

The ringing of the phone interrupted her. And it continued to ring.

"Are you going to answer it?" Beth asked when Julia didn't move.

The ringing stopped at last, only to start up again a moment later.

"I'll get it." Julia reached for the phone.

"No, let me." Beth picked up the receiver. "Hello? Yes, she's right here. Oh, and it was nice meeting you this morning. I hope we get to see you again." She covered the mouthpiece with her hand. "He doesn't sound like he's going to shoot you." She smiled and handed the phone to her mother.

Julia swallowed twice before she was sure she could say a word. "Luke?"

"I think we need to sit down and have a talk." There was pain in his deep voice.

Her heart pinched at the knowledge she'd caused it. "Luke, I…"

Beth was standing next to her, mouthing "Go and see him."

"No more running away, Julia," Luke said in her ear.

Claire had told her that and apparently she was right.

Julia swallowed again. "All right. But I need time to talk with Courtney before I do anything else."

Silence. Then, "Fine. I agree that's important. Very important. I'll pick you up at six for dinner. At your house," he emphasized. "No more excuses."

"Yes. Six o'clock." But her hand shook when she hung up the telephone.

"He's coming here?"

Julia nodded. "But I have to talk to your sister right now. Can you stay here for a while?"

"Of course. No problem." She enfolded Julia in a warm hug. "Mom, I understand a lot more than you think. And so will Andy. Who, by the way, should also be included in this."

Julia raked her fingers through her hair. "I know, I know. And I should be the one to tell him, but…"

"I can do it. No sweat. I'll call him and you can go up and talk to Courtney." She kissed Julia's cheek. "I take it you and the sexy Mr. Buchanan are having dinner tonight?"

"Beth! He's…"

"Very sexy." Beth grinned. "I can see why any woman would fall for him like crazy." She pulled her mother into another embrace.

Julia melted into her warmth. "What did I ever do to deserve kids like you?"

"You were a damned good mom. Now it's time to do something for yourself, too. I'll see if Andy can shake loose of whatever he's doing and we'll hang with Courtney tonight."

"I'll be here, too." Miranda came into the kitchen from the utility room where she'd obviously gone to make herself scarce and gave Julia another hug. "Things will work out. You'll see. It's time for this to come out, anyway."

Beth looked at her. "You knew? About Courtney?"

"Honey, I live in this house, remember? I know exactly when your father moved out and when he moved back in."

"Then—"

"It wasn't my secret to tell." She nudged Julia. "Go on. Go upstairs to her. She's probably a mess, but we'll work through it together."

Chapter 21

"So, is he living here now?" Courtney asked. "In San Antonio?"

Julia nodded. The past few hours were among the most painful she could remember in a long time. Nothing she said seemed to reach the troubled teenager. Courtney swung back and forth between anger and tears. It wasn't an easy time for either of them, but now, both emotionally exhausted, they'd achieved a measure of calm. Julia just hoped it wasn't the eye of the hurricane.

"Yes. He has a great job here."

"Where does he live?" Courtney demanded. "Can I go there? Does he want to see me?"

Julia named the all-suites hotel where Luke was staying for the time being. "But he'll be looking for something more permanent. And yes, I'm sure he wants to see you."

"Are the two of you going to get married?" Courtney wasn't pulling any punches now.

Were they? Good question. She hoped he still wanted her after the incredible mess she'd made of everything.

"I think we're going to take this one step at a time, honey. I've told you things I have yet to explain to him."

"What if he doesn't like me?" She scowled. "What if I don't like him?"

"Let's not get ahead of ourselves." Julia sat on Courtney's bed and she tried to reach for her daughter, but the girl scrabbled away from her. Julia bit back whatever words bubbled up. Such a long way to go yet. "I'm going to have dinner with him tonight. And then we'll arrange for the two of you to get together. But, honey, I know he'll love you. Why wouldn't he?"

"Maybe I'm unlovable," Courtney mumbled.

"Oh, Court."

"Why can't I have dinner with you tonight? Why can't I come, too?"

"Because he and I have things to discuss. This has been a shock to him, too."

"At least now I know why I didn't get to go to those awful dinners with Andy and Beth." She frowned. "Mom, if your—if Charles made your life so miserable, made it impossible for you to tell my father about me, why did you marry him in the first place?"

Why, indeed?

"I'll tell you the same thing I told Beth. My only excuse is I was young, naïve, and vulnerable and anxious to get away from my own dysfunctional family situation. I thought he was the answer."

Silence.

Julia waited.

"So you're not ashamed of me?" Courtney's voice sound so young and defenseless. "How come you never told him about me?" Courtney asked the same question for what was probably the twentieth time.

"Oh, Courtney, no. Such a thing is so far from the truth. I love you. You were the only piece of him I had to hang on to all of these years."

Again Julia tried to hug her, but Courtney wrenched away from her. Julia rubbed her forehead, trying to beat back the rapidly building headache, and looked at her watch. "I'd like to take a shower before Luke picks me up. Will you come downstairs to say hello to him when he gets here?"

"I'll see."

Julia rose from the bed, heartsick and aching. "I'll let you know when he gets here."

But Courtney had already withdrawn into herself.

Half an hour later, Julia walked back downstairs and into the kitchen. She found Andy, who'd apparently arrived during the time she was in the shower, drinking coffee with Beth. She looked at them, twins yet such opposites. The six foot two young man, muscular with sandy hair, was blessed with the kind of almost-rugged good looks women seemed to fall over themselves for these days, Charles's good looks, but with a lot more warmth. Beside him, his sister was such a contrast, petite like Julia, with hazel eyes and dark hair, and a curvy body even sloppy jeans and a sweatshirt couldn't disguise.

What beautiful children she'd been blessed with.

"Why aren't you hanging out with some woman?" she joked.

"I am. My two sisters." He grinned. "They don't get any better than that."

"You know what I mean. What did Beth pull you away from?"

"Nothing." He kissed her cheek. "Besides, there's nothing more important than being here right now." He looked upward. "How's the kiddo doing?"

Julia leaned against him. "Not so good, I'm afraid. I think we have a lot of stormy days ahead of us."

"We'll get through it," he assured her. "Together. Beth told me everything she said to you, and it goes for me, too." He set his mug down. "And also about Dad. Look." He shoved his hands in his pockets. "We've never talked about it and maybe we should have. But Beth and I knew what Dad was like, even as young as we were. He never played with us, never enjoyed us, and never wanted to take us anywhere. If it was bad for us, it must have been hell for you. Deciding on the divorce couldn't have been easy. And bringing Dad back here for those last months was no cakewalk either, I'm sure."

"We're sorry you felt you had to walk away from Luke," Beth broke in. "Mr. Buchanan. We're done with questions and answers for the moment, and Luke will be here any minute. I'm sure you've got a tough evening ahead of you. But there are still things we'll want to know. We want answers, Mom. And we deserve to have them. Courtney, too."

"Yes, you do. You'll get them. And thank you for not ripping my head off, which you have every right to do."

They squeezed her between them in a warm hug.

"We're spending the night," Beth told her, "so we'll be here with Courtney and available to talk when you get home, if you want."

"Thank you." She gave each one of them a quick kiss and hurried upstairs to get her purse and finish her makeup, her stomach in knots and every muscle in her body tighter than a high wire.

But she'd barely reached her bedroom before the phone rang. Her first thought was Luke had changed his mind. Decided he didn't want anything to do with any of them anymore.

She picked up the receiver almost reluctantly. "Hello?"

"That's him, isn't it, you slut?"

The rage in Rod Maguire's voice was so violent, she almost dropped the phone.

"Rod?"

"I know it's him. The father of your bastard. The man you betrayed Charles with." He bit off each word.

Julia took a deep breath, doing her best to steady herself. "I think who I see is no longer your business." Why couldn't he just go away and leave her alone?

"On the contrary. You betrayed Charles, one of the best men I've ever known, in the worst way possible. How he even wanted to be in the same house with you after what you did is beyond me. But he left me specific instructions, Julia. Very specific. And as his executor, I feel duty-bound to carry them out."

She rubbed her forehead. "I think I said everything to you I had to say the last time I saw you. Nothing's changed. Just leave us alone."

"I'll ruin him." The words were virulent. "I'll find his name and I'll destroy him. And you and your bastard brat along with him. Be warned."

The call disconnected with a slam on the other end. Julia replaced the phone with a hand that shook so badly it took her two tries. But she meant what she'd said. Tonight she would lay it all out for Luke and pray Claire and the twins were right. That he'd give her the strength to handle this together. She was through being a coward, through being afraid of a man who was a bully, through letting other people control her life. It was past time to move forward.

Luke arrived promptly at six. Julia hurried downstairs to let him in, but Beth and Andy got there first. She braced herself for an uncomfortable few moments, but obviously she underestimated her older children. Andy pulled the door open to give Luke room to enter and held out his hand.

"Andrew Patterson. Andy. I'm really glad to meet you."

They shook hands and Andy drew Beth forward.

"I'm Elizabeth," she said. "Beth." She studied Luke's face. "Please take good care of our mother. She's been through a lot."

Luke appeared startled. Julia knew this wasn't exactly the kind of reception he'd been prepared for. Nor had she. Again, Claire was right. She should have had faith in her children and Luke from the beginning. Tried harder all this time to find him. Instead she'd wasted a lot of years.

"Julia?"

She was suddenly aware of everyone staring at her. Waiting for her to do or say something. "I'll be right back. Stay right here."

She ran up the stairs, knocked on Courtney's door, and pushed it open. "He's here, honey. Will you come downstairs?"

Courtney was bunched up on her bed, hugging a stuffed animal. "No. I can't see him right now."

"Courtney." Julia reached out a hand. Drew it back. "He'd really like to see you."

"I'll think about it."

Julia waited a moment then decided not to push it. She closed the door and ran down the stairs, forcing a smile. "I'm ready," she told Luke. Then she kissed each of the twins. "Thanks for everything."

"No sweat," Andy told her.

Luke looked up the stairs. "Where's Courtney?"

"In her room." Julia wondered if she'd have to explain the agony of the afternoon to him right now. "I let her know you were here but—" She held out her hands in a gesture of helplessness.

Finally, Luke shifted his gaze back to her. "All right, then. I guess we're ready to go."

"You raised some truly great kids." That was the first thing he said to her when they were in the car.

"Better than even I imagined."

And those were the last words they exchanged during the tense ride to the restaurant.

* * * *

Luke gave his drink order to the waiter while Julia asked for hot tea. She didn't need alcohol to dull wits already pretty scrambled.

"I have a lot of questions for you," he began.

"I'm sure you have. And I'll give you the best answers I can. I promise."

His eyes narrowed. "No sidestepping," he warned. "All the cards on the table."

"Yes. I owe you that."

"Why don't we eat first? You look about the way I feel. Some nourishment might do you some good."

But she barely ate any of her meal. She simply couldn't swallow anything but the tea, which the waiter kept refilling.

He'd managed to find an out of the way place to take her, and she was so grateful he was sensitive to the need for them not to be disturbed. Julia didn't think she'd see anyone she knew, but you never could tell. She was always expecting Rod to pop up like some jack-in-the-box.

"Julia." Luke put his coffee cup down and looked across the table at her. "I think it's time to talk."

"Yes." She closed her eyes and prayed for strength and guidance to get through this. To make him see things from her point of view. For him to forgive her. He might not want either her or Courtney in his life now, but she couldn't stand it if he hated either one of them.

She started with the reason for her divorce and the rest just came tumbling out. She was totally honest with him. Well, almost. She gave him every detail of Charles's illness, unloaded her guilty feelings about his heart attack, and even confessed to looking for Luke more than once.

"I understand the pressure you were under, believe me." He paused. "But I think we still have a lot of unanswered questions on the table here. We haven't gotten to the reason you couldn't let me know what was going on." His voice was calm and even, but there was strain and even anger behind it. "I know Claire told you how many times I called, but you couldn't take a minute to contact me at all? Not once?"

"No." Her voice was so low she almost didn't hear it herself. "I didn't."

"I have a daughter I didn't know about and I've missed thirteen years of her life. You tell me she's going through a rough patch, not unusual for teenagers, but maybe I could have helped." He signaled the waiter and ordered another drink before continuing. "So let's agree you were behind the eight ball during the time Charles was dying at the home you so graciously accepted him back into. But what about after the funeral? What then, Julia?"

"I didn't want you hurt." She whispered the words.

"Hurt?" He picked up the drink the waiter placed in front of him, took a healthy swallow, and reached across the table for her hand. It was the first intimate contact he'd made with her since picking her up. "How on earth could I be more hurt than to be shut completely out of your life after what was building between us?"

And then, like a bad dream, a shadow fell over the table and she looked up to see Rod Maguire standing there. Her first thought was she should stop going to restaurants. Her second was a reminder she was no longer the scared woman she'd been all those years ago.

"Hello, Julia." His voice was like steel. "How about introducing me to your…companion?"

Somewhere deep inside she found the remnants of courage and pulled herself together.

"Hello, Rod." She congratulated herself on her composure. "This doesn't seem like your usual place to hang out."

"The owners are new clients. Sharon and I are having dinner with them." He looked pointedly at Luke. "And you are?"

"Luke Buchanan. And you?"

"This is Rod Maguire." Julia folded her hands in front of her so neither man could see how they trembled. "He was a friend of Charles's and one of his law partners."

"Yes." It was difficult for anyone to miss the distaste in his voice. "Charles Patterson and I were childhood friends. He was a great man and an excellent attorney."

"I'm sure he was." Luke's tone was mild. "How fortunate for him, then, to find a woman of such quality as Julia for his wife."

"Fortunate. Really. An interesting word. Well. I'm sure we'll be seeing each other again." He looked at Julia. "Right, Julia?"

"Nice of you to stop by, Rod." She was through letting him frighten her. Each time she faced him down only made her stronger. "Don't let us keep you from your clients."

He gave her one last scathing look before walking away.

Julia slumped in her seat, taking deep breaths to steady her pulse. A waiter placed a glass in front of her.

"Drink it." Luke's voice penetrated the fog. "Come on, Julia. You're white as a sheet and look like you're about to faint."

When she made no move to do anything, Luke reached across the table and placed her fingers around the glass.

"Drink it, honey. Then we'll talk."

Honey. She hadn't thought he'd ever speak to her in such a caring tone again. It gave her enough strength to lift her drink and take a swallow. The amaretto burned its way down her throat and into her bloodstream, and shook her out of the well of defeat she'd fallen into.

"Good." Luke tipped the glass toward her. "A little more. Then we're getting out of here. I'm guessing the asshole we just saw has something to do with this and I want to leave before I'm tempted to kill him."

Somehow she managed to sit there as he paid the check, then let him help her out of the chair and lead her from the restaurant. When they got into his car, her reserve snapped and the tears she'd been holding back for fourteen years came flooding out.

"I'm glad I have a car with a bench seat," Luke told her, pulling her close to him and cradling her against his chest.

She cried until she was sure her tears were gone and then she cried some more. A storm of such violence, when it subsided she was left with no strength.

Luke tightened his arms around her. "I'd prefer not to do this in a car, but I think if you don't get it out now you'll strangle on it. So let's have it. And don't leave anything out."

"You're right. It's time."

He tipped her face up so she was forced to look in his eyes. "There's no place to hide any more. Whatever it is, I want to hear it all. Okay? Please?"

She searched for a place to start, but once she began it seemed she couldn't stop, like a storm unleashed. Charles's explicit terms, her promise to agree to them to protect her children, the letters still in Rod Maguire's safe. Maguire himself, who'd always hated her and took great pleasure in controlling her life. Her pitiable miserable existence. And the guilt she'd lived with year after unending year.

Luke stroked her face and she was so pathetically gratefully for just the little bit of tenderness, she almost began crying again. He heaved a great sigh and brushed a kiss against her forehead.

"Julia. My God."

"I'm so sorry, Luke. Everything is my fault. And now the children know anyway. Oh, hell." She burrowed against his chest, trying to hide from whatever she might see in his eyes.

He cupped her chin and forced her to look at him. She tried to read him, but there was so much going on in her own mind.

"Listen to me. I'm a lot of things right now. Pissed off. Murderous. Sad. Hurt. The list is endless. But mostly I'm upset you let a man bully you into sacrificing your life because you wanted to protect me. Julia, I'm a grown man who's not without resources, and Rod Maguire sounds like nothing but a penny ante tyrant. Most likely just as Charles was."

"But—"

"No buts. Okay?" His breath was a warm breeze against her chilled skin. "I won't lie to you. I dealt with a lot of emotions today, not the least of which was anger. But there's so much to sort out here. Now I'm thinking about the kind of hell you've lived in for the past fourteen years. This won't be easy but we'll sort it out, honey. I promise you."

She pressed her face against his chest. "I love you, Luke. I've never stopped. I have to make you believe what I'm telling you."

He kissed the top of her head. "I know you do. Same goes here. I guess it's the reason it hurt so much. But we'll get past it."

"I did try to find you a few times," she said in a small voice. "Now I wish I'd tried harder."

"And I could have stopped feeling sorry for myself, said to hell with it, shown up here and taken care of whatever had to be done so we could be together. So we each have regrets." He pressed a soft kiss on her lips. "Meanwhile, we have a lot of damage control to do. Have you told the kids why you've never said anything about this?"

"Yes. Today." A small hysterical laugh escaped her. "I think they were angrier than you or me, if that's possible. Especially when I told them why Rod felt so beholden to Charles. Andy called him the asshole of assholes.

"I couldn't agree more." He kissed her again. "But now we need to make some plans. Maguire will be looking to do his worst. I'm sure it pissed him off the way you stood up to him just now."

"I really don't want him to confront the kids," she whispered.

"He won't." He took one of her hands in his. "We have a lot to sort out, including what's between us. But I think this is enough for tonight. Tomorrow is Sunday. Let's have a civilized brunch. Then we can decide what we're going to say to Courtney. Together. After that, we'll make plans. Okay?"

She gave him a weak smile. "Okay."

* * * *

A light rain misted in the air when they left the restaurant, but by the time they turned onto Julia's street a capricious wind had whipped up a full-blown storm. Yet even through the rain, Julia saw Claire's car in the driveway behind Andy's and Beth's. For some reason they'd turned on every light in the house. Her stomach clenched and a sick feeling rushed through her.

"Something's wrong." She fought to keep herself together. What else could possibly happen tonight?

"Don't borrow trouble yet," he told her. "Let's see what's up first."

"But there's no reason for Claire to be here tonight. She and Brad made plans."

"Let's get inside first before we panic. It may be nothing."

Apparently, someone watched for them, because the front door opened and Andy hurried out with a big umbrella. Luke hunched his shoulders against the rain as he opened Julia's door, then squeezed her between Andy and himself as they ran into the house. Miranda, a strained look on her face, waited for them in the foyer with towels to blot themselves dry.

Julia looked around. Claire and Beth sat on the stairs. Brad leaned against the wall, his hands in his pockets. No one smiled. Julia unconsciously reached for Luke's hand, five pairs of eyes noticing the movement.

"All right. What's wrong? Is it Courtney? Where is she?"

"First of all, don't get too excited." Claire rose and came over to her, giving her a hug. "I'm sure everything's going to be fine."

"My God." Julia trembled. "Is she sick? Did you take her to the hospital? What is it?"

"Mom?" Andy was next to her now. "Don't freak, but she's gone."

"Gone?" Julia thought her heart stopped beating. She squeezed Luke's hand as hard as she could to keep herself together. "What do you mean, gone?"

"I checked on her right after you left," Beth said. "Andy and I thought we'd take her out to eat, but she wouldn't open her door. Wouldn't say anything except tell us to go away. I should have just opened it the way you do. "

Andy picked up the thread. "We waited about a half hour and then I went up. I was ready to break the door down if necessary, but it was unlocked. Her window was open and she was gone."

"B-But how? How did she get out?"

"Over the garage roof, I think," Andy told her. "It's right out her window. Then she can shimmy down the drainpipe."

"They called me," Claire added, "because they didn't want to disturb the two of you until it was necessary."

"Necessary?" Hysteria bubbled in Julia's throat. "My child disappeared and you don't think it's necessary to call me?"

"Julia." Luke reached for her but she pulled away.

Brad uncorked himself from the wall and held out his hand to Luke. "Brad Westbrook. Sorry to meet like this." He turned to Julia. "I went out looking in my car. Figured a kid her age couldn't get too far. And we're not exactly on a bus line here. Claire and the twins started calling her friends."

"Mom, she hardly sees any of them anymore." Beth's face was filled with distress. "They said she hangs out with a weird group."

"I know. We've had huge fights about it."

Luke seemed to rouse himself from whatever shock he was in. "Julia, you need to put on something warm and dry. Why don't you go change and we'll go into the family room and see where we're at. I promise you she's not far away. She's just trying to scare you. Us."

"I can't—"

He touched a finger to her lips. "Yes. You won't be any good if you get sick." He looked at Beth. "Why don't you help your mother? Andy, is there any brandy around here?"

"She likes hot tea," Miranda put in.

"Dump some brandy in it," Luke told her. He took Julia's hand again. "Go on. Put on something comfortable while we work on this."

"Luke, she's been gone a long time."

"I know, honey. But it will work out. I'm sure of it. Okay?"

She finally let Beth lead her upstairs and obediently changed into the sweats her daughter dug out of the closet for her. She was startled when Beth drew her into a fierce hug and began to cry.

"It's my fault," she sobbed. "I should have kept a closer eye on her. I knew she was upset. I should have made her open the door to me."

"Hush." Julia stroked her daughter's hair. "If it's anyone's fault, it's mine. I tried to protect everyone and just ended up making a mess of things."

"I'm so sorry, Mom. I'm just so sorry."

Julia tipped Beth's face up so she could look at it. "Stop it. You have nothing to be sorry about. I should have done something about this situation a long time ago. I was a coward and now every one of us is paying for it."

"D-Does he want to see her?" Beth asked in a small voice.

"Oh, honey, of course he does. He's furious with me because I kept her from him for so long." She released Beth and stepped back, running her fingers through her hair. "Another problem I'll have to deal with."

"Do you... Do you think you guys can work it out?"

From somewhere, Julia found a smile. "I hope so. Right now, we're taking things one at a time. And the first thing is to find Courtney."

Luke was standing in the foyer when they came back downstairs, everyone else hovering in the background.

"The security guard in my building just called me on my cell," he said. "Apparently Courtney's there asking for me."

"Oh, my God." Julia dug her fingernails into her palms to steady herself. "How did she get there? Is she okay? Wait. I'll get my coat and we can go down there right away."

"Hold it." Luke held up a hand. "I'm doing this one solo."

"But—"

"She came to see *me*. Made it her business to find a way to get there. I think I should talk to her alone first. Julia, if she sees you, she'll think I sold her out and she'll clam up."

"But I'm her mother," she protested.

"Of course you are." He gave her a steady look. "And I'm her father. It's time I stepped up to the plate in that role."

"He's right." Claire hugged Julia. "Maybe things were just supposed to happen this way. Maybe it's the stick of dynamite needed to blow it apart so you guys can put it back together."

"Come on, Mom." Andy tugged her toward the kitchen. "I've got tea and brandy for you, and Luke's cell phone number. Let him do this. Okay?"

Julia stood rooted to the floor for a long moment, filled with indecision and panic, and the sense she was losing everything. But then Luke stepped over to her and pressed a brief kiss to her lips. The five people watching didn't seem to phase him, giving her the first real flame of hope.

"I promise I'll call you. I'll let you know when I get there, and then I'll call again after she and I talk. Now go let your friends and family take care of you."

He nodded to the others then headed out into the night and the rain. She could only imagine what disaster awaited when he was alone with Courtney, the daughter he'd just found out about.

* * * *

Luke sat across the kitchen table from his daughter, marveling at how such a wondrous creature had come into his life and at the same time dreading the pain he knew was yet to come. In some ways, teenage girls weren't much different than teenage boys. They were both rebellious, angry, and uncertain. He just hoped he had the sense and strength to get a handle on things before she became a teenager in earnest.

She looked much different than the sodden mess waiting for him in the lobby with the guard when he'd arrived.

"I hope it was okay to call you, Mr. Buchanan." He looked at Courtney. "She claims she's your daughter and wanted me to let her into your place. Is she telling the truth?"

"Yes, she's my daughter."

"Well, I hadn't seen her before and I thought I ought to check with you first."

"You did the right thing. Thanks." He tucked a folded bill into the guard's hand, then nodded to Courtney. "How about we go upstairs? You look too damn wet to be comfortable."

She'd been a combination of surly and scared when he got her upstairs. He managed to convince her she needed to get out of her wet clothes and bully her into a shower. When he was sure she stood under the hot spray he called Julia to tell her Courtney was safe, explained she'd walked in the rain to the gas station a mile away and called a taxi, using her birthday money to pay for it. He'd call again soon but she was not to rush right down there. He asked her to put Claire on the phone, wanting to make sure she and Brad didn't let her out of their sight.

He obviously didn't have proper clothes for a thirteen-year-old girl, so he did the best he could: a pair of shorts, and a T-shirt, and a couple of safety pins. He'd poured hot tea into her and sat in silence, waiting for her to say whatever she'd come to tell him. He hoped he'd be able to give her the answers she was looking for.

It was his fault as much as Julia's. He could have pushed harder. Tried harder. Used Claire as an ally. Somehow bullied her into telling him the hellish situation Julia had trapped herself in. Well, so much water under the bridge now. It was what it was, and they could only move forward.

He'd fixed Courtney something to eat, but she let it sit in front of her as everything rolled out of her. The pain. Everything. Thirteen years worth of it. She'd bombarded him with questions, sulked and then shouted at him, and cried her way through half a box of tissues before finally settling down. Now she finished the last of the sandwich and drained her glass of milk. She wiped her mouth with the paper napkin, crumpled it into a ball, and dropped it on the empty plate.

"So are you gonna hang around or what?"

Her air of false bravado stabbed at him. She wanted so badly to have a father, to have a place in his life, but she'd been flailing at the wind for so long she didn't know quite how to settle down.

"That's my plan," he told her calmly. "Does it appeal to you?"

"I guess. I mean, if you'd like it too."

Her defenses were so sharp they pierced his heart. He and Julia had a lot of fence mending to do, not the least of which was between the two of them.

"Very much." He took a swallow of his coffee.

"Will you move into our house? Live with us?" She spoke without looking at him, as if fearing what she might see on his face.

"That's up to your mother and me. But wherever I live, Courtney, you will be an important part of my life. An essential part. I promise you."

Silence.

"Is she mad at me?"

He didn't have to ask who *she* was. "I think scared and worried is more like it."

"Are *you* mad at me?"

"There's plenty of time for me to get mad at you when we sort this out. I think all parents get mad at their kids at some time or other." He smiled. "How often I get mad and how much will depend on you."

More silence.

"Do you *want* to live with us?"

Did he? Could he forgive Julia so easily? More than his anger was a fierce sense of protectiveness, and a different kind of rage, this one aimed at Charles Patterson and Rod Maguire. He'd take care of the situation in his own way. And if he put everything else aside, he'd never stopped loving Julia. Not even his anger and pain now could disguise his feelings or displace them. So yes, he wanted to live with Julia and Courtney. As a family.

"Yes," he told her. "I do. As soon as your mother and I...fix some things."

"Are you as mad at her for not telling you as I am?"

Luke knew this was an important question. "I don't think mad is the word. Hurt, maybe. And sorry I've missed out on so much of your life. But we have plenty of time now to make up for it."

It took the better part of another hour before Courtney finally ran down and exhaustion grabbed her.

"How about if you bunk in the guest room?" he asked gently. "I'll call your mother and work it out with her. That okay with you?"

Her eyelids were already drooping. "Yeah. If you want me to, I mean."

"You have no idea how much." He hoped his words conveyed how he felt.

"All right, then."

She was asleep seconds after her head hit the pillow. Luke left the door cracked open in case she had a nightmare or got scared in the middle of the night. Then he called Julia.

"She's fine," he assured her when she insisted she was coming right down there. "Go to bed, Julia. And have someone bring you here in the morning. Let me talk to Claire."

But it was Andy who came on the phone. "We'll make sure she gets to bed," he told Luke. "I know you and Mom have a lot to talk about, but Beth and I would like to bring her to your place in the morning and take everyone out to breakfast." He hesitated. "If that's okay."

How many times had he heard that phrase already tonight?

"Yes. Good. Then you can take Courtney home so your mother and I can take care of business."

"Thank you, sir. We'll see you about nine o'clock. I don't think we can keep her away longer than that."

Luke actually found himself laughing. "No, I guess you're right. Nine o'clock it is. And bring some clothes for your sister."

Epilogue

"Luke, could you zip up my dress, please?" Julia called.

The dress was a pain in the rear, and expensive as hell to boot. But the moment she'd tried it on, both her husband and her daughter had insisted it was the one. And for such a special day as Courtney's graduation, she was willing to indulge them. Now she stood in the big walk-in closet struggling to reach behind her.

"Here. I'll do it."

Luke's warm hands brushed hers away and before he tugged on the metal tab, he took a moment to kiss the nape of her neck.

"You smell great," he murmured. "Too bad we're on a time table here, or I'd yank this dress off, toss you on the bed, and ravish you."

"Could you hold that thought until later?" she teased.

"You bet. Then I'll be holding something else." He nipped the lobe of her ear, then pulled the zipper into place.

"We have to leave in ten minutes," Courtney called from the hall.

"We'll be ready," Luke answered. "Come on in and let us see you."

While Julia, Courtney, and Beth did the salon thing that morning, Luke had taken Andy to breakfast. Julia never stopped being amazed at how the twins had bonded with Luke so easily after such a disastrous beginning. Their wedding took place two months after what she'd taken to calling "the disaster weekend." They were married quietly at the house, with only the children, Claire, Brad, and Miranda in attendance. Miranda prepared a feast for them in celebration. And somehow the family structure developed from such a fragile beginning.

Not without its hurdles, however.

A week after their "disaster," on Saturday morning, they were finishing a family breakfast with everyone there including Andy and Beth when Rod Maguire showed up at their door unannounced. Andy happened to be the one who opened the door for him, and from her seat at the kitchen table Julia saw his body tighten with anger.

"We're busy," he said.

"I came to see your mother, so just get out of my way and let me take care of business."

He rudely pushed Andy aside and strode into the kitchen. But Andy was beside him in a second.

"If you came to expose what you think is some big secret, we know everything." His voice sounded so deep and mature Julia wanted to cry.

"You think so?" Rod's voice had its usual nasty edge she'd gotten used to. "Including the fact she's a whore and your so-called sister is a bastard?"

Courtney's face turned chalk white, but Beth reached over and took her hand, smiling encouragement at her.

Luke rose from his chair, his face dark with rage, and stood so close to Maguire the other man was forced to take a step back.

"Here's a couple of things for you, asshole. One. Do not ever speak of this woman or our child in this manner again. And I mean never." He held up two fingers. "Two. Do not ever, and I mean, never, come to this house again under any circumstances. Or approach any member of this family."

"You can't stop me," Maguire sneered. "I'll ruin you. I'll go to Alan Wilson, who by the way belongs to the same clubs I do and serves on a lot of boards with me. I'll tell him what a mistake he made hiring you. Who do you think he'll listen to? And I'll urge him to pass the word along in the industry. By the time I'm finished, you won't be able to get a job selling T-shirts at the county fair." He looked at Julia. "Wait until everyone in this town knows the sordid details of what you did. None of you will be able to hold up your heads again."

"Three." Luke reached into his pants pocket, pulled out his money clip, and extracted a business card he'd stuck in there. He held out the card to Maguire. "This is my attorney. Eugene Walsh. I believe you're familiar with him. He assures me he has more clout than anyone else I can retain. He said he'd be delighted to face off with you in court over a suit for libel or slander, whichever method you choose."

Before Luke could say anything else Julia, rose from her chair. "Luke and I have both talked to Alan Wilson, Rod. He has the whole story. You might be interested to know he doesn't have nearly as high an opinion of you that you seem to have of yourself. And that story? It's old news. Perhaps I should tell everyone why you're so dedicated to Charles's memory. That would make a nice story, too."

Rod's face paled even as an ugly expression gripped his features. "You'd better keep your mouth shut, bitch."

Beside her she sensed Luke's seething rage and she put a hand on his arm. "As should you. You've done enough damage to me and to my family. You can't bully us anymore. So do us all a favor and get the hell out of our lives."

Luke tucked the business card in Rod's pocket. "Oh, and by the way. My attorney will be calling you about the trusts you're managing for this family. Looking out for our interests, so to speak."

"I see. You think you've fallen into a pot of gold and you plan to protect it."

"That's enough." Julia snapped out the words. "Luke doesn't need my money, or the funds left to the children. But *they* deserve it and I won't let you screw them out of it."

Luke clamped his hand on the other man's elbow. "And now, I believe you were just leaving."

Julia was half laughing, half crying when he closed the door. "I should have had a camera to take a picture of his face."

"He's a bully," Luke said. "I know why you didn't fight back when the kids were younger, but it's time to get the monkey off our backs."

Courtney was still pale and shaking. Luke pulled her up from the chair and wrapped his arms around her. "It's okay, kitten. All taken care of. Nobody—and nothing—is going to hurt you. I promise you that."

There were still legal strings entangling them. Julia wanted the fund her money came from liquidated and distributed among the three children, and she was still worried Rod might pull funny stuff with the trusts for the twins. But apparently one meeting with Eugene Walsh had been enough to get things straight. Somehow, Gene even got Rod to hand over Charles's letters he was holding. Luke had given them to Julia and they conducted a little ceremony out on the patio when she burned them.

Building trust with Courtney had taken some time and patience, but Luke hung in there and eventually she began to respond. Even more amazing was how quickly something special had grown between him and the twins. Watching Luke with her children had given birth to an idea. A month after they were married, when Luke was in Los Angeles at a conference, Julia swore everyone to secrecy and flew to Boston to meet with Mark and Jared Buchanan. She hadn't even been sure they'd accept her phone calls, but with her children gathered around her for courage, she'd dialed the numbers. She was sure only curiosity made them take her calls and agree to meet with her, but she'd taken whatever she could get.

They'd gathered in a restaurant at the Boston airport, a meeting that began in hostility but ended with a hint of conciliation. She'd brought pictures, not only of Luke and Courtney but of the twins, of Luke speaking at events, and of their family gatherings. Although they'd called her separately a few times afterward, each time cautiously and with more questions, she hadn't been sure she'd actually be able to heal the breach. Nevertheless, their relationship with their mother was fractured and she'd sensed they were looking for some kind of familial anchor.

Holding her breath, she'd extended the invitation to Luke's fiftieth birthday dinner at one of their favorite restaurants. Not only had his sons come, but also their wives and children. She was sure it was the first time she'd ever seen Luke Buchanan speechless. The evening had produced many moments of strain and unease, but it was a good beginning. Now at least Luke and his sons kept in touch with each other and she and Luke had already made two trips to Boston.

So many changes, Julia mused, as she searched for her shoes. Not the least of which was what everyone referred to as "the move." Luke had insisted she sell the house and they build a new one.

"It's diseased," he'd told her. "No wonder no one's happy in it. No way can we make a fresh start in this place."

Even in a slow market, it sold quickly, along with most of the furniture. They'd camped out at Luke's suite at the hotel during the time the new house was being built at the northwest tip of the city. Luke had insisted Courtney be included in every decision, including the shopping for furnishings, and she'd bloomed under his love and care. Maybe Beth had been right and what her child had lacked the most was a father. Or maybe it was just *this* father.

The Connell Wilson launch had gone so well Bright Ideas client list had grown exponentially. Bigger clients had approached them. They'd hired more staff and moved into bigger offices. But at the end of the day she always came home to Luke and the comfort of his body in bed.

Now, on this special day, Courtney burst into the room, breathless. "How do I look?"

Julia's breath caught in her throat. Her sullen, angry, rebellious child had grown into a beautiful teenager, with acceptable grades and a blossoming personality. The result of Luke's work, she knew, and it hadn't been an easy task for him. Courtney twirled around, the skirt of her soft blue dress spinning with her like a cloud, her shining black hair hanging in waves to her shoulders.

"Gorgeous." Luke kissed her on the cheek. "I'd hug you but I don't want to disturb such beauty."

Courtney laughed. "Daddy, you crack me up. I guess I'll just have to hug you."

And she did, bringing tears to Julia's eyes.

Dimly, she heard the front door open and close, and Miranda hollered up the stairs, "Beth and Andy are here. Y'all comin' down or not?"

Luke smiled at her. "I guess we'd better go."

Miranda waited in the foyer with a camera. "I want plenty of shots to post on my Facebook page."

Courtney's jaw dropped. "*You* have a Facebook page?"

Miranda cocked an eyebrow. "Any reason why I shouldn't? Now everyone get together. That's right. Boy, don't you just look like a fine family."

Julia looked at each of them. "Yes, we do."

And as they stood together posing for Miranda who snapped away, Julia realized that at long last, after so many years of incredible misery, she'd not only found the love she'd been missing, she'd found herself.

ABOUT THE AUTHOR

Known the world over as the oldest living author of erotic romance, and referred to by *USA Today* as the Nora Roberts of erotic romance, Desiree Holt is three times a finalist for an EPIC E-Book Award (and a winner in 2014), a nominee for a Romantic Times Reviewers Choice Award, winner of the first 5 Heart Sweetheart of the Year Award at The Romance Studio as well as twice a CAPA Award winner for best BDSM book of the year, and winner of the Holt Medallion for Excellence in Romance Literature. She has been featured on *CBS Sunday Morning* and in *The Village Voice, The Daily Beast, USA Today, The (London) Daily Mail, The New Delhi Times* and numerous other national and international publications.

"Desiree Holt is the most amazing erotica author of our time and each story is more fulfilling then the last." *(Romance Junkies)*

Learn more about her and read her novels here:
www.desireeholt.com
www.desiremeonly.com
www.facebook.com/desireeholtauthor
Twitter @desireeholt
Pinterest: desiree02holt
Also on LinkedIn and Google+

www.ingramcontent.com/pod-product-compliance
Lightning Source LLC
Chambersburg PA
CBHW031418250626
47155CB00004B/1531